THE
DEMON
DUKE

By

Margaret Locke

"We cannot change the cards we are dealt, just how we play the hand." – Randy Pausch

For J.

I may be your mom, but you've taught me more than you'll ever know.

Play on, kiddo.

CHAPTER 1

BLACKWOOD ABBEY, YORKSHIRE, ENGLAND
LATE OCTOBER, 1813

*Please come home. Your father and brother are
dead. Carriage accident. You are Duke now. We
need you. Come quickly, Damon.*

— Mama

Damon Blackbourne, youngest son of Silas
Blackbourne, Duke of Malford, stared at the
note without seeing it. He didn't need to;
he'd read it a hundred times already. He
balled up the paper and threw it to the floor.

"Home?" he snarled out loud, although the room, as
usual, was empty. "Home, Mama?"

He had no home. None other than Blackwood Abbey,
at least—the cavernous abode to which he'd been
banished seventeen years ago. Seventeen years. More
than half of his lifetime—nearly two-thirds, seeing as he
was now twenty-seven.

He paced the room, a library brimming with books, a
place he'd long claimed as his own. Not that he'd had
competition, given his only company was a few servants.

And Hobbes. Thank God for Hobbes.

A fire crackled merrily in the fireplace, its warmth soothing him. It had turned unseasonably cold for October, a cold that now seeped into his bones, freezing his soul from the inside out.

He stopped in front of the flames, their flickering captivating him. What should he do? He hadn't been to Thorne Hill, hadn't seen his family since that awful day; the day he'd turned ten and his father turned him out.

"No son of mine shall exhibit such evil behaviors," Silas had roared. "You are possessed by the devil. I cast you out. Do not show your face to me again. You are not my son."

Not even the sound of his mother's weeping had turned Damon around as he'd climbed alone into the carriage, numbness enveloping him. It was a welcomed state, the lack of feeling. It had dulled the pain of his back, which bore witness to the intense lashings his father had laid upon him, a desperate attempt to exorcise the demons Damon knew only too well.

His sisters had been mere babes in arms. They hadn't even been present. But Damon would never forget the look on his beloved older brother's face. It was the look of a boy torn—no, a man, perhaps, considering his brother at fourteen no longer had had the body of a child. Moisture had filled Adam's eyes as their father had raged, but he'd raised no voice in Damon's defense, made no attempt to stop the man. Adam had always been too dutiful for that.

Damon sighed. Should he go? Did he owe his mother—or anyone—that?

He'd never gone south, even though he'd come of age years ago. What would have been the point? And what would he have faced? More ridicule? Possibly Bedlam? His father never would have countenanced his return.

Damon had been dead to Silas, dead to everyone, as far as he knew.

Except Adam and his mother, Felicity. She penned letters as often as she could, Adam less often, though both without his father's knowledge. Silas certainly had never written. But Mama told the mundane details of life at Thorne Hill, of how his brother had fared with the estate's management, how his sisters loathed practicing the pianoforte and hated their dance tutor.

He'd never had such things. A tutor came for a while—at whose bidding, he didn't know—but Mr. Jensen had long since left, disturbed not only by Damon's defiant manner but also by his rages.

For Damon had long struggled with his temper. It sometimes superseded even his odd body movements and frequently got him into trouble, which was one of the reasons he avoided company.

"Not like being exiled to Hell would assuage anyone's anger," he muttered as he reached for the glass of brandy he'd set on the side table.

Then it sank in. He was now the Duke of Malford. Unless his father had disinherited him. Was that possible? If so, his uncle, Fillmore Blackbourne, would be Duke.

And yet, his mother had written to him. Why?

Even if he were the legal heir, why would she want him back? Did she not fear he would be worse than before? Though he'd written her once, years ago, of how he'd mastered his demons, the physical ones, at least, in hopes of being called home. Had that been enough to convince her he could manage in polite society?

But he'd wanted the summons then. Not now.

He walked over to the window, staring out at the craggy moors glistening with snow. He knew in his heart what he had to do. For his mama, who'd done the best she could, he supposed, in circumstances beyond her control. For his sisters, whom he only remembered as tiny tykes who loved to pull his black hair. And for himself. To prove once and for all he was no devil. None beyond his own making, at least.

"Hobbes," he bellowed.

A short man with thinning brown hair entered the room. Stiff-backed and with his nose in the air, he was the quintessential butler, who served also as Damon's valet. Though his main role over the years had become that of friend. Despite the difference in age and status, they'd bonded, two lonely people bumbling about in this monstrous abbey, each with no family to call his own.

Still, the man loved to put on airs, to remind Damon both of his status as a ducal family's servant—and Damon's status as Lord. "Yes, my lord?"

"For Pete's sake, Hobbes. It's Damon. Damon." *Or rather now, Your Grace.*

"I know." The grin that cracked Hobbes's cheeks softened his expression. "It merely amuses me to bait you."

Damon smirked. "Ready the horses and coach."

Hobbes's eyebrows reached skyward. Damon nearly laughed out loud, which would have been quite the rarity, at the comical expression on the butler-come-valet's face.

"We're going to Thorne Hill."

At that, Hobbes's jaw literally dropped. He looked out at the snow-blanketed expanse of the abbey's grounds. "In this weather?"

"Why not? If I'm going back home, it's only fitting that Hell has frozen over."

CHAPTER 2

CLAREHAVEN, HAMPSHIRE, ENGLAND
FEBRUARY, 1814

*G*race Mattersley pulled her pelisse robe around her as she settled into the window seat of the library, clutching a book. It would be far warmer on the settee in front of the fire, and yet somehow the window drew her again and again.

She glanced out at the high drifts of snow enveloping her family home. Normally, they'd have spent the entire winter in London for the Season while her brother Deveric, Duke of Claremont, sat in the House of Lords. But this year they'd returned for his wife Eliza's confinement, anxiously awaiting the newest Mattersley. Isabelle had finally made her appearance two weeks ago.

Grace's sister, Emmeline, was likely pacing the hallways, longing to get to town again, bored to tears in the dead of winter with only her sisters as companions. Rebecca, too, was no doubt chafing at the bit, wishing she could be out on her horse, galloping through the woods. But Grace was quite content exactly where she was. Grateful, even, that she hadn't had to disrupt her daily rituals to return to London and all its people.

Her mother, Matilda, though, was anxious to return. "We cannot miss the entire Season, after all. No, not with all three of you out now. And we must show strength in Amara's absence. Yes, yes, we must. Oh, this blasted snow!"

Mama loved every social opportunity, every chance she had to mingle with the highest echelons of London society. She relished hopes of grand matches this year for her youngest daughters, no doubt. Emmeline and Rebecca might be interested, but Grace most assuredly was not.

She flipped a page. How she disliked the Marriage Mart. Last year had been awful. If one more awkward, bumbling viscount or baron asked her to dance, she'd likely scream. Not that she minded dancing. But she did mind the men, with their hopeful, occasionally leering glances. And, oh, how dreadful, having to make conversation with someone she did not know!

What was wrong with her? Many of her friends were eager to find a match. Emmeline soaked up male attention as if it was her due. Even Rebecca giggled in delight when young lords flirted with her. But Grace?

She'd rather her heroes remained literary ones, at least for now. At twenty-two, however, she was nearly on the shelf, as her mother was prone to remind her.

She was expected to marry. That's what highborn ladies did, after all. At least in the Mattersley family. They didn't engage in trade. They didn't design houses. They certainly didn't write novels. No, a Mattersley's duty was to marry well and produce heirs.

"Managing an estate and family will keep you busy enough, my dear," her mother promised.

Grace looked down at the page. She'd read the same sentence three times over. Not that it mattered; she knew the book by heart. Ever since Eliza had brought her a copy last year, Grace read it through at least once a month. There was something about its heroine, Elizabeth Bennet, that spoke to Grace. Her spirit, her independence. Her intelligence. Elizabeth Bennet was a member of the gentry, though, not the nobility. Those of the highest society hadn't fared as well in their representation in this book, *Pride and Prejudice*.

Grace loved the story. But why did illness or injury have to play such a large role in securing a husband? Marianne with Willoughby and Colonel Brandon, Jane with Mr. Bingley. How absurd.

On the other hand, had Eliza not done the same when she'd fallen in that dreadful accident? She'd been unconscious for days, but that event had knocked sense into Grace's brother and made him realize his feelings for this odd American, this distant cousin of theirs, ran far deeper than familial. Not so absurd after all, then.

"Perhaps Mama will suggest I walk in Hyde Park during the rain. Although a cold would redden my nose, I suppose, and no suitor would find me attractive then." She pressed her fingers to her lips; she'd been speaking to an empty room again.

"Always talking to the air, silly goose," Emmeline liked to tease her. It didn't bother Grace; she preferred empty rooms to crowds of people. Crowds made her uncomfortable.

The door burst open and Emmeline ran in. "I should have known you were here, sister," she exclaimed. "I'm so bored. Will this winter never let up?" She plopped down on the settee with a huff, throwing her head back against the piece of furniture in dramatic fashion. "There's nothing to *do!*"

"You could read."

Emmeline glowered at her sister. "Read. Read. I swear I've read every book in here worth reading."

A very unladylike snort escaped Grace. "I highly doubt that, sister. And even if you have, read them again. You could give this one a try." She held up her book. "It's wonderful. You would quite like it."

Emmeline glanced at it. "Eliza told me all about that one. She insists Deveric is her Darcy." She rolled her eyes.

"Better than a Wickham, that's for sure." Grace stood and crossed to her sister. "We'll be off to London soon, dear Emme, and then you shall once again be the belle of every ball." She beckoned with a hand.

Emmeline rose and they neared the fire, holding their fingers in front of the flames. "That was Rosaline Marcheux, and you know it," she said with a pout. "No one could compete with her violet eyes and that sable hair."

"More like a raven's nest, if you ask me. Besides, she ended up with Lord Demville. That old goat; you wouldn't have wanted him, anyway."

"You're right. But I was hoping, so hoping."

Grace linked her arm through her sister's, and they exited the room. "Soon, my Cinderella in waiting, soon."

"Cinderella? As if I'd be caught dead sweeping up ashes!"

Grace could only smile as they headed to the parlor, where Emme said Rebecca had set out a game of cards. She loved her sisters, but in many ways she was their opposite.

Oh well. She could return to Darcy later.

It wasn't as if there was much else to do.

CHAPTER 3

THORNE HILL, HAMPSHIRE, ENGLAND
MARCH, 1814

*D*amon pulled at the cravat encircling his neck. "Why must I wear such an infernal contraption?" he demanded, growling at Hobbes, who stood calmly in front of him, adjusting the folds of black cloth.

"Because it is how it is done, Your Grace, as you well know."

"Stop calling me that. I hate it."

"You are the Duke now, whether you wish to be or not. As I am now merely your valet instead of valet and butler and tutor and . . . "

Damon snorted. "I think perhaps you have come out the better of us in that exchange."

Hobbes smoothed the shoulders of Damon's black evening jacket and stood back to survey his work.

Damon ignored his valet's perusal, brushing his hand through his thick black hair. He picked up a skull head stickpin from the side table and fastened it to the front of his cravat.

"Must you wear that?"

Damon's lips curled up. "Is it not proper mourning attire?"

"It might be, if you were actually in mourning."

"You think I'm not showing proper respect for the dead?"

Hobbes chortled as he gathered Damon's shoes. "I don't think you show proper respect to the living."

Damon adjusted the cuffs. "Why start now? It's not as if anyone ever showed respect for me." He couldn't hide the bitterness in his tone, despite his nonchalant manner.

"Your sisters are very charming, Your Grace, and have taken to you. And your mother—"

"My mother is deep in mourning for a man who banished me from my family. It's hard for me to overcome that, no matter how much she professes her regrets." He gave Hobbes a hard look.

"True," was the valet's only response. "I shall leave you to dinner, Your Grace."

"Call me that one more time, upstart, and I shall send you in my stead."

Hobbes backed through the doorway, hands held up in mock surrender. "Better you than I, Damon. Better you than I."

DAMON STOOD at the top of the stairs, girding himself for yet another family meal. It was quite an adjustment, having to set his schedule according to others' needs, according to propriety and tradition. At the abbey, he'd eaten when he'd wanted to, often just snatching bits of meat or bread from the kitchen before heading off for a run or back to his beloved book-filled sanctuary. He didn't much care for the formal dinners observed at Thorne Hall but was doing his best to assimilate.

Why, he didn't know. Why *was* he here, working to protect the estate of the man he'd hated, who had hated him? Why had he returned to this place, where painful memories lurked around every corner? Sometimes his body ached just remembering.

At least he had Cerberus, his cat. And Hobbes. His friend hadn't enjoyed the long journey here anymore than the feline had, but having both with him helped ease the stress of all the newness.

Damon had underestimated the challenges. Running the estate was not the difficulty; it was navigating the intricacies of society. It wasn't as if he were starting from scratch—he'd had ten years under his father's watchful eye, after all, Silas drilling him time and again on manners and expectations, titles and traditions. And he had Hobbes. Hobbes had come ten years ago to instruct him in the ways of a gentleman, a "gift" from his mother.

"Whatever for?" Damon had spat upon Hobbes's arrival. "They will never have me back, and even if they did, I wouldn't go!"

He'd given his jerking, twitching behaviors full rein in hopes they'd drive off this man some fifteen years his senior, convinced Hobbes's true purpose was that of a spy to determine if Damon ought to be committed to an asylum.

Then again, Hobbes hadn't initially cared for him, either, resentful of being sent to the ends of the Earth, or at least of England, to tend to a wild young man little more than half his age.

But both had grown to respect each other: Damon for Hobbes's ability to ignore his rages and movements, for Hobbes's refusal to treat him as anything less than a full peer, and for Hobbes's wry sense of humor in poking fun at both of their situations, abandoned to each other in the middle of nowhere.

Hobbes, meanwhile, expressed sincere admiration for Damon's intellect. "You are far superior to your father and brother, my lord, in nature and ability. Never did care for His Grace, if you don't mind my saying, and Lord Adam, though a pleasant enough chap, simply did not apply himself to life, content to float along behind others."

But still, despite the instruction, despite everything Damon had learned since his return to Thorne Hill—and he'd thrown himself into mastering every aspect, determined to excel, to prove his father wrong, to prove to himself he was more than his affliction—his insides quaked at the thought of making his appearance in London.

He would not show it, however. Never would he let others beat him down again.

Laughter floated up the stairs, jarring him from his thoughts as his two sisters entered the hallway below. Spying him, Lady Persephone, or Sephe, rather, called up in her clear, pleasant voice. "Damon! Are you coming?"

His other sister, Lady Cassandra, tossed him a grin, one eerily similar to his own. Cassie's light blue eyes, mirrors to his, flashed at him as he descended the stairs. It was always a shock to see her; were she not obviously much younger, she and he might have been mistaken for twins.

Thank goodness he had taken after his mother in looks. Had he looked like his father, that big barrel of a Viking descendant, nightmares would have dogged him every time he looked in the mirror. Sephe had their father's blonde locks, but her blue eyes spoke of their mother's influence. Those ice-blue eyes were considered a hallmark of the family, for all four of the Blackbourne siblings had them.

These two women are why I am here.

Damon descended the stairs, the side of his mouth cocked up in his customary grin. He had missed them in his own way. What would it have been like to grow up together? To have had a family he could count on? Though these past months had allowed them to get to know each other, the connection was too new for him to put much faith in it.

Two years ago, at eighteen, Cassie had refused every offer during her first Season, because she wanted to wait for her sister, who was two years her junior.

"I need Sephe to be out so we can take the London Season by storm, together," she'd insisted.

His mother grumbled over that—"The expense! And what if she'd missed a most excellent match?" But the love for her daughters shone in her eyes every time she looked at them.

It shone for him, too. But he didn't trust it. He didn't trust her. His mother regretted the past, regretted not standing up to his father, regretted the lost years with her son. She'd said as much many times since he'd arrived, her eyes haunted, shadowed with that look of fear he himself had often borne as a child. Had his father raised a hand to her, too?

If the bastard weren't already dead, I'd kill him myself. He'd fantasized over the years of doing to his father what the man had done to him, of beating the man to a pulp. He'd dreamed of returning from Blackwood Abbey and presenting himself to his father in triumph, proving he'd become every inch a man and more. He'd longed for it, that sense of revenge.

And yet he'd fought it, too. The world might believe him to be the devil he'd been called, but a part of him, buried deep within the recesses of his own heart, wanted to prove he was different from Silas Blackbourne; that the evil in the old man's mind hadn't warped his, as well.

It had, of course. How could it not? A ten-year-old boy sent to live in the wilds of northern England for something he couldn't control? How a parent could simply rid themselves of a child like that, Damon didn't know. He himself had grown quite attached to the cook's daughter, the little girl he'd held when she was just a babe. He'd watched her grow up, moving from winsome toddler to young schoolgirl, delighting in her milestones along with her mother. He missed her, that young girl, and she wasn't even his child. How could his parents have sent him away?

He knew their answer. Knew his father had been convinced Damon was possessed, had had an evil in him.

"What else could explain it, boy?" his father had roared. "Be grateful it's only Yorkshire and not an asylum."

What else *could* explain the jerks of Damon's body, the tossing of his head and the flaring of his nostrils, over and over again? The blinking of his eyes and the grunting that flared up, especially when he was angry or scared? How he hated himself, how his own body betrayed him, taking on a life of its own. His movements had scared the servants, had scared even his little sisters. Whispers of demons and curses had floated around him for as long as he could remember.

It hadn't always been like that. Sometimes the feelings had calmed. Sometimes he'd had complete control of his body. But when he hadn't, it'd been a nightmare, a nightmare of emotions and urges he couldn't suppress. No remedies applied had made any difference, though his father had paraded numerous physicians past him. Nearly boiling-hot baths, bleeding by leeches, and antispasmodic pills of dubious content had made not a whit of difference. One of the doctors had called the painful twitches "tics," and Damon a "ticcer."

His father had called him much worse, horrible names too awful to repeat. "No son of mine will be so out of control, so lacking in self-discipline, so beleaguered by such irregularities!" Silas had shouted on more than one occasion.

How often had his father beaten him black and blue with a switch, commanding Damon to stop? If Damon had had any lasting control over his own body, did his father truly think he wouldn't have? What boy would have continued with such "nasty habits," as Silas termed them, if he'd had a choice?

His mother had wept each time she'd applied salve to Damon's back, held him close and whispered words of love into his hair, even as he'd railed against her, against his father, against everyone. Against himself.

"I know, my son. I know the truth. You can't help it. I know." She'd repeated the words to him time and again.

But the only time she'd said such words to Silas Blackbourne, he'd shouted her down with such ferocity she'd never attempted again. And she hadn't stopped Silas from sending Damon away.

He walked into the main dining hall. His mother, seated at the far end, was a pale and shriveled version of the woman he'd known as a child. His heart constricted. What was left of it, that was.

"I am so sorry, Damon, my love." Over and over she'd said the words the day he'd arrived at Thorne Hill. Often had she repeated them in the months since. Part of him wanted to fall at her feet like that lost little boy and beg her for love. Wanted to forgive her when she professed her grief and guilt over his childhood.

The other part wanted to run. Return to Yorkshire. She was no mother. Was she not at least half as much a monster as his father? She'd let him go. And only when he'd written of his victories over his movements, insisting they were now well controlled and had been for some time, had she hinted at the possibility of reconciliation. "Perhaps when Adam is Duke," she'd written once. But never again.

Now *he* was Duke, his father and brother gone in one fateful, unexpected moment.

If only Adam had married and had had an heir. Then Damon would still be at the abbey, still be in all that was comfortable and familiar.

"Damon." His mother greeted him warmly, though her face looked wan in her widow's weeds.

"Mother."

His sisters sat down, ignoring the tension in the room. Or did they not feel it? How he envied their light-hearted approach to the world. How different their childhoods had been.

"The weather is warming," he said as the first course was laid. "I suppose it is time. Tomorrow, we pack for London."

His sisters burst into furious conversation with each other; his mother smiled, animation lighting her face for the first time in a long while.

Only he, apparently, was marching into the gates of Hell.

CHAPTER 4

REXBOROUGH BALL, LONDON
EARLY APRIL, 1814

*G*race squeezed nearer to the wall, surveying the crowded room from her cramped corner. Bodies moved around each other as everyone jockeyed for position. It was the first grand ball of the Season, a mad crush at the Marquess of Rexborough's expansive London estate. There was hardly space to dance, though the orchestra played gaily.

If only she could go home. Her sister Emmeline danced by with Lord Everton, a vivacious smile lighting her face. Even Rebecca's eyes sparkled with happiness as she carefully executed her steps opposite the handsome Marquess of Emerlin.

Why could Grace not feel the same excitement?

Matilda, standing next to Grace, beamed at her other two daughters, delighting in their successes in snagging eligible men so early in the evening.

"They're merely dancing, Mother. No need to plan the weddings."

The dowager duchess sniffed. "At least they're dancing. You have begged off three invitations so far."

"Lord Oglesby has two left feet, quite possibly three, if my toes have any say. Lord Featherstone is old enough to be my grandfather. And Lord Emerlin only asked because you wished him to. You know he's had his sights on Becca for waltzing."

Her mother aired her face with the elaborate fan in her right hand. "I suppose it wouldn't be a bad match. Though he is so much her elder."

"A marquess and the eventual heir to a dukedom. Not such a bad match, indeed. And ten is not so many years. Many a young lady has married a far older gentleman."

Matilda Mattersley opened her mouth as if to respond when a commotion started amongst the ball goers. They gave a collective gasp as a man entered the room. He was clad entirely in black—black pantaloons, black coat and waistcoat, even an ebony shirt and cravat. Thick black hair tousled wildly over his forehead. Two young ladies next to Grace tittered.

"He is of fine countenance," one gushed.

"Who is he?" said the other.

A matron broke in, speaking sharply. "Did you not hear him announced? That's the Duke of Malford." She made the sign of the cross. "They say he is a devil. They call him the Demon Duke."

"Really?" the first girl exclaimed.

The older woman slapped the girl's knuckles with her fan. "Don't even think about it, Alice. Come, let us seek some lemonade."

The girl obediently followed the matron, no doubt her mother, through the mass of people.

"The Demon Duke," Grace murmured.

The man moved farther into the room. His grin was wicked, but his shoulders tight, his eyes . . . sad. Did he notice how people edged away? How whispers raced across the room? How eyes peeped at him while pretending not to do so?

How could he not?

Sympathy flooded through Grace. "He doesn't look devilish to me," she said to her mother. "He looks uncomfortable. Like he wishes he were anywhere else but here." How she could relate.

Matilda sucked a breath. "However he looks is not your concern. The Duke of Malford is not an option."

"I do not think you have anything to fear, Mother. A man such as that would never be interested in a mouse such as me."

A smile leaked through the dowager duchess's pursed lips. "A mouse, indeed. It's good to see this mouse knows to stay away from a cat. He looks rather feral."

He is a panther, sleek and black. With the mien of a lion.

"If you'll pardon me, Mama, I am in need of the retiring room."

Grace slipped from the room. With everyone's attention on the Duke, this was a good time to sneak away to the library, as she'd done at Rexborough balls a time or two before.

She pulled a book from the shelf. *Ah yes.* Aesop's fables. She settled in near a window, her thoughts on the man in the ballroom.

Hadn't Aesop said it was the mouse who saved the lion?

THOUGH HE AFFECTED an air of nonchalance, Damon's cravat dug into his neck, his hands itched inside his gloves, and as gasps echoed through the room and the weight of what seemed a million eyes fell on him, he wanted nothing more than to leave. Especially since it was not his lovely sisters at his side, but his appearance that had them tittering.

They'd all thought him dead.

"Your father told everyone you'd passed away," his mother had confessed, shame wringing tears from her eyes. "I've had to admit it wasn't the case—but one look at you and they'll know. They'll know you are a true Blackbourne."

So he'd died all those years ago—and now had come back to life. At least in the eyes of the *ton*. A sneer slipped across his face. Let them think that. Let them call him the Demon Duke. He knew the talk. He knew his return to London had set the gossip mill grinding, that the very mystery of him had sparked numerous rumors since the family's arrival in London last week.

Cassie tutted at a wide-eyed debutante who stood as if transfixed in front of Damon. "He doesn't bite."

The young woman skittered off, her eyes bulging, though whether in response to him or his sister's rather rude comment was unclear.

His eyes sparkled. "You needn't defend me."

"It's just silly, all these people acting as if you're some kind of ghost."

"Or monster," he said.

Sephe snickered from his other side. "Monster. Posh. You are perfectly delightful, as the last several months have proven." She linked her arm through his. "Although I *am* sorry for this attention, Damon. I'm sure you can't enjoy it. If only Mother—"

"Our mother cannot be here because she is still in mourning. I know. That is why it has fallen to me to escort you through the Season."

"Well, it's possible Aunt Martha could have done that," Cassie admitted. "I think Mother wanted to make it up to you by letting you take your rightful position in society, wanted to show that we as a family accept you."

Damon's jaw clenched. Fury snaked up his back. He didn't have to be here? He could be home, in solitude, instead of at the center of attention amongst people he didn't know, people who gaped at him as if he were Lucifer himself?

"Though likely she would rue the current attention," Sephe said. "I doubt it shall last long, however." She raised her chin as if to bolster her assertion.

It was true the tittering had died down somewhat. Several young dandies eyed the sisters appreciatively. No one could deny the Blackbourne ladies cut fine figures. Cassie, her coloring so similar to Damon's, was clad in a cream gown trimmed in black (fitting for half-mourning, or so he was told) that enhanced the blue of her eyes. Sephe had opted for a lavender confection that made her complexion shine and complemented her nearly white-blonde hair to perfection.

"Do I need to stay by your sides the entire evening?" Damon muttered, hot beneath the gazes of those around him. Or perhaps it was the numerous candles ablaze above them. The room was overly warm, but that was no surprise considering how many people occupied it.

"I see Cousin Daphne," Sephe cried out. "I didn't know she would be here. I thought she was still in Bath!"

A tiny young woman with dark hair smiled from across the room as she gave Sephe a wave. The older man standing next to her, however, was not smiling. He fixed his eyes on Damon, scowling fiercely. The longer the man stared, the ruddier his complexion grew.

"That's Uncle Fillmore," Cassie said.

"I know." Damon grimaced. The man looked so much like his father it was like seeing a ghost. Ironic, perhaps, considering it was Damon who'd allegedly returned from the dead. His whole body went rigid as his uncle approached. Though shorter and smaller than Damon, the man's demeanor radiated hostility. Did his uncle mean to do him bodily harm?

It wouldn't have been the first time. Fillmore, in fact, was the one who'd encouraged Silas to send Damon away. Damon had overheard them arguing about it in his father's study, years ago.

"The boy is a menace," his uncle had insisted. "A plague upon this family. You do not want his like contaminating us."

His father's response had been inaudible.

"He must go," his uncle had persisted. "Perhaps . . . an accident. With his rages and afflictions, no one would question that."

"Are you telling me to *murder* my own son?" Damon's father had roared.

Apparently whipping me within inches of my life is acceptable, but killing me is not, Damon had thought. *I suppose I should be grateful you draw the line somewhere, Father.*

He had sat, shaking, in the hallway. Surely the jerking of his head, the clearing of his throat, the occasional noises he emitted without his knowledge weren't enough to damn him as unfit to live. Were they? Was he truly so evil his own family would rid themselves of him?

Damon stared at the man in front of him. His hands itched to close around Fillmore Blackbourne's throat, to take out all of his anger and hurt and disgust on this shadow of his father before him. He clenched his fists, his teeth grinding as he willed control to return.

"Damon," his uncle bit out with a terse nod.

"I believe you should address me as Your Grace," Damon responded evenly.

Fillmore's face reddened even further. Perhaps he

would succumb to an apoplectic fit and spare Damon this unpleasant interaction.

"You shouldn't be here," his uncle growled in a low voice. "You shouldn't exist."

Daphne put a hand on her father's arm. "Father," she chided, casting apologetic eyes toward Damon.

Sephe and Cassie moved between their brother and their uncle at the same time, forming a wall.

"Uncle Fillmore," Cassie said quietly but firmly. "This is neither the time nor the place for such a public display. And any disparaging words you say to your nephew— our brother—cast aspersions on us all and reflect most poorly on you."

What backbone his sister possessed to face down this man a good thirty years her senior. Her ardent defense touched him. He had endured such castigation before; his sisters most certainly had not. Had they decided to distance themselves, he'd have understood.

Fillmore leaned around Sephe to address Damon, icy daggers emanating from his eyes. "You should not be Duke," he hissed. "You are not a Malford."

Damon's brow rose. "Why, dear Uncle—are you suggesting my mother cuckolded my father?" The corner of his cheek slid up into a sardonic grin. "I would be careful what you say. Men have called each other out over lesser offenses. And not that you would know, but I am a crack shot. I've had lots of time to practice."

His uncle's face paled. He dusted off invisible flecks from his coat before nodding at Damon, as if that would put the bad blood of the past few moments—or past decades—behind them.

"I am thirsty, Father," Daphne said in a calming voice. "Shall we find some refreshment?" She looked to Cassie and Sephe. "Perhaps you would like to accompany us?"

Damon breathed a sigh of relief. He needed a chance to escape, to be alone.

"By all means," he said to his sisters. "I would like to explore the gardens as it is. I have heard they are among the finest in London."

With that, he excused himself. His insides shook, but his outward demeanor revealed nothing. He tipped his head politely to the various matrons and young debutantes who gaped at him and nodded to several gentlemen. All the while, his mind screamed: *Get out. Find some space. You're going to start again. You're going to start.*

A peek through the windows showed the gardens ablaze with lantern lights. A number of couples strolled along the paths. *No good. Run. Flee. Don't show them. Don't show them.*

As quickly as he could, he raced down the nearest hallway, seeking a place of respite. He tried the nearest door, hoping not to surprise a couple *in flagrante delicto* or disturb his host. To his delight and relief, the door swung open to reveal a rather expansive library, numerous wooden bookshelves covering the walls, each crammed full of titles. *Thank God.* He slammed the door behind him and stood, trying to catch his breath.

The tics exploded with a ferocity he'd not felt in years. His head jerked repeatedly to the side and his nose twitched uncontrollably. It had been ages since his body had reacted in such a manner, but he gave it free rein. Any more suppression would make it worse. He flexed his hands, waiting for the surge of adrenaline to work its way through his body.

Years of practice had given him mastery over the tics, for the most part. The urge to move in such random ways rarely struck. In fact, the compulsion to repeat the odd mannerisms only reared its head in times of great stress. Such times had been rare at the abbey, so much so that he'd truly believed the tics gone.

No such luck. During the first few weeks at Thorne Hill, as he'd worked to assimilate with his family and master the running of the duchy, the old feelings had returned. Not often, but enough. He'd hoped it was merely a reaction to being back in that space, in those rooms in which he'd been beaten and shamed so many years ago.

Apparently not.

He stared into the flames of the large fire blazing in the fireplace. At least the fire was oblivious to the battle raging within him. He paced, body spasming, squeezing his eyes shut as he waited for the anger to dissipate.

After a few minutes, the tension eased. He breathed slowly, deep breaths in and out, like he'd taught himself years ago. Just when he thought he had complete control again, a soft voice spoke from behind him.

"I'm sorry. I thought you should know you're not alone in the room."

CHAPTER 5

REXBOROUGH BALL, LONDON
EARLY APRIL, 1814

*D*amon whirled.

A young woman sat in a cushioned nook near the window, dressed in a rather simple gown of pale green. Gorgeous sable hair swept up in a simple chignon highlighted her elegant neck. Kind chocolate brown eyes watched him, and her lips curved into a delicate smile. She set the book she'd been reading on her lap.

"I hate it when my sisters surprise me when I think I'm alone, so I thought I owed you the same courtesy."

"Who are you?" Damon demanded, his mind racing. She'd seen him. She'd seen him at his worst, when his body wasn't under his control and he'd twisted and turned as if demon-possessed. Apprehension flooded through him. What if she revealed his secret, that the tics that had plagued him as a child were not completely gone? What if it started again—the accusations, the avoidance?

She rose and approached him. No repulsion reflected in her eyes. "Grace Mattersley. Sister to Claremont."

"Claremont," he repeated, stalling as he tried to place the name. So many blasted titles to remember. A Christian name teased at him. Derrick? Or Deveric? Yes, that was it. Deveric Mattersley, Duke of Claremont.

"Damon," he said, cocking his chin in the air to disguise his unease. To go on the attack was often the strongest defense, was it not? "Blackbourne. Duke of Malford."

Damn. He should have simply said Malford. That's how it was done. Not giving one's Christian name, not as member of the *ton* and with certainty not as a duke. He might be rusty, but he remembered the rules. Most of them. Still, she'd introduced herself by *her* given name. Was it any wonder he'd done the same?

He did not like how off-kilter this stranger set him.

Grace—*Lady* Grace—smiled, revealing dainty white teeth. "It is a pleasure to meet you, Your Grace. But I'd best leave you to yourself, lest we be discovered here together."

She was right; it wouldn't do to be caught in a compromising position with a young lady of the *ton*. Even one as delectable as this.

A satisfied smirk spread across his face. "Well, if I had to be caught with *someone*."

He inched toward her, coming to a stop a mere hand's span from her face. Her chest rose and fell, nervousness emanating from her.

"What?" His smirk turned into a sneer, her obvious discomfort upsetting for some reason. "You wouldn't wish people to know you were associating with the Demon Duke? For that's what they call me, as I'm sure you have heard, now that you know my name."

He ogled her up and down in an intentionally rude fashion. *What are you doing? Why are you trying to frighten her?*

So that she would run. So that she wouldn't want anything more to do with the odious Duke of Malford. Because his body wanted everything to do with her and that was unacceptable.

"Would you?" he added, his voice sharp. He expected her to cower, to back away. That was what most others did when he brought out his beastly side.

She didn't.

She looked him full in the face, those chocolate eyes nearly sucking the soul out of him. Warmth radiated from them—not sensual, but rather sympathetic, as if she knew what he was doing and felt sorry for him.

Sorry would not do. It would not do at all.

Quick as lightning, he swooped in, his hand wrapping around her neck, his face dipping down until he brushed his lips across hers. He waited for a moment, gauging her response. He wasn't such a monster that he would truly force a woman; he merely wanted to shake her up a little. And give her reason not only to keep their meeting a secret, but also to keep far away from him.

Beautiful young debutantes were not in his plans for the future—no sense pining after something he could never have. And he couldn't ever have someone like her. How could he marry someone, perhaps even have children, if there was the chance said children would suffer from his affliction? No, far better to maintain the monkish lifestyle to which he'd become accustomed.

And yet, as her lips opened shyly beneath his, as she leaned into him, other parts of his body waged war against his well-thought out plan. He wanted to inhale her, to absorb her, to touch and caress every part of her soft, delicious, and strangely unafraid body. He deepened the kiss, his tongue flicking out to taste her mouth. Would she run in fear now? Reject him for this depraved behavior? His heart constricted at the thought.

She made a soft sound, half sigh, half whimper, and opened her mouth more fully. Their tongues wrapped in liquid embrace, and he ran his fingers into her hair, clutching her to his body.

The logs in the fireplace settled, and the crackling noise startled him back to reality. He broke off the kiss and stepped away, his fingers going to his mouth.

"I—" he began, but stopped. What could he say? He wanted to apologize, to beg forgiveness for his brutish behavior. He wanted to kiss her again. He wanted her to think him awful, so he wouldn't be tempted by those heavenly eyes and luscious mouth. He wanted her not to despise him, not to reject him like so many others. What was wrong with him? The surge of emotions overwhelmed him. He needed to run, to flee, to clear his head. Again.

"Don't worry," she said as she moved toward the door. "Your . . . secret . . . is safe with me."

"Secret?" He whirled to face her again. *Damn.* She had seen. She'd seen his tics. Of course she'd seen. How could she not, with how he'd been carrying on?

She touched his arm briefly, the lightest bit of reassurance. "It was a pleasure to meet you, Your Grace."

With that, she exited the room, closing the door behind her.

CHAPTER 6

*G*race leaned against the wall, her racing heart robbing her of breath. She'd nearly fallen from her seat when he'd burst into the library. She'd hoped to have the room to herself, to read and to avoid the crush of people in the main ballroom. She'd get an earful from her mother later on, perhaps her sisters, as well, but she hadn't had it in her this evening to engage in small talk and smile and simper.

She'd finished several of Aesop's familiar tales and started *The Count of Oltranto* when the door had whipped open and the devil himself had entered. Not the true devil, naturally, but that man, Malford. Damon Blackbourne. So sinfully handsome in all that black, and with such a look of wrath on his face. Was it any wonder she at first believed Lucifer himself had come calling?

And then the poor fellow had had some sort of fit. What else could she call it? His fists had clenched, his cheeks had spasmed as he'd attempted to control his body, but his neck had jerked and his whole form had seemed to pulse to an unheard rhythm.

Perhaps she should have been frightened, witnessing him move in such a way. Her old nurse would have crossed herself and whispered against demons. But Grace wasn't scared. Instead, sympathy had burst upon her for this large man fighting what appeared to be a hard battle. The desperation in his eyes when he'd finally seen her, like that of a cornered deer, had mirrored the entrapment she often felt.

But this man was no meek deer. He was the panther she'd first thought him to be, sleek and black, untold power hidden in those ferocious blue eyes. And then he had pounced, kissing her when she'd least expected it. She ought to have been outraged, she supposed. He had no business being so familiar with her person. And yet, he'd given her a choice. He would have stopped. She'd sensed his momentary hesitation.

What had come over her? It wasn't as if she'd never been kissed before, but this kiss had been different. Somehow, in that instance, it had felt right. *Maybe Mama is correct. Maybe those novels* do *have a bad influence on me.* She exhaled. It wasn't as if the man was Fitzwilliam Darcy, despite his brooding demeanor. She didn't know him at all—he was as likely to be a scoundrel as a hero. Wasn't he?

She'd heard of him before tonight, of course. Emmeline had regaled them with tales of the mysterious new Duke of Malford, returned from the grave. Nobody knew where he'd been or what he'd been doing these last seventeen years.

There was no doubt he was a Malford; those blue eyes gave it away. He looked a great deal like his mother, actually. What had happened? Why had he been away?

"Some say he went mad and was locked up in an asylum. Or was banished for unnatural acts," Emmeline had exclaimed in the carriage.

"What kind of acts would those be?" Grace hadn't been able to help herself; she'd had to ask, merriment crinkling her cheeks.

"A lady never speaks of such things."

"Especially when a lady knows not what those things are."

Matilda had hushed them, but that hadn't stopped Emmeline and Rebecca from whispering amongst themselves.

With those rumors and the violent physical convulsions she'd witnessed, why hadn't she been frightened? Grace didn't know. Her instinct had been to soothe, not to scream. The poor man had seemed lost and bewildered. As she so often did herself.

And then that kiss. She traced her lower lip with her finger. To her surprise, part of her—a large part—wanted to go back into the library and kiss him again, to experience once more the electricity, the magnetism that had flowed between them for one brief moment.

Smoothing her skirts, she made her way to the main ballroom, grateful the door behind her hadn't opened and the mysterious Malford hadn't emerged. She adjusted her hair, which his hands had loosened from its pins. The man would not appreciate her sympathy, nor her vision of him as some sort of wounded animal. Men preferred to be viewed as strong and invincible. Lord knew her father had never admitted fault.

"Grace! Where have you been?" Rebecca rushed to her side. "You're missing all the fun. I've danced with Lord Brisbane and Lord Evensham, as well as Lord Emerlin. And what of the Duke of Malford? Clad all in black, like a vengeful spirit. And that skull pin!" Rebecca shuddered. "You missed it. He nearly came to blows with his uncle in this very room!"

Grace frowned at her sister. She hadn't seen whatever

altercation Becca referenced, but still. "A vengeful spirit? What nonsense! The man is in mourning for his father and brother, you goose. I was right here and saw him myself. He's as human as the rest of us."

Rebecca dismissed the subject with a wave of her hand. "If you say so. Did I tell you Lord Emerlin has asked to waltz with me? Two dances in one evening. Mama will be so scandalized!"

She grabbed Grace's hand and pulled her through the crush, weaving toward the other side of the room, where Emmeline stood with her friend, Lady Adelaide. It took every bit of Grace's willpower not to look behind her, to see if her duke had appeared.

DAMON SANK into the settee in front of the fire, threading his fingers through his hair. What had just happened? He'd come into the room seeking respite and refuge, a place to let his body have full rein. And had ended up kissing the most heavenly female he'd ever laid eyes on.

Had Hobbes been here, he surely would have greeted such an assertion with a snort. "It's not as if you've spent much time around women, living in that God-forsaken abbey," the man would likely have said.

Regardless, no one had caught his attention the way the little mouse reading in the library had.

Mouse? Where had that come from? She was no mouse; she was a beauty. A lioness. But something in her quiet demeanor, not to mention that she'd been hiding in the library, suggested she didn't consider herself such. He'd guess she far preferred a quieter, simpler lifestyle. Or was that hopeful thinking?

He shook his head. What had gotten into him,

imagining a nice, quiet life, with a nice, quiet wife? With *Grace Mattersley* as his wife? Good God, the unsettling events of the evening—of the past months—were clearly having a most deleterious effect. They'd unbalanced him. There was no other reason he would be thinking of Grace Mattersley as an option, much less a marriageable one.

But she wasn't afraid of you. She saw you, really saw *you, and wasn't afraid.*

"That doesn't matter. By tomorrow, my uncle will have spread the tale through all the corners of London," he muttered. Even if families still welcomed him into their homes—an homage to his very respectable mother and sisters, no doubt—they would never entertain the thought of one of their daughters marrying him. It just wasn't done.

He sank lower in the settee. How long could he hide before his sisters got worried? Or worse, how long before some incorrigible rakehell tried something as atrocious as kissing one of *them* in a darkened room? Damon scowled. It had been some time since he'd had to think of anyone but himself. He stood up, adjusting his waistcoat as he reluctantly prepared to rejoin the ball.

Duty called.

CHAPTER 7

REXBOROUGH BALL, LONDON
EARLY APRIL, 1814

*G*race tapped her foot, impatient as the strains of a waltz started up. She was ready to return home. She'd been ready an hour ago, but hadn't wanted to make a fuss and drag her sisters away. They were enjoying themselves. No doubt Emmeline had danced with nearly every young buck here and Rebecca had hardly lacked for partners. Grace had refused all requests, making such excuses as she could. Now she stood against the wall, watching the hands of the large, ornate clock at the north end of the room. How much longer would she have to stay?

Malford had reappeared after their library encounter, but did his best to avoid her. Or perhaps to avoid people all together. He'd occasionally check on his sisters and then disappear again. To where, she wasn't sure. If she ventured to the library, would she find him there again?

What was wrong with her? She shouldn't be watching for him. This wasn't her normal behavior, daydreaming about a mysterious man. *Kissing a man wasn't normal behavior, either, and that didn't stop you.*

Chastising her inner devil, she crossed her arms, glowering at the dancers. A young gentleman who'd been making his way to her stopped mid-stride at her expression, the confident smile draining from his face. He turned and walked the other way.

She put a hand to her lips to stifle the giggle threatening to escape. Who knew she had such power as to halt a man in his tracks?

A slight clearing of the throat came from her right side. She looked up into the Duke of Malford's fierce face. It was far more likely that *his* dark expression had sent her potential suitor scurrying, not her own meager grimace.

"Might I have the pleasure of this dance, Lady Grace?" He gave her a gallant bow and held out his hand.

All attention was riveted on Malford. And her. Her skin prickled, no doubt flushing that horrid puce she detested when she found herself the object of scrutiny. She should refuse him, should not risk more interaction with him this evening. Her mother's nearly apoplectic expression, visible from across the room, confirmed it.

Grace had never been the type to defy societal expectations. Not openly, at least. While her inner thoughts often ran wild, her outward appearance, her behaviors in polite society, were never such as to stir up commentary. No scandal had ever been attached to her name, unlike her sister Amara.

Dancing with the Duke of Malford would no doubt alter that, especially as no one had seen them introduced.

A noticeable hush fell over the room. Goose pimples erupted on her skin. She loathed being the center of attention. She should refuse him and end this.

But doing so would surely draw *more* attention. Unfavorable attention. On him. He hadn't asked anyone else to dance, she was sure of it. And she wasn't about to shame him with a public rejection, not after what he'd endured.

Plus, dancing with him meant she could touch him again. And, oh, how she longed to touch him, to prove this was real, not an imaginary dream. She'd kissed this man. She *wanted* to dance with him, truly wanted for the first time ever to waltz with a man.

Exhilaration burst through her, the sweet sizzle of defiance catching her off guard. Let them talk. She would accept. She would show kindness to this man. Surely no one could fault her for kindness? And if they did? Let that be on them.

"With pleasure, Your Grace," she replied, placing her hand in his.

His nostrils flared and his eyes widened.

If only she'd answered with some other word. Pleasure brought his kiss back to her—as if she would ever forget it—and her breathing hitched.

His lips twitched into a sly grin. Before she could say anything, he swung her into position, his hand around her waist, his other hand clasping hers. He held the correct amount of distance between them—no one could accuse them of impropriety, beyond the scandalous nature of the waltz itself—and yet she felt as if she were on fire, as if they were the only two people in the room, as if she'd melt into a puddle on the floor should she stop looking into his eyes. Quickly, she turned her head toward the other dancers.

"Chicken," he teased, gripping her hand more tightly.

Across the room, her mother held a hand to her throat, horror etched across her face. Emmeline swung by in the arms of some marquess or other and winked at her. A most inappropriate laugh threatened to burst forth at such disparate reactions from two of the people with whom she was closest in the world. She bit her lip to keep it from escaping, startled when Dam—*Malford*—made a noise, almost like a groan.

She looked up at him. He had closed his eyes, but opened them again, piercing her with the full force of those magnetic blue circles.

"What is it about you, Grace?" he said, shocking her with the use of her Christian name. Had he noticed his error? He whirled her into the next turn, deftly maneuvering her around the other dancers.

"You dance quite well, actually," she blurted out.

His body tensed and his eyes cooled, although he didn't release her.

"For an uncultured savage, you mean?" he bit out. "It amazes what one can learn watching one's sisters' dance instructor, if one puts his mind to it. And they've borrowed me often for practice these last few months." A harsh sound, almost a bark, escaped him. "So you see, wild dogs *can* learn new tricks."

"That's not at all what I meant. Not in that way, at least. I know you've had a different upbringing. But surely you know that is not your fault." She tilted her head. "To call yourself a savage seems unduly harsh."

He gave what she could only term a snort and looked away. "Don't you know? Don't you know of me? I thought everyone knew how my father, my mother, sent me north because I was rotten. Evil to the core."

Now it was Grace's turn to snort. "I'm sorry, Your Grace, but your trials and tribulations have perhaps played a larger role in your life than in mine. No, I have not heard much of you before tonight."

That wasn't exactly the truth, given her sisters' conversation in the carriage. Plus, a week or so past, Emmeline had read something in the daily paper about a duke returned from the dead, who'd grown up in the north, even though his family lived west of London.

Grace hadn't paid attention to the details, however. She'd been immersed in Shakespeare's sonnets and had tuned out her sister's incessant prattle, as she often did.

Malford stared at her, nonplussed. She'd surprised him. Good. Why she took delight in that, she didn't know. But she did. Likely he was used to being the one to set people off balance.

"In any case," she added with a casual wave, "I set no store in gossip. I'd rather hear the truth from the horse's mouth."

He chuckled, an unexpected but pleasant sound. "You're calling me a horse?"

Grace's face burned. "Of course not. You know what I meant."

He nodded as the music ended. "Indeed, Lady Grace. Too bad. I rather fancied myself a thoroughbred."

"Or a stubborn ass."

Her hand flew to her lips. She'd said that aloud? How her mother would chastise her; women did not speak so plainly in the company of gentlemen. They certainly ought not to speak so rudely. Before she could utter an apology, Malford threw back his head and laughed, a burst of amusement that drew every eye to them again.

He bowed before her, delight crinkling his eyes. "I appreciate an honest woman," he said, raising her gloved hand to his lips before pressing a kiss to it. "Thank you for the dance."

With that, he strode toward the ballroom entrance, signaling his sisters and calling for his coat.

Grace watched him go, despite everyone gaping at her. Surely they were wondering how she, the notorious wallflower, had snagged the attention of such a man. And what had she said to make him laugh so?

She twirled a curl with her finger. Let them wonder. It wasn't their concern, anyway.

CHAPTER 8

BLACKBOURNE HOUSE, LONDON
APRIL, 1814

A grin crept onto Damon's face the next morning as he sat for breakfast at Blackbourne House, the Malford town house in Hanover Square. He buried his head in the papers lest his sisters notice, but they were too busy chatting about the ball to pay attention to him.

After his sisters exited the room, his mother approached, dressed from head to toe in severe black, a black that mirrored his own garb—though each wore it for different reasons.

Despite being in mourning, Felicity Blackbourne had insisted on accompanying the family to London. "I shall refuse all social events," she'd said. "But I want to be there to show my support for Damon as head of this household. As Duke of Malford."

She paused now before him. "Damon." Her voice cracked. "I'm sorry for what happened yesterday evening with Fillmore. Cassie told me. I did not know he would be present. The last I knew, he was still in Bath. We do not communicate much."

Damon nodded before turning back to the paper.

"And I am sorry," she added, her voice catching, "for all of it. For your father. For not doing better by you. For what you suffered."

Did she mean the beatings at his father's hand? Or his own movements and rages?

Did it matter? The only reason he hadn't completely closed himself off to his mother was she had written. Not often, but enough to show she still cared.

She'd never visited, though. No one had. Blackwood Abbey had long festered as the neglected Malford estate; it was cavernous and run-down, and so far north that nobody had wanted to bother with it in years. As it was not a manor on which tenants depended for aid and protection, but rather an old abbey dissolved during the reign of Henry VIII and given to some Malford duke or another, it had languished, attended to by a skeleton staff, for the last two hundred years.

He nodded stiffly, unsure of what to say. She had made other overtures in the last few months since his return. When he hadn't responded much one way or the other, she'd shrunk back into herself, taking refuge in her mourning for Silas and Adam. She'd made sure the steward devoted hours to instructing Damon on managing the Malford estates and the details of the dukedom, but had mostly kept to herself.

Tears filled her eyes and one streaked down her cheek. He reached and wiped it off, blue eyes meeting blue. More tears spilled out as she sobbed.

"I . . . I wanted to be stronger, Damon. I wanted to keep you here. But a part of me thought perhaps it would be better for you away. He wouldn't . . . he couldn't beat you if you weren't at Thorne Hill. I had hoped that for you it would be easier, without eyes always on you."

Damon swallowed. He'd never thought of it from that

angle, that by sending him away, his mother might have actually thought she was helping him. He'd only felt the hurt, the pain, the devastation resulting from the ultimate rejection, that of a child by his parents.

It was true that once in Yorkshire, he'd had freedom he'd never known. No one had beaten him. No one had mocked him. If the servants had, it had been behind his back. But frankly, he doubted it. They had taken to him, delighted to have someone new in their midst. A master.

Mrs. Hardy, the housekeeper, and her husband, Joseph, who'd served as a jack-of-all-trades at the abbey, mending items and caring for the few horses, had taken him under their wing and become his surrogate parents, more loving than any he'd known. Especially his own.

"I want you to know—I *need* you to know that I am sorry. So very sorry. I don't ask that you forgive me, but you need to hear this: I accept you fully, as Duke and as my son. In the few short months since your return, you've mastered everything thrown at you, excelling in all aspects. I am proud of you."

She swallowed and his throat bobbed likewise, a surge of emotion flooding through him. But before he could respond, she spoke again, her fingers fidgeting with the lace at her sleeve cuffs. "I'm worried, Damon."

"About what?"

"About Fillmore. About what he might do. He was so angry last autumn to hear you were still alive. And that you were coming home. He seemed to think he would become the next duke after the passing of your father and A—Adam." A sob choked off his brother's name.

Damon rose and enfolded her in a brief, awkward embrace. "Rest assured, I do not fear my uncle. Men like him, all bluster and no action, are two a penny."

His mother ducked her head as he released her, worry creasing her brow. "I hope so, my son. I hope so."

Chapter 9

*H*ad it truly been a week since the Rexborough ball? A week since Grace had kissed a man—and not any man, but the Demon Duke himself, Damon Blackbourne, Duke of Malford?

Not that he was any sort of demon. She knew better than that. All week long, her sisters had discussed the gossip around him, tidbits they'd gleaned from the papers or from their morning calls. Some said he'd killed a man as a boy and that's why he'd been banished. Others claimed his mother had cuckolded his father, who couldn't bear the sight of her bastard son, so he'd sent him away. Far-fetched rumors insisted he turned into a bat at night and stole the souls of young virgins. She had struggled to hold her tongue at such tripe.

But hold her tongue she had. Her family would take immediate notice if she talked about Malford at all. They'd questioned her enough after the ball. How had she known him? Why had he wanted to dance with her? About what had they conversed?

She'd simply shrugged, ignoring the first two questions. "We talked of the mundane things everyone speaks about: the London weather, the health of the King, the theater."

None of that was true, of course. Thoughts of the duke streamed through her mind at inopportune times, but she had revealed nothing in the days since. Her sisters would mock her mercilessly, given how often she teased them about pining over potential suitors.

"Do you not know?" her mother had cried the morning after the grand event. "Do you not understand the scandal this could cause? What notion did you take into your head to accept *him* after refusing all others? You must not do so again. Indeed, no, you must avoid the Duke of Malford at all costs, for your sake as well as the family's. Think of your reputation. Of *our* reputation."

Grace's mother had carried on for another several minutes, though Grace had ceased listening.

She adjusted the bonnet on her head, shaking off remembrances of her mother's endless chastisements. She took great pleasure in reliving that evening as often as she could in her mind. Surely that was typical behavior for someone who'd experienced such a kiss? She was allowed ruminations, wasn't she?

It was a fruitless yearning, however. As exciting and, yes, handsome as the man was, he was not suitable. Of that she was well aware, especially given her mother's lecture after the ball. Her family would never approve of such a fellow—he was too unknown, too wild, too much of a black sheep.

Perhaps that's why you keep thinking about him, silly goose; he's exactly what you could never have, so it's easy to let your fancy run free. There's no possibility of anything becoming real.

It wasn't as if her family couldn't endure scandal. Her eldest sister, Amara, had suffered greatly for her illicit tryst in a garden with an engaged gentleman. But she and the family had weathered the storm, Deveric having done his best to minimize the damage. Then Amara had run off with a sea captain last summer, to everyone's dismay. Yet the Mattersleys had carried on, though Matilda was quick this time to lay blame at the absent Amara's feet, lest her actions taint her sisters' prospects.

Had it worked? The only one of her sisters who'd married was Cecilia, a number of years ago, though even the youngest, Rebecca, had been out for two years already. Rebecca, like Grace, professed no rushed desire to marry—but what of Emmeline? She, at least, made no bones about desiring a match.

"I haven't found anyone to my liking," Emmeline had declared with a toss of her head at the end of last Season, but a touch of sadness had lingered in her eyes.

Both of her sisters had had a steady number of dance partners at the Rexborough ball, however, much to her mother's visible relief; if gossip still abounded about the Mattersley family, it seemed not to have dimmed the women's prospects. Not that a dance a marriage proposal made.

When Grace's eldest brother had married their distant American cousin Eliza two years ago, there'd also been talk. No one had known of Claremont cousins in America, and Eliza's mannerisms and way of speaking were considered odd. But with her bright, happy personality, she'd quickly endeared herself to everyone who met her. It hadn't taken long for Deveric to fall deeply in love with her.

The match had delighted Grace and her sisters. Deveric had suffered much during and after his first marriage. Their mother, however, had not approved.

At least at first. Matilda Mattersley may not have accepted the American upstart right away, but they'd reached peace with each other, especially given the changes in Deveric. He was no longer the overly solemn, rigid man he had been. For that Grace was also thankful.

She missed Eliza. If only the American were here in London. But Eliza hadn't wanted to subject Isabelle and her older siblings, Frederick and Rose, to the London air or the bitterly cold weather that had enveloped the country.

Eliza staunchly defended Grace's love of books and her desire to write, and for that reason and many more, Grace loved her. Eliza was as much a fan of novels as Grace and they often discussed *Sense and Sensibility* and *Pride and Prejudice,* two most excellent works Grace herself had read countless times.

Eliza had met the author, a Miss Jane Austen, in London some time ago. Although Miss Jane did not wish it widely known she'd penned those works, preferring instead to publish them as being written by "a Lady," she'd welcomed both Eliza and Grace into her home at Chawton. They'd spent several comfortable afternoons chatting with each other.

Someday Grace, too, wanted to write novels. Oh, she couldn't match the wit of Miss Jane Austen, but to put pen to paper, to create characters so intimately familiar and yet so different, to control the happenings and morals of her own tales? Nothing sounded more thrilling.

"Are you ready?" broke in an eager voice from behind her.

Grace turned to find Emmeline hopping down the stairs, her cheeks already ruddy despite the fact they hadn't yet stepped foot outside.

"I am so excited," Emmeline continued, without

waiting for Grace to answer. "Aren't you excited? I so love visiting the Egyptian Hall!"

"Even though you were there just last Season?"

"Indeed! I am sure there are many new things." Emmeline's expression grew dreamy. "Can you imagine? Visiting *Egypt*? La, everything there is so *exotic*."

Grace pursed her lips. "I suppose. But did you ever consider that to the Egyptians, *we* might be the exotic ones?"

"That's silly. We are the most civilized society on the planet."

"Tell that to the ancient Romans."

Emmeline batted her on the arm with her gloves as Rebecca entered the room.

"I don't suppose we could ride horses in Hyde Park?" their youngest sister asked in a wistful voice.

"Tomorrow," Emmeline said. "You've promised all week to accompany me, and so you shall!"

AFTER AN HOUR looking at Bullock's curiosities, Grace wished to return home. Not that the objects and the animals weren't intriguing, but her head ached and she relished the idea of a short lie-in. With a good book. A new book, perhaps. They were close enough to Hatchard's; surely her sisters wouldn't mind if she disappeared down the street for a few minutes.

"I shan't be gone long," Grace insisted.

Emmeline frowned. "At least take Mary; you know very well you cannot go alone." Mary was Rebecca's personal maid, who had accompanied the women to the Hall as per their mother's request.

"Then *you* shall be without a maid," Grace protested.

"Yes, but Rebecca and I shall still be together, safely

in this Hall, whereas you cannot possibly venture out onto London streets unaccompanied. It isn't done."

Grace sighed as she headed out the door, Mary close behind her. It wasn't done. It *wasn't* done. Oh, what she wouldn't give to be a man sometimes. Men could go where they wanted when they wanted, instead of following such silly rules of convention. Grace knew the rules were there to keep women safe—unsavory types occasionally preyed upon ladies in town, even ladies of good repute, if they were on their own. But from here to Hatchard's, in the middle of the day? Mary, at least, was wise enough to follow at a short distance behind as Grace moved at a rapid, angry pace, no doubt not wishing to disturb the Mattersley daughter's fit of pique.

Upon entering the beloved bookstore, Grace paused to inhale the smell of the books. Her eyes feasted on the shop's rich offerings, the sumptuous leather-bound volumes, the plainer pamphlets, the maps. Mr. Hatchard nodded in greeting; Grace was a familiar presence in his shop.

"Good afternoon, Mr. Hatchard," she called out, her good mood restored now that she was among the rows of books. "Have you got anything new for me today?"

Mr. Hatchard smiled. "Yes, Lady Grace, I believe I do. Have you read Frances Burney's new novel, *The Wanderer?*"

Grace clapped her hands in excitement. "No, indeed, but I would surely like to. I did so enjoy *Camilla.*" She raced toward the volume the shop's proprietor extended to her. As she reached for it, she stopped, hand in mid-air.

A gentleman stood in the back of the shop, dressed head-to-toe in black, his finely tailored coat enhancing the breadth of his shoulders, the leanness of his middle. She swallowed. Surely it couldn't be?

The Duke of Malford looked up from the book in his hand and tipped his hat in Grace's direction.

"Good afternoon, Lady Grace." He flashed her a devilish grin.

"Good afternoon, Your Grace," she responded automatically, though her heart began to race. What was he doing here? Did he know? Did he know how he had affected her? How she had thought of him every day—and night—since the ball? How she had thought of that kiss?

She was as moonstruck as Emmeline's friend Lady Adelaide Guernsey over a man. And oh, how she hated it. Heat rushed to her cheeks even as she broke off her gaze, looking fixedly at Mr. Hatchard. Thankfully, the bookshop owner made no comment regarding her flustered behavior.

Malford sauntered over to her. "What have you chosen, if I may ask?"

Surely he'd heard Mr. Hatchard? Why was he asking such an obvious question? "Um, the latest by Frances Burney. I doubt you would know of her."

His eyebrows knit together. "Why ever not?"

Grace gulped. He could and most likely *had* misconstrued her comment as an attack on his education. Having grown up in Yorkshire, he'd not attended Eton, much less Oxford, as most noble sons did. Why did she continually make such *faux pas* in his company? "Because her stories mostly appeal to women, I think."

"Tsk tsk, Lady Mattersley," he responded, a gleam again entering his eyes. "I greatly enjoyed her *Camilla*, although I rather preferred *Cecilia*, to be honest."

"You've read Fanny Burney?" Grace wanted to bite her lip over the inanity of that comment. What was wrong with her?

Mary moved into her line of sight, the maid's curious eyes watching the exchange. If only Grace could send the girl away. She did not want anyone observing her reactions to the Duke of Malford, spots of pink no doubt illuminating her cheeks, considering how they burned; the flustered movements of her fingers as she clutched the book in her hands; the way her breathing had accelerated to the point where it must be noticeable.

Drat it all, why must Mary and Mr. Hatchard be here? Or perhaps the better question was, why must Malford? The feelings he aroused in her were nothing like she'd ever felt before—and quite a bother, truth be told.

Mary moved several inches closer.

Malford ignored the maid, his sole focus on Grace.

"There wasn't all that much to do at Blackwood Abbey," he confessed, looking directly in her eyes. "At least it had an excellent library."

"Oh, that sounds wonderful."

His brilliant blue eyes lulled her, mesmerized her.

"It is. Rows upon rows of books of every sort, fiction, history, economics, law. I daresay it could rival Hatchard's. No offense intended, sir," he added, nodding toward the shop's proprietor.

"None taken, Your Grace. It was always my honor to serve your mother when she frequented the shop."

"That explains the trunks of books which made their appearance twice a year. I suppose I should thank her for that, at least." His smile did not reach his eyes.

Mary stepped forward. "Mi—milady. Perhaps we ought to return to the Hall?"

"Ah, the faithful maid here to rescue her lady from the evil wolf." He grinned so widely that his incisors did, in fact, render him rather wolfish.

He tipped his hat to them both. "It was a pleasure,

Lady Grace. I myself am off to read Lord Byron's *Corsair*. I hear it is quite the tale. A youth rejected by society because of his actions."

His grin faltered ever so slightly. His eyes looked sorrowful. Grace longed to comfort him, but any action on her part in front of Mary and Mr. Hatchard would most definitely be noted. She didn't need stories making their way back to her family.

"Indeed," was all she could think to say. "I should be going. Good day to you, Da—Your Grace."

His eyes dropped to her mouth for a second before he passed by and walked out the door.

"It is now," he called over his shoulder. "A good day indeed."

CHAPTER 10

WHITE'S CLUB, LONDON
MID-APRIL, 1814

 week later, Damon stood outside White's on St. James's Street. He'd never been in, although naturally he'd heard about the famous gentleman's club as a boy.

Having spent the greater portion of the day listening to his sisters discuss the merits, or lack thereof, of nearly every member of the *ton*—for his edification, his mother had insisted—Damon thought nothing sounded better than an evening in the company of gentlemen who would leave him alone. He'd considered staying at home and hiding away in the library, but he had the sneaking suspicion his sisters would have found him even there.

His mother assured him he was a member of the exclusive club. She'd called in a favor from the Duke of Arthington, whose father had been an old family friend, to secure the thirty-five members' approval necessary for membership.

It must have been some favor, to overcome my reputation. The Demon Duke, indeed. Well, he could play the role. Doing so would likely keep others at bay, anyway—if, indeed, anyone wished to approach. Adjusting his cravat, he climbed the few steps and confidently crossed through the entrance, seeking solitude and solace for a few hours.

Inside, a number of gentlemen loitered—many sat alone, reading the paper while sipping on some sort of alcohol. Brandy or whiskey, no doubt. Others bantered back and forth over games of cards. As he walked through the main room, smatterings of conversations about horses and guns and certain debutantes echoed around him. Younger bucks compared notes as to which houses boasted the best female companionship in all of London. At this, he gave a wry grin.

No one paid him much attention. Oh, a few eyes had looked up when he'd walked through the door, but by and large he was left to himself, discretion and privacy a welcomed code at White's.

Settling into a chair, he had opened Byron's book to read when a gentleman from across the room approached. "Pardon me, Your Grace," the man said. "I do hate to be so forward, but do you remember me?"

Damon looked the man over. Sandy brown hair, hazel eyes, a friendly expression. Nothing familiar. "I'm sorry," he said. "I'm afraid you have the advantage, sir."

The man nodded. "It's been years; I understand. I'm Peter Wainscott, of Delview Manor."

Delview Manor bordered Thorne Hill to the east, didn't it? An earl, perhaps? Or a viscount? Damon clenched a fist, pressing it into his thigh. He should know his own neighbors, shouldn't he? Then again, learning the basics of the estate, the ins and outs of polite society itself, had swallowed up all of his time while he'd been at Thorne Hill.

"Viscount Huntington," the man added, his expression hopeful that that might help.

"Again, my apologies. It's been a long time since I've been . . . south."

Why was he apologizing? He outranked the man. Still, guilt rode him that this Huntington recognized him, whereas he had no memory of the man.

Lord Huntington grinned, a friendly gesture that set Damon somewhat at ease. "I understand. I didn't suppose you might recall, but we used to play together as boys. Occasionally, when your family invited mine to dinner."

A vague memory hit Damon of a snowball fight and tunneling through snowdrifts with a sandy-haired boy long ago. "I remember a snow castle . . . " he began.

"—Yes." Huntington nodded enthusiastically. "Remember when we pelted my sister, Julia, with snowballs? I thought your father was going to thrash the both of us."

He did. At least me. Later on, once you'd left. Shaking off that bitter thought, Damon gave a wan smile.

"Anyway, I was delighted—astonished, really—to hear you were back," Peter pressed on. "I was so saddened to hear that you had died, and, well, obviously—" He faltered.

"Obviously I hadn't."

"Yes, right." Huntington cast his eyes at the fireplace, his fingers fidgeting with the edges of his waistcoat. "My condolences on the loss of your father and brother."

None are necessary. Not for my father, at least. "Thank you."

"If you would care to join us, we're playing whist." Huntington motioned to a table of men in the corner.

Damon was about to decline the invitation—he truly did prefer solitude this evening—when a man sitting in a chair near the gamblers caught his eye.

His uncle.

Fillmore Blackbourne's attention was riveted on Damon, fury purpling his face. The man gripped a tumbler of dark liquid in his right hand. His knuckles were so white, it was a wonder he hadn't shattered the glass.

Huntington cleared his throat, drawing Damon's focus again. The viscount looked to Damon's uncle, then back to Damon. "Perhaps I—"

"Please, return to your friends. I'm afraid this is not the night for me to join you."

Huntington's face relaxed. He was no doubt grateful to have been excused, especially as Damon's face knitted itself into a snarl.

"Perhaps another time," the viscount said before moving off.

Damon merely nodded, no longer paying attention to his childhood companion. His eyes fixed on his uncle, who rose from his chair and approached him with a rather unsteady gait. The man was clearly in his cups.

"*You!*" his uncle shouted as he neared his nephew. "You shouldn't be here. This is a club for refined gentlemen. Not for the devil himself."

Damon remained sitting. "The devil himself? You do me too much of an honor, Uncle." His voice was calm, disinterested, even, but his blood boiled with rising anger in the face of this attack.

"*Get. Out!*" Fillmore roared, his face heavy with rage. "You have taken everything else from me. You may not take this!"

A man to Fillmore's right put his hand on Fillmore's shoulder. "Lord Fillmore," the man said in a quiet but firm voice. "That's enough."

Fillmore shrugged off the man's hand, glaring at the newcomer. "He is an usurper. A monster! You should see! You should see him when he is possessed. A demon inside that boy, I tell you! He should have stayed in Yorkshire. He should have *died. I* am the one fit to be Duke, not he!" Flecks of spittle flew from Fillmore's mouth as he shouted for all the room to hear.

Damon rose from his seat and stood nose to nose with his uncle, or rather nose-to-balding-head, given the man's shorter stature. The muscles in Damon's neck spasmed, the urges to jerk nearly overwhelming him. But he would not. Not here, not in front of this man. He took one long, deep breath, drawing himself up to his full height. He towered over the older man.

"Say another word, Uncle, and you shall meet me at dawn. The only reason I have not called you out already is because of my family. *Our* family."

Fillmore's face paled. *Coward.* His uncle looked down at the glass in his hand. Taking a quick gulp, he set it on the table next to where Damon had been sitting. With a final glower at his nephew, he stalked toward the door, guided by the man who'd checked him a moment ago.

So much for peace and quiet, and anonymity. Well, he hadn't exactly been unknown upon entry, but at least he'd been left alone. Now the focus was on him, although a few gentlemen returned to their own activities at his stare. He looked at the book in his hand. Why bother? There was no respite here, not now.

The man who'd escorted Damon's uncle to the door reappeared. "Arthington," he said, extending his hand to Damon.

Ah. James Bradley. The Duke of Arthington. The very man who'd gained him access to this club.

"Malford," Damon answered. "But then, I suppose you already gathered that."

Arthington nodded. "An unfortunate incident," was all he said.

Damon immediately liked him for that; it was clear

the man was offering him privacy and not expecting any further explanation.

"Yes, well, perhaps it was too much to hope to be accepted here," Damon said before he could stop himself. Damn, that was not the kind of thing to admit to a stranger. But his emotions were roiling, his anger increasing toward his uncle, toward his father, toward this life he'd been denied and now wasn't sure he wanted. He clenched his fists as the familiar urges assailed his body anew. *No. Not here. Not now.*

"Nonsense," Arthington said, flashing his slightly crooked teeth in a grin. "Would you care to join my friend Emerlin over there—" He gestured toward a tall, waifish man with a shock of black hair. "—and me? We are bound for Watier's."

"Thank you," Damon said, genuine appreciation curling through him, even as he focused on controlling his body. "Another time, perhaps. I must be going." He tipped his head at Arthington, who returned the gesture.

"Anytime," Arthington said as Damon strolled out the door.

Once outside, Damon sucked in huge gulps of the nighttime air, willing his body and his mind to settle. Turning north, he walked, counting and re-counting to the sum of eight as he went. When that didn't work, he broke into a run. If anyone were paying attention, they'd no doubt remark on the peculiar behavior of the Duke of Malford. Better to incur gossip for running than for head spasms that would surely mark him as a candidate for Bedlam. He pushed his body to its limit as he raced through the narrow back streets toward Hanover Square.

Running had always helped. Something about putting all of his focus and energy into placing one foot in front of the other, of pushing his heart and lungs to the brink, forced his mind to let go, to calm down, to give up the urges to move in other, less regular ways. He'd discovered that in adolescence, when the movements had been at their worst.

He'd thought at first they'd worsened because of the shame, the pain, the guilt, the despair, and, yes, the loneliness at having been banished from his home. From his family. His siblings. His mother. The frequency of his bizarre movements, his need to control and organize his surroundings, had increased exponentially in those first few months. But after a while, he'd noticed patterns. Or perhaps not patterns, exactly, but a rhythm. There were times when the need to move plagued him not at all, and times during which nothing helped except to let his body do what it needed to do. Sometimes the movements seemed connected to his inner state; other times not.

He'd wondered at times if his father were right. Maybe he was possessed by demons; maybe he was plagued by devils. What other explanation could there be for these bizarre behaviors and thoughts with which he suffered? He'd even thought at times, in the worst of the dark days, those long cold winter nights with no companions except a fire and a book, that perhaps he would be better off dead.

Then it had begun to improve. Why, he didn't know. Was it because he'd found ways to cope, ways to soothe the manic body rhythms? Running worked. Reading often worked, too, as long as he was absorbed in the material. And animals. Animals in particular soothed him like nothing else, and he'd spent many a happy hour at the abbey with the stable hand's dogs and the stray cats that hovered about.

His heart pounded as he rounded the corner to Hanover Square and came to the rear entrance of his town house. At the mews, he cursed. He'd forgotten about his carriage. He'd have to send someone for it.

He bent over to put hands to knees as he gulped in large amounts of air. It had worked, though, this fierce physical punishment; his control had returned. As he strode through the rear entryway, still breathing heavily, a loud meow hit his ears.

Cerberus, his three-legged cat, charged down the hallway at him. His mother wasn't fond of having animals in the house, particularly in London, but Damon had insisted. If he must be here, attempting to live up to his new title amongst people he didn't know, people inspecting his every action, he at least needed the one thing that adored him completely, no judgment, no reservations. He leaned down and scooped up the cat, which lavished head butts on his chin.

The animal had appeared out of nowhere one day, lounging about on the front steps of the abbey as if he owned the place. From that day on, he had.

The ease with which the feline got around was surprising, considering his lack of a front leg. It was unclear if the cat had lost the limb in some sort of injury or had been born that way. The absence had never slowed Cerberus down, however; the cat acted as if he were every bit the equal of his four-legged brethren, undaunted by any challenge that crossed his path.

It's exactly what Damon had needed; a fellow companion who was different, but lived life as if he were the same as everyone else. Such a regal feline, with his long, black hair and piercing amber eyes, had deserved a moniker on par with his bearing. Cerberus, the name of the three-headed dog who guarded the gates to Hades, seemed appropriate for a three-legged cat, somehow. And amusing.

The cat followed him everywhere, even on runs, although by far his favorite activity was curling up in Damon's lap in Blackwood Abbey's vast library. Leaving

Cerberus at the abbey once he'd received his mother's summons simply wasn't an option.

The cat lapped at the sweat on Damon's neck, and he chuckled, setting the feline down.

"I know," he said, as the cat watched him with those wide amber eyes. "I need to bathe."

Walking farther down the hallway, he whipped off his coat and waistcoat and called for servants to draw him a hot bath.

"Tomorrow," he muttered to himself as he climbed the stairs to his chambers. "I will run again tomorrow. I should not have given that up."

Fillmore's face, veins popping with fury, leapt to mind. The man clearly bore a monstrous grudge against Damon. It seemed quite possible he might resort to violence to achieve the end he'd wanted so long ago. Damon would have to remain on the alert.

He paced the length of his bedroom as he waited for the servants to fill the large bathtub in the dressing room beyond. When the knock came to signify all was ready, he shed his clothing without waiting for Hobbes (he'd never liked the idea of a valet dressing and undressing him, anyway) and slid into the steaming hot water, sighing in relief as the aches and stresses of the day oozed out of his pores.

His head back, he studied the chocolate brown walls. A boring, staid color. No life to it. Unless it was the rich, chocolate brown of a certain Grace Mattersley's eyes.

He hadn't seen her anywhere in the past week after their two brief, although intense, encounters. Then again, he'd attended few social affairs. Having Cousin Daphne in town, and her mother's sister, Aunt Martha, to serve as chaperone, had provided his sisters with another social outlet, letting Damon off the hook, thank goodness.

It was a relief not to have to rub elbows with the *ton* every evening, especially since he remained an object of great interest. On the other hand, solitude had its drawbacks. One of them being that a certain chocolate-eyed, well-read mouse was nowhere to be found.

Cerberus plodded into the dressing room and leapt onto a stool to the side of the bathtub. The cat stared at the water disdainfully, as if wondering why anyone would ever subject himself to such torment, then began cleaning its face.

"I miss my mouse," Damon said to the cat, which ignored him as it groomed itself. *Or I miss the game of cat-and-mouse.* Their encounter at the bookstore played in his head—and, without question, the unexpected kiss at the Rexborough ball.

It was strange to think so often of a woman. Of one woman in particular, in any case. Even in the wilds of Yorkshire, Damon had garnered plenty of female attention.

"It's the eyes," Hobbes had often commented with a roll of his own. "Or maybe that wicked grin you wield."

In his youth, Damon had a few times enjoyed the charms of a certain dairymaid from the neighboring farm. In recent years, however, he'd mostly kept his distance. He didn't need the complications women brought—not with his affliction. Still, the village girls had sought his attention, giggling when he'd passed. Until they'd heard the rumors about him.

The same had happened in London at first—appreciative glances from ladies of all ages. But tales of the Demon Duke must have spread quickly, spurred on no doubt by his uncle. Debutantes might still watch him out of the corners of their eyes, but their mothers ensured their daughters gave him a wide berth.

As an eligible duke, young and with all his teeth to

boot, his mother had sworn he'd garner a plethora of female attention. His sisters, too, decreed he'd be fought over in the marriage mart.

Not that he wished to marry.

But, still, their predictions had proved wrong.

On the streets, men and women either stared openly or, more often, avoided his gaze. It wasn't so much the cut direct, perhaps, since he tended to avoid eye contact, as well. Not out of shyness or uncertainty, but because he had better things to do with his time—and his mind— than worry over the silly workings of London society.

But Grace was different. She hadn't been scared of him, even in the library, even when he'd tried to intimidate her. He'd thrown her off balance in the bookshop, appearing where she'd likely never expected to see him, but still she'd held her own. There'd been enough time for her to hear the stories about him, if she hadn't known them already. She could have refused to acknowledge him, could have excused herself immediately. She hadn't. Most surprising, with her, Damon didn't feel judged on his eccentricities. She'd seen them and still interacted with him, still seemed as affected by him as he was by her.

With her, he felt electric. On fire. Alive.

Perhaps it was the mouse that had captured the cat.

CHAPTER 11

HYDE PARK, LONDON
LATE APRIL, 1814

*G*race set down her pen and straightened her back, relishing the view of the Serpentine. It was a bit chilly to be in Hyde Park so early in the morning, but she'd needed to get out, to escape for a while. At home at Clarehaven, a small lake nestled in the northern corner of the estate, and she'd often ridden there to find solitude and write. The inner grounds of Hyde Park, though not as remote, had proven surprisingly quiet, given the hustle and bustle of London. It was a place she'd found much to her liking.

She hadn't come by herself, naturally; a maid was situated nearby, along with a footman, but as the two seemed quite engaged with each other—the young serving girl kept making calf eyes at the marginally older footman—it almost felt as if she were alone. Oh, how she relished the quiet, broken only by the delightful birdsong of a few thrushes, tits, and finches. Occasionally, a horse nickered—someone out for a morning ride along Rotten Row, perhaps—but for at least a little while longer, she could imagine she had the park to herself.

A family of ducks made its way out of the water onto land, the mother anxiously ensuring each baby followed along in line. Occasionally, one of the tiny ducklings attempted to hop to the side, but its efforts didn't last long, as the mama duck quacked at it and nudged it back in place.

Oh, little duckling. You and I are kindred spirits, both desiring a different path but forced into a straight line, following along dutifully with our siblings.

Not that, as the privileged daughter of a duke, her given path was a difficult one. She'd seen enough from the insides of her carriage of the unseemly side of London life, had read enough tales of woe, to be grateful that was not her lot. But if only her life weren't so prescribed. She was expected to comport herself properly at all times, marry well, manage an estate, and produce male heirs. Nowhere in there were allowances for wanting to pursue other passions.

Wife and mother. Those were to be her primary occupations. Her own mother had seemed perfectly content raising her brood of children. Indeed, two boys and five daughters, as well as the entire Clarehaven estate, was quite a household to manage, even with help from nurses and nannies.

Grace ran a finger over the edge of the paper, the corners of her mouth tipping down. Seeming content and being content were often two entirely different things. And when it came to marriage, Matilda's unhappiness had been evident in her rigidity, in the dourness that had permeated the entire family. Especially after their father had opted to spend more and more time in London, leaving his wife and children at Clarehaven.

Their father had taken a mistress in London, perhaps more than one. He'd indulged freely in women and spirits, living the dissolute lifestyle commonly accepted among male members of the *ton*.

She looked out over the waters. That was one of the reasons she had little interest in marriage, unless she could form a true love match, like that of her brother Deveric and Eliza. Or of Darcy and Elizabeth.

Unbidden images of Damon flooded her brain. His dark, tousled hair, his piercing blue eyes, the sharp edge of his jaw. How striking he was in complete black. It wouldn't surprise her to learn he always dressed thusly, in mourning or not. It suited him, giving him a dangerous air. An air he seemed to welcome. An air that fed the flames of imagination of those around him. The Demon Duke.

"The Demon Duke, indeed," she said with a huff. Perhaps he dressed so, acted so, because it kept people at arm's length, where she suspected he preferred them. He didn't truly think himself possessed, did he? Emmeline had giddily related the tales Fillmore had spouted the night of the Rexborough ball—tales of Damon's fits that had overset Grace's mother.

But not her. Though he'd manifested his anger in physical ways with the tossing and jerking of his body, that didn't mean anything, did it? Deveric often leapt upon his horse to pound out his own emotions. Needing a physical outlet was not so uncommon for a man.

In any case, it hadn't frightened her to see Malford in such a state. Why, she didn't know. Perhaps it should have.

A baby deer limped out of the woods nearby, the mother not far behind, keeping a watch over her offspring. The fawn must have been injured at some point, though it hobbled along determinedly. Malford reminded her of that deer, a wounded animal needing tenderness and care.

One of Deveric's dogs had been caught in a trap once at Clarehaven. The poor animal had lain there, wounded and bleeding, in desperate need of help, but anytime anyone had tried to near it, it had snarled and snapped with all the ferocity it had, preventing anyone from coming to its aid. Deveric had had to shoot it to put it out of its misery.

Damon was like that snapping and snarling dog, although he didn't show it. He maintained that stoic, uncaring façade. But she had seen it. She had seen the inside, however briefly, and it made her want to hold him, to tell him it would be all right if he'd let people help. Let her help.

She closed her eyes. Whom was she kidding? Why should it be she who could help, she who disliked the crush of society nearly as much as he did? *Because I understand it.* The war within oneself. That desire for love and acceptance so at odds with the need to be one's true self.

The mother deer and the fawn disappeared back into the woods. Grace glanced at the paper on which she'd written precious few words, then to her maid and the footman. She caught only the flash of a dress hidden partially behind a tree, and heard a giggle, then a telling silence.

She should probably chastise them. They were supposed to be accompanying her, protecting her. But who was she to begrudge them momentary happiness? The memory of Damon's face, so close to hers, and then his lips caressing hers, danced through her brain again. A silly grin crossed her face at how cautious his touch had been, though he'd set out to intimidate her. If he were a demon, he was a gentle one.

A crunching along the nearby foot path startled her out of her reverie, and she turned to find none other than the Duke of Malford running down the path at full speed. Alarmed, she hopped up. Was someone pursuing him? He ran right past, then stopped and reversed, breathing heavily as he nodded toward her.

"Why, good morning, Lady Grace." He paused to gulp in more air. "I, er, would not have expected to find you here."

Her forehead creased in alarm. "Are you all right, Damon? Is someone chasing you?"

His mouth quirked up at her use of his Christian name, an accident on her part, given her concern and the fact that she'd just been thinking of him in rather intimate terms.

He brushed the hair from his forehead, which was beaded with moisture. "I am quite fine, I assure you, *Lady Grace*," he said, teasing evident in his address. "I enjoy exercise. I find it calms my mind and body."

The rapid rise and fall of his chest eased into a more regular rhythm. He wore only breeches and a black shirt—no waistcoat or overcoat—and rather plain black shoes similar to those her footman wore. The sparseness of his attire, plus the sweat that molded it to his skin, rendered the lines of his physique readily apparent. A shiver ran through her at the leanness of his legs and his narrow hips. She jerked her gaze to his arms, startled by their surprising muscularity. Perhaps he boxed?

A chuckle escaped him. "My eyes are up here, Lady Grace. Though you are welcome to look all you like . . ."

Horror dropped her jaw as her cheeks burned with embarrassment. She opened her mouth, but nothing came out. She'd been caught red-handed ogling a man.

The side of his mouth twitched into a wicked grin. "As long as you return the favor," he added, dipping his gaze pointedly to her chest.

Grace laughed. She ought to be outraged and chastise

him for being less than a gentleman, but that hardly seemed fair, given she'd just openly admired the leanness of his middle.

"Of course, you *are* wearing more clothing than I." He gestured to her pelisse, his eyebrow crooking up mischievously. "You could always remedy that."

Grace's mouth fell open once more. Was she truly standing in Hyde Park exchanging potentially suggestive—no, make that overtly suggestive—conversation with the Duke of Malford? She, who'd always been somewhat of a wallflower, however voluntary the wallflower position had been?

Had the maid and the footman noticed her interaction with Malford? She glanced in their direction. No trace of the maid's skirt remained. Grace's eyes widened. Had something happened to the pair?

"Don't worry," Damon said. "They are happily entertaining each other. I could see as I ran by." He winked at her. "I averted my eyes to give them some privacy."

Grace giggled. She actually giggled. Giggling like a silly schoolgirl was something she'd never been prone to. She rather detested such behavior, actually. And yet here she was, giggling as if she were one of the many vapid young debutantes she despised.

"They ought to be keeping an eye out for my welfare," she managed to say once the laughing fit had subsided.

"True." Damon's eyes darkened. "But if they were here, I couldn't do this." He strolled forward, slowly enough to give her plenty of time to back away. She didn't. When he stopped, mere inches from her body, a surprisingly pleasant smell tickled her nose. A very masculine smell. He stood, his eyes locked with hers, waiting to see what she would do.

A wise woman would back away, would break the

tension. Young ladies of the *ton* did not engage in salacious behavior, much less in broad daylight. They weren't doing anything salacious, however. Yet. Her eyes traveled over his face, taking in the deliciousness of his high cheekbones, the devilish arch in his brows, the ferocious intensity of his blue eyes. Eyes that bored into hers.

Her breath hitched. Surely he wasn't going to kiss her, not here, not in the morning light where anybody could happen upon them. Verbal play was one thing, but a physical encounter would be every bit improper. She should take a step back. She should move, break away. But it was if his eyes held her captive. His own breath caught as he lifted his hand and ran the backs of his fingers along her cheek. Her lids closed at the softness of his touch. Memories of the library flooded back, of his lips on hers. Oh, if only he would lean in and kiss her anyway, the consequences be hanged.

Her eyes flew open at the boldness of the thought. His squinted in amusement, as if he knew what she was thinking. Then his attention dropped to her lips, a hungry look on his face. A hunger matching hers. Thank goodness she wasn't the only one affected.

He dropped his hand but didn't move back. Neither one said anything.

"Milady?" broke in a voice from a near distance. Startled, Grace turned to her left, where the maid stood, her hair slightly mussed. The footman stood next to her, uncertainty written on his face.

Grace's hand flew to her lips. She backed away from Damon, avoiding his eyes. "I—I—" she stammered.

"Lady Grace is fine," Damon said, stepping away as well. "We were merely discussing her—" He glanced down at the pen and paper on the ground. "Writing."

The maid nodded hesitantly at her mistress.

"Tis fine, Dora," Grace agreed. "His Grace and I are acquainted."

Dora turned back to the footman and they moved off a short distance, granting Grace a modicum of privacy.

"I owe you an apology," Damon said in a soft voice.

"Whatever for?"

"For speaking to you so baldly before. It is not how a gentleman treats a lady. I beg a thousand pardons."

Grace's skin erupted in goose bumps at thoughts of their earlier conversation.

"I am unaccustomed to dealing with ladies. Much less those of your high status." He exhaled, running his fingers through his hair. "It is clear," he started, then broke off, turning his head away. "It is clear I do not comport myself well around you. I shall not trouble you with my presence again."

Before Grace could say a word, he turned and ran down the path, his legs flying as if all the Hounds of Hell were chasing him.

CHAPTER 12

LAMSHILL BALL, LONDON
EARLY MAY, 1814

*T*wo weeks. It had been two weeks since he'd seen her; two weeks since that morning in Hyde Park, when he'd wanted nothing more than to strip her down naked and lie with her in the soft grass.

What had Lady Grace Mattersley done to him? He hardly knew her, and yet he thought of her all the time, of her luscious brown eyes, intelligence sparkling in their depths. Of her soft manner. Of her matter-of-fact, less volatile approach to the world.

Maybe she wasn't as composed as she appeared. He'd flustered her in the park, to be sure, with his ungodly behavior, and even in Hatchard's, her hands had betrayed some level of agitation. Though she'd hardly batted an eye at his strange movements at the Rexborough ball.

She showed no fear of him. Why was that? Others had always given him nervous glances, at least at first, though thankfully not the servants at Blackwood Abbey.

When the movements had been at their worst, when

he was perhaps twelve or thirteen, Mrs. Hardy, the abbey's housekeeper, had steadfastly ignored them, treating him as if he were the same as any other boy. She'd rarely acknowledged, in fact, that he was master at all. He'd loved that about her; that to her, at least, he was no better—and no worse—than anyone else. It was a heady feeling after his father had drilled into him for so very long that he was a Malford; though he may not be the heir, Malfords behaved in certain ways. Malfords were better than those around them. And Damon was every kind of evil because he was not living up to the family name.

Tonight was another grand ball celebrating Napoleon's surrender and abdication to Elba. Damon had wanted to beg off, but his sisters had their hearts set on attending and Daphne's aunt had taken ill. He would have to chaperone.

Would Grace be there? He half hoped she would, half hoped she wouldn't. He'd studiously avoided events he'd thought she would likely attend as he tried to wrestle his emotions under control. Why on God's Earth had he spoken so explicitly to her in the park?

On the other hand, she *had* been investigating his body. And had laughed along with the conversation. Still, he'd been careful when he'd gone running to avoid the place in which he'd last encountered her, in case she returned to write again.

What did she write? Journals? Letters? How *did* noblewomen spend their time? His sisters evidently found plenty to do to occupy themselves. Social calls took up a great deal of their days, as did shopping. Damon enjoyed neither venture.

Besides running in the Park and reading his books, he immersed himself in managing the estate, in understanding the accounts, and in planning future investments. Thank heavens that, for all his other faults, his father had done a decent job with keeping Thorne Hill not only solvent, but also prosperous. Bookkeeping and estate management were proving more pleasing than Damon had thought possible. The organized rows of numbers and logical calculations soothed the part of him that craved order.

His brother, Adam, however, had griped in his infrequent letters at the responsibilities he'd been expected to assume.

"I've never been clever at sums. Not like you, brother," he'd written on more than one occasion. "How do you do it, adding so quickly in your head?"

Numbers had always come easily, unlike many other things. Physical self-control, for one. Even as a boy, Adam could sit still for hours. Not Damon. He had to move, to utilize his limbs. He had to release the energy, lest it do so on its own in other, less acceptable ways. A difficult dilemma here in London, given he was bound to encounter persons he'd much rather avoid if he took to the streets.

Once or twice he'd returned to White's, glad not to have encountered his uncle a second time. According to Cassie, Fillmore's gout had flared up once again, and he was homebound. Damon couldn't say he was sorry. The man was detestable, an unpleasant reminder of Damon's very unpleasant past.

While at White's, he'd spent a pleasant evening with Arthington and his friends: the Marquess of Emerlin, the Duke of Cortleon, and the Earl of Stoneleigh. They'd whiled away the hours talking horses and books—topics on which Damon could expound. And politics. Damon cared not for it, but as a duke, he needed to learn.

Each man proved surprisingly pleasant. None pried into his private affairs, but welcomed his opinions as he gave them. He'd actually enjoy spending time with any of them again.

"When Claremont returns, we shall have to go carousing. Engelsfell, too." Arthington clapped his hand on the table for good measure at his assertion.

Damon went still. Claremont? These gentlemen knew Claremont? Grace's brother? It shouldn't have surprised him; the *ton* wasn't all that large of a group, and the men and women of similar age a smaller circle still.

"You think Her Grace will let her husband go carousing?" Emerlin's mischievous grin revealed dangerously charming dimples. No doubt the ladies went wild for him.

The Earl of Stoneleigh took a swig of his drink. "You think he would want to? Unlikely. He only wants to be with his wife and children."

"Ah. You have me there," Arthington said. "Deucedly bad, this marriage thing. Though if one has to marry, may it be someone as lovely as Claremont's American."

"Hear, hear!"

They each drank a toast to that, though Damon had no familiarity with this Duchess of Claremont. The Duke, however, was evidently besotted with her.

Fueled perhaps by the brandy, Arthington shared numerous tales of Claremont's sisters. Amara, the eldest, had endured some sort of scandal, though now she was married and gone. Cecilia had married some time ago, and she and her husband rarely came to town. All four men agreed Emmeline could charm the most dissolute rake while trying to marry him off to someone or other at the same time.

"And Lady Rebecca's knowledge of horseflesh rivals my own," Emerlin said, his eyes growing soft when he spoke her name. His mouth twisted, however, when he added, "Though she is of such tender youth."

Neither gentleman mentioned Grace. She remained an enigma.

"And the Lady Grace?" Damon had to ask. How could he not? The beauty was always on his mind.

"I am not well acquainted with her." Arthington said. "A bluestocking, I believe. Always with her nose in a book."

"Nothing wrong with reading," Lord Emerlin broke in. "It would behoove you to give it a try, Arth."

Arthington cuffed his friend on the head, eliciting chuckles. Arthington and Emerlin's friendship was obviously a deep one.

Ah, the privilege of knowing someone cared about you that much. He and Adam had had that, as children. Being ripped from Adam had hurt as much as being torn from his mother. More, perhaps, in that he'd played with Adam on a daily basis, whereas Felicity Blackbourne had often busied herself with other matters.

He grieved for his brother. He truly did. Not because of Adam's recent death—they hadn't seen each other for seventeen years, after all. No, he grieved for what had been and what now would never be. They'd exchanged the occasional letter, but Damon had not known Adam, the man. And Adam had not known him. When their father was dead and Adam was Duke, they'd welcome him back into the family. Adam had said as much in his last letter.

So much opportunity lost. Though could he ever fully forgive them for exiling him to the north? At least they hadn't forced him into an asylum or had him killed, as had been Fillmore's wish. And still was, apparently.

A shout from the street pulled him out of his reverie and back to the sights and sounds of London passing by the carriage window. His sisters sat across from him, conversing with Daphne, who sat to his side, but all three paid him little regard, used to him being lost in the depths of his own mind.

The coach came to a halt outside a grand mansion on the edge of Grosvenor Square. *Who was hosting this ball again?* No doubt every other member of the *ton* knew exactly whose home this was. As the door to the coach opened and his sister Cassie made to step out, she whispered, "The Earl and Countess of Lamshill."

How well she was getting to know him, to realize he'd be at a loss. Names didn't stick in his head well, not like numbers, especially when there were so many different titles attached to them.

He followed the women out, nodding to the coachman, who drove off to stable the horses for a few hours while the ducal family was in attendance.

Lights blazed from the front entrance, a thousand or more candles in chandeliers casting a yellow glow on the attendees gathered below. Ladies in similarly styled dresses—some of colorful hues, but many more of the pastels and whites he was coming to loathe—chatted in small groups as the butler announced the new arrivals.

"His Grace the Duke of Malford, the Ladies Cassandra and Persephone Blackbourne, Miss Daphne Blackbourne," the butler dutifully intoned as Damon and his female companions entered the ballroom. All eyes moved to them, but lingered for a shorter amount of time. The scandal of his appearance was dying down. Thank God.

His sisters greeted acquaintances, exclaiming at each other's gowns, though they all looked the same to him: white muslin after white muslin. Numerous young bucks eyed his female relations; he'd better not go far, especially as a particularly bold lothario walked up to Sephe and not so discreetly ogled her bosom.

He stalked toward her, ready to call the man out, but

Sephe was already delivering a sharp rebuke. The would-be Romeo cast a dark look at her, one that turned to fear when he spied Damon, and slunk off to the other side of the ballroom.

"Glad to see you can fend for yourself, sister," Damon said.

"Indubitably," Sephe replied, casting him a sweet smile. "Which means you needn't hover all night long. I will be fine. We shall be fine. We know what not to do."

"Don't disappear with a man into the gardens, don't let a man escort you alone to a different room in the house, don't dance with the same man more than twice in the evening, and maintain a proper distance in the waltz at all times, if indeed one dances a waltz at all," Daphne rattled off in a monotone. She looked around the room, thereby missing Damon's amused grin.

"Seriously, brother. Go and enjoy yourself," Sephe insisted. "Play cards. Dance. Speak with, I don't know, a woman. Live a little. You spend far too much time cooped up in the study at home, or in the library. I've never known anyone so immersed in books as you."

He did.

GRACE PINCHED her nose between her fingers, wishing for the hundredth time she'd stayed at home. She'd considered pleading a headache, but her family would have seen right through it.

"You only get headaches when it's time to go somewhere," Emmeline had pointed out just last week.

So Grace had dutifully dressed in her favorite ball gown, one of a pale green hue with darker, bolder green embroidery enhancing the hem and bosom. She'd always been partial to green. *Until you saw eyes of a blue lighter than the sky.*

She brushed the thought off, then touched her hair, which Bess had styled into a flattering chignon, with wisps of hair curled to frame her face. She had even agreed to a dollop of Rigg's Liquid Bloom for her lips, though nothing heavy enough to merit disapproving comment.

Would this Season never end? It had been one social event after another. Theater outings, afternoon tea, carriage rides along Rotten Row, and balls. This was the third ball in two weeks, and she'd scream if she had to dance one more minuet.

She should give it an effort. Her mother so dearly hoped this would be the year she made a match. And a number of the gentlemen were pleasant enough. She'd danced with Lord Ratheby last week and Lord Derwood earlier tonight. They'd been able conversationalists and had even expressed admiration for novels. Both men were clearly interested in furthering their acquaintance, especially since Lord Ratheby had come calling unexpectedly that very morning. Grace *had* used the headache excuse then. He was a fine man. He just wasn't a particularly interesting one.

Blue eyes under swooping black eyebrows popped into her mind. She pinched her lips and shook her head, attempting to shake the image loose. She hadn't seen Malford since their encounter at the park. Was he avoiding her? Or had they simply not attended the same functions?

She shouldn't care. Given his actions in the library and his speech in the park, his intentions weren't honorable—if he had any sort of intentions toward her at all. The man didn't seem to know what to do with her; half the time it was as if the Devil himself were trying to seduce her, the other half as if he couldn't wait to get away from her.

Emmeline danced past with Lord Tarrington—their second dance of the evening. Emmeline's eyes flashed and the young viscount watched her every move.

Grace sighed. It was all so confusing. Why couldn't she be interested in the right sort of fellow, if she had to be interested? Or better still, why couldn't she leave it all behind and return home to Clarehaven, to her spot by the lake, where she could create characters and weave stories that ended exactly the way she wished them to?

Because there was clearly no controlling the Duke of Malford. And even if . . . even *if* he expressed a more formal interest, her mother would never approve. Under normal circumstances, a duke would be a more-than-ideal match, a coup, in fact, even for the daughter of a duke. But not *this* duke. Not the Demon Duke.

More whispers and gossip about him had reached her in the recent weeks. Some said he'd shot a man over a card game. Others, that he rode a beast of a horse pell-mell through Hyde Park, leaping bushes and forcing spectators to rush out of his way, lest they be trampled. Emmeline's friend Adelaide insisted his eyes had turned orange and glowed in a possessed manner when he'd encountered Lady Sarah Trumble at Gunther's last week.

Grace didn't believe any of it. First off, what would a devil be doing getting ices at Gunther's, anyway? And secondly, she just knew he wouldn't intentionally harm anyone. He'd had the chance to harm her, twice, and he hadn't. He hadn't exactly behaved as a gentleman, 'twas true, but it was clear that although he might have a temper, he wasn't a violent man.

Why did her thoughts always return to the Duke of Malford? As if she knew him well enough to judge his character. As if she knew him at all. And yet she continually scanned the crowd, hoping for a glimpse of him.

Rebecca elbowed her at one point. "Is there someone special you seek?"

Grace pulled at the edge of her glove, not meeting her sister's eyes. "No. I'm merely in want of some air."

Luckily, Rebecca's friend Lady Agnes asked her something at that moment, sparing Grace further questioning.

"His Grace the Duke of Malford, the Ladies Cassandra and Persephone Blackbourne, Miss Daphne Blackbourne."

Grace's whole body tensed at the announcement. He was here. He was actually here. Her eyes feasted on him as he conversed with his sisters, occasionally flashing one of them that cheeky grin. His face turned dark, dangerous, when a young man approached Sephe. The man quickly left.

She drank him in, those long limbs and that black hair. His square jaw. Those mesmerizing eyes. How could all the other women not be looking at him, too? A few debutantes cast discreet glances his way, but by and large the room ignored him.

He probably preferred it so. He was likely as uncomfortable as she, trapped in close quarters with all these people. A kindred spirit, someone else who preferred solitude to hours in a cramped room with nothing else to do but paste on a smile and listen to endless prattle.

Or did she merely hope he were so? Had she begun to fancy him her own personal Darcy, like Eliza with Dev? Had she blurred the lines between fantasy and reality without knowing it?

"That's the danger of novels," her brother Chance had teased her last year, sometime before he'd taken his commission. "You lose yourself so much in them, dear sister, you might come to believe the characters and stories are real."

She peeked once again at Damon. He stood off to the side, arrogance and indifference writ across his face as he perused the room. He could have easily been Darcy's twin, all brooding and boredom. And discomfort.

And was she Elizabeth Bennet? Was she waiting for him to profess how ardently he admired her? She pinched herself. *Ninny*. Though Austen's hero appealed, this wasn't a fairytale and she wasn't writing the ending.

She smoothed the curls off of her forehead, curls Bess had painstakingly achieved with a hot iron. Thank goodness the maid hadn't burned her, as had happened on a previous occasion.

Perhaps she could sneak out to the gardens. She'd have to take someone, unfortunately; ladies did not enter the gardens alone. But it was unlikely any of her companions would want to leave the ball yet; it was still relatively early in the evening and the dancing had hardly begun.

The strains of Mozart echoed through the room and she closed her eyes, soaking in the beautiful sounds.

When she opened them again, Malford stood before her.

CHAPTER 13

"H—hello," she stammered. "I was . . . I was enjoying the beautiful music."

"Yes. Beautiful." His stare was intense, not acknowledging the musicians in the least.

Her cheeks burned. If only her skin wouldn't betray her every time he was in the vicinity!

He bowed formally and extended a hand. "May I have the pleasure?"

A noise came from Rebecca, still at Grace's side. Of course she remembered Grace had danced with Malford once before, at the ball a few weeks ago. Glances from those around ensured others had not forgotten, either.

It was not unseemly, however, to dance with him again. It had been only the once, sometime distant, and now once more. Emmeline's eyes flashed to hers, as if to say, *It's not the number of times. It's that you're the only one with whom he dances. And only the waltz.*

Was that true? Had he not danced with other debutantes at events she hadn't attended? *Were* there any events she had not attended, given how many invitations her mama and sisters had accepted on her behalf?

Thank goodness her mother was not here tonight; Matilda had caught a cold and had chosen to remain at home to rest. That was a good thing, as Grace engaging with Malford for a second time would likely have sent her mother into full pneumonia.

"You are not to associate with him, Grace," her mother had commanded after the Rexborough ball. "We need no further scandal to taint this family, and Malford is nothing but scandal. Those eyes. That devilishly black form." A sharp exhalation followed the words. "No, he will not do, duke or not!"

Matilda Mattersley's words echoed in Grace's mind, but they produced not the usual acquiescence, the normal retreat on her part, but rather, rebellion. Defiance. She'd spent much of her life as the dutiful daughter, a model of propriety and obedience. It'd been expected. It'd been needed, for Amara's sake and that of the entire family.

But Amara was gone. And Grace no longer wanted to serve everybody else. She wanted to please herself.

Nodding at Malford, she let him pull her onto the dance floor. Once there, he assumed the waltz position, settling himself an appropriate, perfectly decorous distance from her, and lightly positioned one hand at her waist, the other clasping her hand loosely. It was everything that was proper.

As proper as this new dance could be, at least. Many matrons still clucked about the waltz, deeming it unseemly. But more and more balls included at least one or two. Even Almack's had recently approved it.

They began moving to the music. Neither spoke a word. Grace stared at his chest, her eyes following the intricate weaving of his black cravat, the startling specter of the skull pin holding it in place. What should she say? So many times since that morning in Hyde Park, she had wanted to see him, to assure him he'd done nothing wrong. So many times she'd wanted to assure herself.

She peeked up. His eyes, bluer than the heavens, fixed on her face. He wasn't smiling. She inhaled sharply.

"I can't seem to stay away from you, Lady Grace," he finally said. His nostrils flared. She waited for him to continue, but he didn't. He watched her, devoured her, like a lion with its prey.

"I—I . . ." She swallowed. Who was this simpering miss? She may not be the most comfortable in mixed society, she may be a wallflower, but it was by choice, not because of lack of backbone. She straightened her shoulders and tried again. "I see no reason for you to do so."

The hand on her back pulled her in closer, not enough to raise eyebrows, but enough that the heat radiating off of his body enveloped her.

The corner of his mouth quirked up. "I haven't had much practice in dealing with the fairer sex, I admit." A muscle flexed in his jaw. "I shall work harder to behave like a proper gentleman in your presence."

But I don't want you to! I want you to pull me closer, to kiss me, to never let me go. Grace gasped at her own thoughts. Damon's face blanched at the noise and he loosened his grip.

"I'm sorry!" she cried, clasping his hand tightly. "It was something I was thinking, Your Grace. Not you, my lor—Damon."

Hearing his name on her lips, his grip on her waist tightened again and he drew her in until their bodies nearly touched, whirling her around the floor. Anyone paying attention now would consider his closeness unseemly. But she couldn't bring herself to restore the appropriate amount of space between them. No, not when his nearness did such queer things to her insides.

What was it about this man?

"I have missed seeing you," he whispered in her ear. "Everywhere I go, I look for you, even though I know I shouldn't. I fear you have bewitched me."

She stumbled, caught off guard by his words. Her eyes flew to his, which were hungry, wanting. Would he kiss her? Would she let him? Here in the middle of the ballroom?

He didn't. His eyes darkened, and he took a noticeable step back, restoring the proper distance between them. As the music came to an end, he muttered, "But I am not good for you. No one needs to be subjected to my demons, least of all you."

With a stiff bow, he nodded to her and walked off without another word out of the ballroom. All eyes followed him before returning to her, curiosity, pity, and judgment radiating from faces everywhere.

Grace stood rooted to the floor. What had just happened?

DAMON BRACED himself against a balustrade outside the entranceway to the garden, breathing in the cool night air. He fought the tumultuous emotions rocking through his body. He'd sworn he was going to leave her alone. He was right; he was no good for her, not with his obnoxious behavior during their previous encounters. And yet he couldn't help it. He was like the proverbial moth to the flame, though she was the one who was going to get burned.

He longed to turn around and walk back in, sweep her in his arms, and dance with her again. Or better yet, spirit her away down a dark hallway, find a room, perhaps a library, and share a stolen kiss or two. Or more. His body tightened at the thought of Grace in his arms, her dress undone, her head thrown back in pleasure. He groaned.

"Malford. Is that you?"

Damon willed his body under control. Hopefully it was dark enough in the gardens that whoever was speaking wouldn't notice the billowing of his pantaloons. He turned toward the voice. *Oh, thank God, a familiar face.* "Lord Emerlin. A pleasure."

Morgan Collinswood, Marquess of Emerlin, gestured toward the ballroom. "Too crowded for you?"

"Something like that."

Damon's cryptic answer elicited a laugh from the fellow peer, whose dark hair and light eyes reminded Damon a little of Adam. And himself. "And you?"

"A certain female is determined to secure another dance with me. As we've already danced twice together, it's best we not engage in a third. And since *no* doesn't seem to be in her vocabulary, I opted for the coward's route: escape."

A bush rustled nearby as a couple emerged from one of the garden walks. The woman's face radiated happiness, the man's complete bliss.

"I do believe we've just witnessed the betrothal of the Earl of Esslington and the Lady Beatrice d'Avignon," Emerlin whispered.

A fierce longing swept through Damon, so powerful it was as if he'd been knocked from a horse. If only it had been he and Lady Grace in that garden, he and Grace about to share the happy news.

It didn't make sense. It wasn't logical. He hardly knew her. So why was every fiber of his body drawn to her, as if she were the puzzle piece he hadn't known he was missing?

Because she had seen him. Truly seen him. And she had not rejected him—not in the library, not at the ball, not in the bookstore, not this evening, though every eye was on them. He'd never experienced such open acceptance in his life. How could he let that go?

He knew suddenly what he must do. The answer was painstakingly obvious. And terrifying. He couldn't. He shouldn't.

Demons be damned.

Fear be damned. There was only one logical solution.

Damon Blackbourne, the Duke of Malford, must go courting.

CHAPTER 14

*G*race rode home in the carriage in complete silence. Not that her sisters were quiet; they chatted gaily, exchanging notes on rumors they'd heard and social events for the next week. Grace said not a word, but nobody questioned it; they were quite used to her silences.

What they didn't know was that she was angry. Angrier than she'd been in a long time, as a matter of fact.

How dare he? How dare that oaf dive in and out of her life, pulling her in like a fish on a hook, only to toss her back at random moments? That wasn't how a suitor ought to go about things. Not that Damon was her suitor; he'd made it quite clear he wanted to be anything but.

She clutched at her pelisse as she descended from the carriage, using every bit of restraint not to stomp up the stairs and thereby command unwanted attention. She ground her teeth as she entered her bedroom and as Bess helped her out of her dress. She narrowed her eyes as she put on her nightgown, used the tooth paper, and brushed out her hair. And she fumed as she crawled under the blankets.

She stared at the ceiling. One small tear leaked out of the corner of her eye. She'd had enough of Damon Blackbourne, Duke of Malford, and his rude behavior. She wasn't going to attend to him ever again.

No, the Demon Duke was not for her.

"MILADY, you have a caller," the butler announced at breakfast the next morning. *What?* Grace normally eschewed morning calls, preferring to use the time to read or write. Occasionally, she met with friends for visits to the Royal Academy or to take tea or to stroll through one of the pleasure gardens. But she far preferred the east-facing seat in the library, where she could bask in the sun's warmth while immersing herself in what she loved most: words.

Emmeline and Rebecca looked at her, questions in their eyes. Before they could comment, before she could fret she was only in morning dress, the butler called frantically, "His Grace the Duke of Malford," as Damon sailed into the room, a single white rose in his hand.

Emmeline's eyes widened into huge circles. Rebecca broke out into a toothy grin before Emmeline yanked her by the hand toward the door. Both women curtsied quickly to Malford, murmuring greetings before racing out, claiming they had a social call across town.

Traitors.

Grace glanced at him, coolness in her eyes. She said nothing.

Da—*Malford*; she would *not* think of him by his Christian name—approached her, his expression turning from confident and eager to uncertain in the space of a few seconds. Good. He could at least sense she was less than thrilled to see him.

"Grace?" He handed the rose to her.

She took it, but commented, "The correct way to address me would be as Lady Grace Mattersley, Your Grace."

He stepped back, his head snapping up, visibly stung. Now he knew what it felt like to receive the hot and cold treatment.

"I beg pardon, Lady Grace." He paused, as if debating his next move. "I wanted a chance to explain my erratic behavior toward you. I was hoping you might consent to a ride with me through Hyde Park?" He gestured toward the door. "My barouche is waiting outside."

"I could not possibly go for a ride with you alone, Your Grace."

"Indeed not. The carriage is spacious enough for a maid to accompany you. Or your sisters, if you would like."

At that, her mouth dropped open. He was willing to discuss his behavior in front of her sisters? What was he about?

She should decline. Truly, she should. Had she not vowed just yesterday evening to have nothing again to do with the Duke of Malford? And yet, her curiosity drove her to say, "Very well. I'm sure Emmeline and Rebecca would be most pleased to visit the Park. Once we have all changed for such an outing."

"If they haven't already departed, that is."

Her eyebrow rose.

"Since they had a previous engagement. The one that caused them to run out of the room upon my appearance."

Grace couldn't help but laugh. "I have no doubt, Your

Grace, that my sisters are right outside that door, listening to our every word."

A scuffling noise and the sound of swishing skirts proved she was right. She stood, her chin firm, her resolve set. "Perhaps once in the park, we might let my sisters take in the air for a while. On their own. A maid shall come along, naturally, but she may sit up with the driver."

Mother would never approve. I shall do it, anyway. I must solve the puzzle of this Demon Duke, must know what demons chase him so.

A smile crossed his face.

"Surely riding with you in the middle of Rotten Row in an open-air barouche with a driver *and* a maid would not be objectionable," she continued. "But rest assured: I want answers." She gave him a mischievous grin before pointedly adding, "Damon."

EMMELINE ATTEMPTED to engage Damon in polite conversation as they rode to the park an hour later. His curt answers, while not impolite, soon dissuaded her and she turned instead to Rebecca, commenting on the fashions worn by the people riding or strolling past.

Damon rubbed his hands along his black breeches, his pulse racing. Nerves. Grace sat next to him, garbed now in a simple dress of a peach hue so luscious, it made him want to nibble on her, but she remained quiet, looking out at the scenery as it flew past. Other than the small smile she initially gave him, her focus remained outside of the barouche. *So much for his ability to charm.*

What was he doing? Why had he decided he needed to court Grace Mattersley? Not that one carriage ride meant a betrothal, but that was the direction in which he was headed if he continued to single her out. Which, undeniably, had been his intention when he'd arrived at Claremont House. Now, sweat beaded on his forehead and his hands itched to move. He couldn't possibly want to offer for Grace, could he? He, who'd sworn never to marry because he'd be an unfair burden on any woman?

That's what you mean to determine: whether or not you even like *her, whether she's suited to you.* He was attracted to her, no doubt about it. Being near her and inhaling her light scent, a subtle floral, perhaps violet— much less intrusive than the perfumes many other women wore—had him wanting to bury his face in her hair, to pull out the pins and let those glorious mahogany tresses flow over her shoulders. He wanted to nibble the length of her neck from her shoulder to her ear and then capture those succulent lips with his. His loins tightened at the thought, and he turned back to the conversation between Emmeline and Rebecca, desperate to keep his physical desires under control.

"I don't see why Mama won't let me ride my own horse alone in Hyde Park," Rebecca lamented.

"It's not seemly, and you know it, Becca."

Rebecca crossed her arms over her chest. "Then I cannot wait to get back to Clarehaven. At least there I have *some* freedom."

Grace made a noise at that. "I thought you were enjoying the attention from eligible suitors? Especially a certain Lord—"

"I am," Rebecca broke in, before her sister could finish the name. Flushing, she cast a quick glance at Damon. "I simply miss my horses."

"You should come to Tattersall's," Damon said. "I am sure you are a better judge of horseflesh than many men."

Emmeline's brow puckered. "Surely, Your Grace, you

know Tattersall's is an unacceptable place for a woman to visit?"

Rebecca elbowed her.

Damon grimaced. Lady Emmeline was correct, naturally. He'd never given much thought to the restrictions placed on ladies. He had enjoyed an unprecedented amount of freedom, growing up without the constraints of going away to school, much less the judgment of peers. He'd thought he'd missed out, but there had been benefits to his youth that had been denied to others, particularly those of the female sex. What a misfortune to live constantly under such strict societal dictates. His fingertips dug into his thigh. He was subject to those dictates now, as well.

"You are right, Lady Emmeline. Forgive me, Lady Rebecca. I am not yet well versed in the ways of city life."

"City living and its restrictions have never appealed to me," Grace interjected. "All these silly rules."

Lady Emmeline gaped at her sister before quickly shutting her mouth, clapping with excitement as they entered the southeast gate of Hyde Park. "I do so adore strolling through the park. It is such a beautiful place."

"With that I agree," Damon said. He had run here every morning since the encounter with his uncle at White's. It had done wonders for his physical and mental well-being. Not that these ladies needed to know his secrets. Grace turned and gave him a nod. Could she, too, be remembering their private encounter here?

"Ooh! Ooh!" Lady Emmeline exclaimed. "I see Lady Adelaide! Look, Rebecca. And Lady Jane Marlowe is with her." She waved at her friend. "Would you mind very much if Rebecca and I walked a stretch, so that we might spend time with our friends? Not that we don't enjoy your company."

Grace pressed her lips together to contain her

amusement. "Go ahead, dearest sister. I do not claim to be the best companion. Nor does His Grace seem the type to bend one's ear with mindless chatter."

Damon chuckled. "Please," he said to Emmeline and Rebecca as he signaled for the driver to stop. "I would not wish to deprive you of superior company."

As Emmeline and Rebecca exited the carriage, helped by the driver, Damon looked to Grace.

"We didn't even have to find a reason to get them to leave," she said.

The driver returned to his perch beside the maid, Dora, and set the horses into a slow walk. As the carriage rumbled down Rotten Row, Damon pulled at his gloves. *Uncomfortable things.* What to do? What to say? How *did* one go about courting? Or whatever one called this.

"Thank you for accompanying me today," he offered. "You look quite lovely."

Grace's cheeks pinked and she turned away, watching the trees for a few moments. When he said nothing else, she gave a loud sigh. "You promised to explain."

"Explain?"

"Yes, explain! You promised to tell me why you seek me out, but then once you find me, you do all you can to get away. It's as if you're playing a game of cat and mouse, and I can't say that I care for it." The words came out a whisper, but steel undergirded them.

Damon sat, nonplussed by her frank assessment. It was refreshing to have her speak so plainly, rather than wading through layers of correct behavior to determine her true feelings. Cat and mouse, she'd said. When he'd first seen her, he'd thought her a mouse. Not today. She looked him straight in the eye, no demurring miss. Beneath her shy manner lay a backbone of iron.

"You are right. The problem is, I can't explain it."

She crossed her arms and gave an actual harrumph,

much like a child angry at not getting her way.

Damon snickered. "You look adorable."

Grace glared at him, challenge in her eyes.

"I can't explain it," he said, "because I don't understand it myself. I am drawn to you, there's no denying that. But I don't know why."

Silence filled the barouche, the only sound that of the horses' feet clopping.

"You do know how to flatter a woman." Grace's mouth pinched into a wry grimace.

"That's not—what I mean is, I've spent most of my life alone. I am not accustomed to dealing with people on a daily basis, much less those raised among the rigid strictures of the *ton*. I'm adjusting as much as I can, having been with my family for a few months and now having to circulate here in London. But I don't enjoy it. I feel uncomfortable at nearly all times. Vulnerable."

Grace's eyes widened at his confession. She likely hadn't expected him to speak so directly after his previous hedging.

"I have struggled with body movements for much of my life." He studied the carriage floor as he spoke. He didn't want to see her face, even though she'd already seen his movements. If her expression turned to revulsion once he acknowledged the tics . . . but she said nothing, so he pressed on before he could stop himself.

"They were much worse when I was a child. The movements—the ticcing—came almost all the time then." He ran his fingers through his hair, seeking the strength to continue. "I learned over time that if I ran, if I pushed my body hard, they sometimes eased. Anger and fear exacerbate them."

Grace laid a hand on his arm, and he turned to her, every muscle in his body rigid. Her chocolate eyes met his. In them lay no judgment, merely sympathy. Was that worse?

When she did not speak, he went on, "As I got older, the movements mostly stopped. I don't know how or why. I thought perhaps I had learned to control them. But, as you saw, when I am provoked, they can reappear."

The whinny of a passing horse distracted him momentarily. He sucked in a breath and closed his eyes.

Grace's soft voice wafted to his ears. "I am honored you feel comfortable sharing such an intimate detail with me, Your Grace. Damon," she said. "But I still don't understand why."

"Why? My father said it was because I was possessed by the devil, that I was evil, that no person moved in such unnatural ways. He did his best to beat the demons out of me." A harsh sound erupted from his throat, halfway between a laugh and a groan. "It didn't work."

"That's not what I meant," Grace said. "I meant I don't understand why me." She ducked her head, her fingers fidgeting with a button on her sleeve. "I am not the kind of woman who turns heads. Nor do I wish to be, truth be told. I am happiest when reading or writing. People often make me uncomfortable. So when you say you are drawn to me, I struggle to understand why."

He leaned toward her, tipping her chin up with his finger until their eyes met. "You turn mine. All those other men are idiots if they don't see it." His gaze dropped to her lips. "I admit, when I first saw you, I thought you a quiet mouse. But you are no mouse. You are a lion tamer." He stroked his fingers along her cheek, reveling in the softness of her skin. Not bothering to check if anyone might be watching, he leaned in and brushed his lips against hers, once, twice, before moving back. "And I am starting to suspect I am the lion."

"A panther."

"I beg your pardon?"

"A panther is how I saw you the night you burst into the library. Dressed all in black, sleek and sinewy, with barely leashed energy and power."

"Sinewy? Is that a word a proper young English miss should use to describe a man?"

Grace grinned, her cheek creasing with a charming dimple. "I am learning, sir," she said, "that I am far less proper than I myself had suspected."

He laughed, a full-blown laugh of the kind he hadn't enjoyed in some time. "You do surprise me, Lady Grace Mattersley. And therein lies your answer."

"My answer?"

"As to what draws me back. It is exactly that; you surprise me. I may not have grown up in the midst of this society, but few things that people do truly surprise me. I find human behavior fairly predictable. But you? I'm never quite sure what you are going to say or do next."

"Do you mean like this?" She leaned in and gave him a quick kiss. Upon sitting back, she winked—*winked*—at him.

Instead of answering, he drew in close again, clasping her head between his hands before he swooped in, his lips claiming hers in an explosion of need. She gasped, then wound her own hands up through his hair, her lips opening under his as they moved together.

She tasted like sugar. No, smoother, like honey. Like the sweetest dessert he'd ever known. He couldn't get enough. He groaned as she moved a hand to the back of his neck, holding him close to her. He nibbled at her lip and she responded in kind, their breath mingling as need shot through to the heart of him.

"I do say!"

CHAPTER 15

HYDE PARK, LONDON
EARLY MAY, 1814

race and Damon sprang back from each other. She looked to the source of the voice outside the carriage, exhaling in relief. Her brother's friend, the Duke of Arthington, rode next to them on a fine thoroughbred.

He tipped his hat. "Not that I blame you, Malford, but might I advise a bit of discretion? Gossipmongers lie in wait everywhere, hoping for just such a happening as that. Luckily for you, perhaps, it is not quite the fashionable hour, and so only I have witnessed—"

He flashed Grace that snaggle-toothed grin. "That is, I witnessed nothing beyond a chaperoned young lady out for a pleasant ride."

He kicked his heels into his horse's side, touching his fingers to his hat before riding on ahead of them.

Grace spun toward Damon, whose stiff shoulders hinted at regret. *No! He would not pull away now!* Before he could say anything, she put a finger on his lips. "Don't you dare apologize. Apologizing takes away from the experience, and I shall treasure that kiss. Always."

His shoulders relaxed. "I admit, I like your plain-spoken ways. It's rare a woman would confess to enjoying such a thing, is it not?"

"It is? Wherever did you hear that? My older sister and my new sister-in-law have both waxed profusely about the delight they take in kissing their husbands." And in doing more than kissing, not that she would reveal that to a gentleman.

"Indeed?" He arched an eyebrow. "One might question the company you keep."

She elbowed him, though without any real force.

After a few moments of companionable silence, she said, "I suppose we ought to turn back now. My sisters must be wondering to where we have disappeared."

"I have a feeling they haven't given us a second thought, but if you wish to return home." He signaled to the driver.

"I don't. I would keep on riding right out of town if I could." Oh, how true. How she longed to escape the confines of London, though then she could not spend more time with this man, so refreshingly different than others of her acquaintance. Unless he came with her . . .

He pushed a piece of hair behind her ear. "Tell me of your life. I want to know what it was like to grow up normal."

"Again, sir, I am not sure I qualify as normal. But if you insist." She spoke to him of Clarehaven, of her love for reading. Of her siblings.

"I wish I'd had the opportunity to know my siblings," he said.

"I love my sisters and brothers, and they me. I cannot imagine life without them, especially being ripped away from them. I am so sorry, Damon." She paused. "Though I've never felt quite in step with them, either. I don't want the things young ladies are supposed to want, don't enjoy the things young ladies are supposed to enjoy."

"I could say the same of me."

"You don't enjoy needlepoint and harp playing and practicing perfect posture?"

He laughed, a full-bellied sound. The minutes flew by as he shared his own experiences, first at Thorne Hill and then in Yorkshire. When he talked of the vast library at Blackwood Abbey, Grace's heart pounded.

"Oh, how I would love to see it! I am already green with envy. All of those books in one place, ripe for the reading."

"You would travel to Yorkshire for the sake of a private library when there are numerous ones here in London?"

She cocked her head. "Yes, I believe I would. Blackwood Abbey sounds absolutely heavenly. The lake, the forest. The old, crumbling buildings. It seems the perfect setting for a Gothic novel and a bit like Clarehaven. Minus the crumbling, perhaps."

He chuckled. "Have you ever traveled north?"

"No. We have no relatives there, only to the west. And as a lady cannot travel on her own, I have had no opportunity. The farthest north I have ever been is Birmingham."

"A shame. There is a beauty in the isolation, the sweeping moors. Not that all of northern England is deserted. York is a thriving town."

"Did you get to York often, then? I thought you said the abbey was some twenty miles removed?"

"Occasionally. To seek new books or . . . to find companionship." He broke off, pulling at his cravat.

To what kind of companionship did he refer? Perhaps she was better off not knowing. A lady didn't ask such things.

"It sounds like you miss it." Her brown eyes shone

with sympathy. "I miss Clarehaven, too. It is so much more soothing to the spirit than the loud, dirty bustle of London."

"I agree."

"When the Season is over, will you return to the abbey? Or must you now stay at Thorne Hill?"

"My mother would like for me to reside with the family. But Thorne Hill holds many unpleasant memories for me."

Grace touched a hand to his arm. "I am sorry for the loss of your father and brother. That must be so difficult. I lost my father years ago, but my sister Amara . . ." She grew quiet. "Amara disappeared only last summer."

"Disappeared?"

"She eloped with a sea captain. The gossips had their way with that, to be sure. Though as we've heard nothing, not a single letter, I fear them drowned." Grace fingered the edge of her pelisse, pulling it closer around her, though the air was pleasantly warm. "I guess that is something we have in common, then. Scandal. And loss."

DAMON LONGED to pull her into his embrace, to have soothed the pain in her eyes as she'd talked of her sister, but he heeded Arthington's warning. The path had indeed grown more congested as they neared the park entrance again.

"I do not mourn my father," he said. "He was a horrible man. If anyone were the devil, it was him." The words were low, gruff. "And yet, I have always wondered. I know of no one else who shares my affliction. Perhaps he was right. Perhaps I would have been better served in Bedlam."

Grace gasped. "Surely you don't believe that."

"I don't know what to believe. I would like to think that I am no monster, that my father was wrong, and yet sometimes, Grace, my temper rears its head so fiercely that I scarce know what is happening. And as you know, I am not cured." His jaw clenched, aching with the longing to be a normal man, one who could pursue a lady such as Grace Mattersley without guilt or reservation.

"Perhaps there is no cure. Perhaps there needn't be. Many a man has a temper. My father did. Yet I've seen how gentle you've been with me, even when you had opportunities not to be. Even when you were pushed beyond your limits, as you said."

Lady Rebecca waved to them as they approached, Lady Emmeline at her side, still engrossed in conversation with two female companions. He nodded in return, his whole insides protesting that his time alone with Grace was ending.

"This has been a most peculiar conversation," he said. "We do not seem to observe the formalities, the politeness in topics, do we?"

She gave him one of those beautifully wide smiles. "No, indeed, sir. And for that I am most grateful."

Rebecca raced to the side of the carriage, her hand clutching her bonnet to her head. "My goodness, you have been absent for nearly three-quarters of an hour."

Grace sucked in a breath. Had it truly been so long? Would others comment?

But Becca continued as if their lengthy absence were nothing of import. "We have had the most delightful time," she exclaimed. "The Duke of Arthington stopped and let me examine his horse. We even discussed the best way to cure mallenders. He says he shall tell his stable master of the ointment I recommended."

Emmeline approached at a more leisurely pace, clearly loath to leave the company of her friends. As she followed Rebecca into the barouche, she said, "I do hope you and His Grace enjoyed your time alone, sister."

Grace's cheeks blistered, and from the heat rushing to his face, even his must have taken on a slight glow. Had Arthington said something? Surely not; he'd been riding in the opposite direction after their encounter.

Emmeline arched an eyebrow in silent question, but pressed no further as they made their way to Claremont House.

Upon arrival, Damon helped each sister from the carriage, his hand lingering on Grace's waist longer than strictly proper. He'd enjoyed himself immensely. How much lighter his soul was now that he had shared about his affliction with Grace.

His lips thinned into a line. Suppose once inside, she reconsidered and decided she no longer wished to associate with someone such as him? Suppose she had played along in the carriage and was only waiting until she could make her escape?

He flexed his hands, clenching and unclenching them. *No.* Thoughts such as those had bedeviled him his entire life. He wasn't going to give in to them now.

"It was a pleasure," he said to Grace, soaking in the beauty of her dainty features.

"My pleasure, indeed," she replied. "I hope to see you again soon, *Your Grace.*" She curtsied before him, then flashed him a rather impudent grin.

He gave her a formal bow, watching until she disappeared into Claremont House before climbing back into the barouche.

Soon couldn't come soon enough.

CHAPTER 16

CLAREMONT HOUSE, LONDON
EARLY MAY, 1814

"Where have you been?" Matilda Mattersley, Dowager Duchess of Claremont, stalked toward her three daughters, a scowl on her face.

"We were riding with the Duke of Malford, Mama," Emmeline offered.

Matilda's scowl deepened. "Why did you not confer with me before setting out with such a character?"

Grace stuck out her chin, anger rising. "What do you mean, with such a character?"

Matilda stacked her hands on her hips. "You know exactly what I mean. We have discussed this before. The Duke of Malford is at best an unknown, at worst a danger. He returns after having been presumed dead for years, without explanation? From *Yorkshire*? What could he have done to have been exiled for so long to Yorkshire?"

A shiver went through Matilda at the mention of Yorkshire. To her mother, it might as well have been the bowels of Hell.

"And his mannerisms!" Matilda went on. "Dressing all in black—"

"—He *is* in mourning, Mother," Rebecca put in.

"—Engaging in a public dispute with his uncle—his highly respectable uncle, I might add—keeping to himself. And wearing skulls. Skulls!"

"It is mourning jewelry," Emmeline said. "I have seen the like."

"Ach, be gone with you!" Matilda waved toward them, and all three women turned to ascend the stairs.

Thank goodness for the dismissal. With Grace's blood boiling this much, she'd start a row with her mother if she remained.

"Not you, Grace," the dowager called as Grace made to leave the room. "Attend me in the parlor."

Grace wanted nothing more than to ignore the order, for that's what it was, but followed after her mother dutifully, a lifetime of training too hard to ignore. Once they had entered the parlor, Matilda shut the door behind her and then whirled on her daughter.

"What is the meaning of this?" she bellowed, smacking her lips as she gestured toward Grace.

"I—I don't know what you mean."

"Oh, you don't? Lady Gilderspoon was here not less than twenty minutes ago, having just returned from a drive through the park. Do you know what she told me?"

Grace's stomach flipped, and she pressed a hand to it to steady herself. Surely that old bat hadn't witnessed the kisses she'd exchanged with Damon, had she?

"I knew it! You know exactly to what I am referring! She saw you with your hand on Malford's arm!"

Grace's shoulders relaxed. Thank God, that was all. Thank God.

"He is not suitable for you, Grace," her mother said.

Fire raced up Grace's spine. "Why ever not?" she

demanded. "You yourself have wanted me to marry for some time, to a man of appropriate station. I could hardly do better than a duke, now could I?"

Matilda's mouth dropped. "Tell me there has been no discussion of a betrothal."

"Of course not, Mother," Grace snapped. "I have only known the man a very short time."

Matilda drew up her shoulders. "You may not speak to me thusly, Grace Lavinia Mattersley! A child respects their elders."

"I am sorry, Mother. But I am also no longer a child. Besides, did you not feel the same way about Eliza when she first appeared in our lives? You were determined she would never marry Deveric, and now look at you, besotted by your grandchildren and quite warm with Eliza herself."

Matilda's face softened at the mention of her grandchildren. "That is true," she conceded. "But also different. Deveric is a man and whether we like it or not, men weather scandal better than women. Also, Eliza was a blank slate, an American with no known background. Malford, on the other hand, has quite the reputation, and none of it favorable."

"None of it? With whom have you been speaking, Mother? I have not observed anything untoward in his behavior." *Besides those two kisses.* But she would not mention those.

Matilda sniffed. "I am of old acquaintance with Lord Fillmore Blackbourne, Damon's uncle. He has told me of Malford's wild behavior as a child, of his unpredictable temper and physical . . . difficulties."

Grace folded her arms over her chest and huffed. "And you believe the word of a man who's just learned he's no longer heir to the title and its wealth? A man who would accost another in such a public setting as a ball?"

"Fillmore Blackbourne has no need of wealth, I am sure. The whole family is well off. Not that we should be speaking of such matters. It isn't proper." Matilda studied her daughter for a long while.

Grace returned the stare, refusing to be cowed.

"Who have you become?" her mother said at length. "You are not the Grace I know."

Grace walked over to the window, looking out at the street below. "Because I am not being docile and quiet, do you mean, Mama? Because I dare to speak out on behalf of something, someone, I believe in?"

Silence echoed behind her.

"I cannot countenance your acquaintance with him, Grace," Matilda finally said.

"You do not know him."

"Nor do you. I ask that you think of the family, of your sisters who are seeking suitable partners. Amara did enough damage."

Grace snorted. "What about Chance? He cut a wide swath through London society before taking a commission to fight Napoleon."

"Again, he is a man. Some things we can change, but how we were born is not one of them."

Matilda's footsteps echoed as she exited the room. Grace remained where she was for a long while, watching the carriages move along the street, men and women making their way toward whatever afternoon pursuits they sought.

"Exactly, Mother," she whispered. "Exactly."

DAMON RODE HOME, at peace for the first time in a long while. He'd truly enjoyed the ride with Grace's sisters, who were both delightfully charming in different ways. But Grace—Grace was special. Was it possible he'd found someone who could accept him for who he was? His mother and his siblings cared for him, but they were family. Blood relations. Not that the blood connection had mattered to his father.

It was too early to know for sure if he and Grace were a match, wasn't it? But they'd forged a connection in the carriage and not merely in the physical sense, although his desire for her was nearly overpowering. Her lustrous brown hair, her intoxicating eyes, that dimple when she smiled. How were suitors not beating down her door?

On the other hand, she *was* rather unconventional. Not that he had much experience with ladies, but she certainly wasn't like any other society miss he had met in his month here in London. Thank God. Other women looked at him with fear.

Or desire. A few widows and even one married woman had made overtures at several points. A casual fling would not offend their sensibilities, they'd intimated, so long as it was kept private. He had declined each offer. He was not interested in being something someone had to hide. He'd had enough of that already.

Grace was different. She had no use for the conventions and restrictions accepted by everyone else. Not that she showed that outwardly. Her behavior was impeccable, so much so that at first she blended into the background. The perfect mouse. Now he understood that was intentional; she'd rather observe than be observed, rather have the freedom to be with her own thoughts than deal with the demands of others.

How admirable that she'd found a way to be herself in such a restrictive setting as the aristocracy. Her path wasn't completely clear, however.

"I long to publish a novel," she'd confessed, "but my mother will not hear of it. She insists it isn't to be borne, a Mattersley publishing a novel, though many English women, even those from titled families, have done so."

If Grace were his, he'd let her write to her heart's content.

If she were mine.

The once-radical notion that he could form a true connection with someone and be accepted for exactly who he was no longer seemed an impossible dream. But what were Grace's thoughts on an attachment? She hadn't spoken against marriage, yet from listening to her this afternoon, it was clear she viewed it as one more restriction. Could he convince her otherwise? Did he want to?

After arriving home and leaving the carriage and horses to the care of the stable hands, Damon entered the foyer, satisfaction bringing a lightness to his step. He was almost looking forward to the dinner at the Marquess and Marchioness of Framington's tonight. Would Grace be there? Why hadn't he asked?

The lightness lasted until he rounded the corner into the library. His uncle sat in Damon's favorite chair near the window, hands on his cane, the blackest expression on his face.

"Uncle," Damon said in curt greeting. He strode to the desk and removed his gloves, pouring himself a tumbler of whiskey.

Fillmore gave him a baleful stare.

"Would you like something to drink?"

"No." His uncle shifted in his seat, careful to keep his foot elevated on the small stool in front of him. Too bad his gout hadn't incapacitated the man more fully.

Damon sat in the chair behind the desk and propped his feet on its edge, knowing that was likely to set off his uncle. Fillmore Blackbourne had never approved of such casual behavior. Damon sipped the whiskey and waited.

"How dare you?" Fillmore roared. "How *dare* you?"

"How dare I what? Exist? I suppose you should take that up with my mother and father. Oh, wait. He's dead."

Fillmore's face reddened to the point Damon seriously wondered if his uncle's head were about to explode. "How dare you cut off my funds?"

"Oh, that."

His uncle, he'd recently learned from his solicitors, had long received a sizable number of pounds from Silas annually as a form of allowance. With Fillmore owning the smaller but well-producing Arbour Manor near Bath, Damon saw no reason for his uncle to continue to need such a hefty sum. It was a drain on the Malford coffers. Plus, there was the matter of Fillmore's treatment of Damon, both then and now. It'd not only been easy to cut off the funds, he'd relished it.

Fillmore pushed himself to his feet and hobbled over to stand in front of Damon, spittle flying from his mouth as he addressed his nephew.

"I am a Blackbourne!" he cried. "More Blackbourne than you have ever been or ever shall be. It should be me managing the estates, not you, you rotten excuse for a human being!"

Damon's blood boiled. It took all he had not to rise and strike the man. "Indeed. But you are not Duke; I am. I make the decisions. And the sums you've required, especially in the last year, far exceed what could possibly be necessity. I don't know why my mother put up with the increase. I'm assuming, rather, she didn't know."

Fillmore snarled. "I am a man of honor. I settle my debts."

"Ah, so that is it. You have run up gambling losses?"

His uncle blanched. "A bad run at the tables, but my luck will turn. It always does." He leaned onto the desk, propping himself up on one hand. "I am the rightful

Malford heir. Not you. You low-down bastard. I will have what is mine."

Damon swung his feet down and stood up, bracing his fists on the desk and leaning forward so that his face was mere inches from his uncle's. "You may think whatever you wish about me, *dearest* Uncle, but mind my words: slur my mother's name by calling me such again, and you will be dead at dawn."

A cry from the entryway alerted Damon and Fillmore to his mother's presence.

"Damon," she said, her eyes beseeching.

Damon's fingers itched to close around his uncle's throat, but instead he gave his mother a stiff nod.

Fillmore backed off a step, his face paling. Beads of sweat dotted his brow. "You are the devil's spawn," he shouted, thwacking his cane across the desk. "Your father should have killed you years ago."

His mother charged in, ablaze with fury. "You will leave our home. You are no longer welcome here," she commanded her brother-in-law.

Fillmore's eyes narrowed into slits. "I will have my retribution," he vowed as he made his way to the door. "I will have what should have been mine."

Damon's mother collapsed into the chair Fillmore had occupied, tears streaming down her face. Damon remained where he was, his knuckles white against the desk from the pressure placed on them. He held still, fighting the urges surging through him. He would not twitch, would not tic. Not in front of his mother. He jerked his head once, hoping she'd not notice.

"I should have called him out," he finally muttered as he sank back into his seat, his leg bouncing underneath the desk. At least she couldn't see it. "I should have demanded satisfaction for the offense against my honor. Your honor."

"No, Damon," his mother said. "You need not stoop to his level."

"A gentleman defends his honor, does he not?" Damon snarled. "Not that I would know, having had no one to teach me."

Felicity Blackbourne sucked in a breath. "I take responsibility," she whispered, sorrow evident in her voice.

Damon slammed his hand on the desk. "It was not you, Mother. It was *him*. My father." He spat the name. "And my uncle."

"I should have tried harder, should have insisted—"

"So that he could beat you, too?"

She winced, her shoulders tightening.

"*Did* he beat you? Did that bastard beat you, too?" His voice had risen to a roar, and the muscles in his neck spasmed. *Not now. Not now.*

His mother rose and crossed to him. She laid a hand across the top of one of his, still balled against the desktop. "He is gone now, Damon. It does not matter."

"It matters to me! Did he beat Adam?" Damon paled as a worse thought hit him. "Did he beat the girls?"

"No, no, never."

"Then why?"

"Because . . . because I told him my father had also made movements like yours when he was a child. I said it to defend you, to show it wasn't your fault. To show it wasn't something evil. But it only made him angrier. He was furious I hadn't revealed that beforehand. He thought I had deceived him." She sighed. "But how was I to know? How was I to know that one of my poor children might also be afflicted in such a way? If I had—"

"You wouldn't have wanted me?" His voice caught.

She rested a hand on his cheek, her eyes growing moist. "Heavens, that is not at all what I meant. I love you, Damon. I always have. I only wish I could have spared you the pain you needlessly endured all these years. It is *not* your fault. I failed you."

Damon circled the desk and enfolded his mother in his arms. His own cheeks grew wet as they held each other. "The fault lies outside of both of us, Mother."

It lay with the true demons: Silas. And Fillmore.

CHAPTER 17

PALL MALL, LONDON
EARLY MAY, 1814

*G*race hesitated outside the entrance to Harding Howell & Company, dreading having to enter the drapers. She'd much rather visit the unfamiliar bookshop a few doors down, but Emmeline had decreed they needed new gowns. "We cannot keep wearing the same tired old things. We simply must look our best this Season."

Grace was so weary of the social whirl, the constant demands to attend the theater or dinner parties or, heaven forbid, another ball. Why did people feel the need to constantly *be* with one another? Was it so awful to want an evening or two with nothing more to do than curl up with a good book? Or perhaps even retire early instead of staying up all hours of the night?

As Emmeline passed through ahead of her, Grace lingered in the doorway, casting furtive glances down the street.

"Would you like to go?"

"What?" Rebecca's voice had startled her.

"To the booksellers. Would you like to go?"

"You know I would."

Emmeline was already fingering through fabrics, paying no attention to the fact that her two sisters still remained outside.

"Go. Take Bess. Emmeline and I won't leave the shop until the both of you have returned, and since she and I are here together, we are suitably chaperoned."

How much the restrictions placed on women's movements irritated Grace. Who would it hurt to wander down the street alone and look at a few shop windows? Surely no ruffians lay in wait on a bright, sunny afternoon, especially not in this part of town?

She'd rather go by herself, but Emmeline and Rebecca would never allow it. She looked into the drapers. Bess was now examining fabrics alongside Emmeline, and was as completely entranced. When Rebecca called her over to accompany Grace to the bookshop, Bess's face fell before she quickly smoothed it over.

Guilt settled on Grace's shoulders like a heavy shawl. If only she didn't have to pull the maid away from something she enjoyed.

What choices did servants have with their time, after all? Fewer than she did. That was a sobering thought; she lamented her own constrictions, but she faced fewer than many of the people she lived with day in and day out.

Should she stay for Bess's sake? *I'll only go for a moment or two. We'll be back in plenty of time for Bess to see the fabrics.*

"Thank you, Bess," she said.

The maid bobbed her head, and the two made for their destination.

Grace had never been in this shop. It was quaint, stacked to the rafters with books. Volumes even lay piled haphazardly in a few of the aisles. The place charmed her instantly. How had she not heard of it before?

She strolled the aisles, running her fingers over the book spines. Bess, with her permission, had opted to stay near the front of the shop. At least there, the maid could look out the window. Did Bess not care to read? The thought saddened Grace. How could anyone not love the worlds books opened up?

She pulled an ancient copy of *Gulliver's Travels* off the shelf and was thumbing through its pages when a deep voice spoke in hushed tones quite near her ear. "Lady Grace. What a pleasant surprise."

She whirled around and nearly fell into Damon's arms. He stood mere inches away, a wolfish grin on his face. Had Bess noticed him? Grace tried to peer around him, but the man was so big she couldn't see anything but his chest and shoulders, delineated nicely under a well-fitted coat. Black, unsurprisingly, as was his undershirt, though Grace suspected it was not mourning that drove his sartorial choices. He'd affixed a skull stickpin to his cravat, as usual, though this one was winking.

"Your—Damon. I didn't expect to find you here."

"We seem to frequent the same places."

"Indeed." Balls. Bookshops. The park.

Their repeated encounters shouldn't surprise her; though London was a large city, members of the *ton* and indeed those of ducal families moved in smaller circles, frequenting the same social affairs, the same entertainments. The same shops. As she and Damon were both book lovers who preferred to eschew company for the sake of printed words, did it not make sense they should find each other in a bookshop again?

She looked at the large volume clasped in his hand. "Oh, what are you reading?"

He held up the book. "Edward Gibbon's *History of the Decline and Fall of the Roman Empire*. Volume One.

I've always wanted to read the set, but we didn't have it at the abbey." He gestured toward the tome she held. "And you?"

"*Gulliver's Travels.*"

He wrinkled his nose. "Never cared for that one."

"No?" She set the book back on the shelf.

"You don't have to take my word for it," he said with a chuckle.

She walked a few steps away, running her fingers along the titles.

He followed.

His nearness was overwhelming, intoxicating, and she wanted to inhale deeply to absorb the delicious, masculine scent of him.

"I trust you." She gazed into the clear blue of his eyes.

"Those are perhaps the sweetest words anyone has ever spoken to me," he said, his voice husky. He reached forward and traced the edge of her ear before dropping his hand back to his side. "Forgive me. I cannot seem to resist touching you when I am in your presence."

Grace should make her excuses and leave. That's what her mother would want. For the sake of the family. But as she soaked in his face, his smoldering eyes, she couldn't. She didn't want to. Her fingers trembled. Oh, to reach out and caress him, to run her fingers through his ebony hair, over those admittedly devilish eyebrows, along his high cheekbones, and across those lips, those sensuous lips.

Would anyone notice? The aisles were narrow and packed with books. The proprietor hummed to himself as he filed books an aisle or two away, but she couldn't see him. Could Bess see her? She bit her lip in indecision.

"Am I disturbing you? Should I leave?"

"No, no," she blurted out. "I just . . . that is . . . my mother has forbidden me to see you."

"Forbidden? What, would she have you wear a blindfold, lest I cross your view at any given social event?" His tone was light, but the derisive undercurrent unmistakable.

"I—No. She fears your reputation might damage my sisters' chances of making suitable matches."

Damon's mouth contorted in a grimace. "That bad, am I?" He settled the book under his arm and turned to go.

She grabbed at his elbow. "I didn't say *I* felt that way," she cried.

He turned to face her, her hand still on his arm.

"I don't! You know I don't. But I don't know what to do. I don't want to hurt my family," she said, her voice softer.

He stepped back, separating them, his face shuttered. "That is something you have to decide for yourself. Whether the Demon Duke is worth the risk."

She jutted out her chin. "It's not as if we are officially courting. There are no promises between us."

He closed the distance between them instantly, leaning his head down so that their lips were mere millimeters apart. No part of them touched.

"Are there not?" His blue eyes trapped her brown ones. She dared not breathe. "Do you think I have ever pursued another woman the way I have pursued you? Do you think I have come calling on anyone else?" He scoffed. "Given my peculiarities, do you think I've ever dared to let anyone in, to share any of my secrets? Do you think I've risked that, or would risk that, with anyone else, Grace?"

She swallowed. "No," she whispered.

"Say it again."

"No," she said in a firmer voice.

He heaved a heavy sigh. "I would like nothing else

than to take you in my arms, right here and now, and show you just how much I am courting you."

His eyes dropped again to her lips and then lower. "I would kiss you, yes, but I want to do so much more. I want to run my fingers through your hair, that gorgeous mahogany mass. I want to undo the buttons on the back of your dress. Slowly. Very slowly. I want to kiss your spine after every inch revealed. I want to slide my hands in and around your sides, feel the smooth satin of your skin, feel your—"

She put her hand to his lips, trying to stop him, trying to stop the flood of images and heat his words evoked. He licked her fingers, then pulled one into his mouth, sucking on it ever so lightly. The most curious current of sensation spread through her, down to her core. She gasped.

He released her finger and stepped back, dazzling her with an absolutely devilish grin. "I do hope you are attending the Smythington ball. I look forward to dancing again with you. And you alone." Turning, he strode out of the shop without a backward glance, leaving Grace standing, her mouth agape.

"Lady Grace," Bess called, hesitancy in her voice. "Are you ready, milady?"

Had Bess been watching her with Damon? Hopefully if she had, she hadn't seen anything untoward, with Damon's back to her, blocking much of the view. But would Bess tell her sisters? Her mother?

Grace squared her shoulders. As she'd insisted to her mother, she was no longer a child. She needed to stop acting like one. If Damon Blackbourne, Duke of Malford, wished to court her, the only sound reason for her to refuse him would be if *she,* not her family, didn't wish him to.

Did she wish him to? The purpose of courtship was to

secure an engagement. An engagement which led to marriage. Marrying meant giving herself to a man, subjugating herself to his whims and desires. It meant loss of what little independence she had. Didn't it?

She'd thought so, until Eliza. Eliza and Deveric proved marriage could be a happy thing, a union of souls, each with their own freedom within the arrangement. A happy ever after not confined to the pages of a novel. But Eliza and Deveric loved each other. Mutual love was what made the difference between a happy marriage and one such as her parents had endured.

Could Grace love the Duke of Malford? Could he love her?

She was attracted to him, of that there was no doubt. But attraction was no basis for marriage. And their acquaintance had been of such limited duration, love was not yet part of the equation. It could be, however. Yes, given time to better know each other, time to form a true attachment, she might love Damon Blackbourne.

She wouldn't marry for anything less.

But what of her sisters? As much as she'd like to dismiss her mother's protestations out of hand, the harsh reality was, reputation mattered. If she were to marry the Duke of Malford, what further damage might it do to the Mattersley name? Or was it sullied enough that they needn't give it further thought?

Damon ought not to sully it, however. The Demon Duke, indeed. What rubbish. He was a fine man, a gentleman through and through—more so than many a peer of her acquaintance. People merely needed to see that, to see him in a new and different light. To give him a chance.

Like the chance they never gave Amara?

"Milady?" came Bess's voice again, closer.

"I am coming," Grace called.

How could she explain her length of time there, her dawdling, that she had no book in her hands? She looked to the nearest shelf. Damon had at some point set the Gibbon book on it. She took up the leather-bound volume. She would purchase the set for him and give it to him at the next opportunity. A single woman presenting an eligible man with a gift was unheard of, scandalous, even.

Maybe her sister Amara wasn't the only one capable of stirring things up in the Mattersley family.

CHAPTER 18

*T*he following Saturday, Grace sat patiently in front of her dressing table as Bess styled her hair into an elaborate coiffure. Normally, she read as the maid worked, without a care as to what the final result would be. Today, though, she studied herself in the mirror. How did Damon see her? She'd never given her looks much thought before. She wasn't unattractive, she supposed, but wasn't as lovely as her sisters, either. How could brown hair and eyes compare to Emmeline's lovely blonde and green? Or Rebecca's ebony and bright blue? Grace had always felt the odd one out. Though her eldest sister Amara's eyes were darker, like hers, they were shot through with a rich hazel green, and honeyed streaks laced Amara's chestnut hair, streaks Grace's tresses lacked.

It was hard to believe her oldest sister was gone. *Wherever you are, may it be a happier place, dearest sister.* Life had never been the same for Amara since being caught half-naked with an engaged bounder who'd then fled to America.

The scandal had devastated her mother, who'd vowed to do all she could to protect her daughters from anything like that again. Hence Matilda's protests about Damon. But how could her mother give credence to Fillmore Blackbourne's opinions, a disgruntled relative who insisted erroneously he'd been cheated out of a birthright that was never his?

Bess fussed with attaching a simple string of pearls around Grace's neck.

"Do you have the earbobs?" Grace asked.

The maid went to fetch them, an approving smile spreading across her face. Grace never wore earrings. She'd never seen the need. But tonight she wanted to look special. For Damon. And for herself.

"Here they be, milady." Bess helped affix them to her ears. "Do you wish a hint of Pear's for the cheeks? Perhaps Rose's lip rouge?"

Grace nodded. "Why not?"

Bess applied the cosmetics with a deft touch, so as not to make Grace appear a bird of paradise. Standing back, she let Grace examine herself in the mirror.

A beautiful young woman stared back at her. The creamy ice blue of her gown enhanced her delicate complexion and made her brown eyes glow with rich warmth. Its bodice was lower than any she'd ever worn, her breasts rounding out of the top in a way her mother would no doubt disapprove of. The dress itself was quite simple in style, but the blue had been overlaid with a sheer fabric woven with silver thread throughout. When she moved in the candlelight, the dress sparkled.

"Oh, milady, you shall be the belle of the ball! A true diamond of the first water."

Grace touched her neck self-consciously, smoothing a curl there. "I rather doubt that. But thank you, Bess. I appreciate your efforts."

Bess flushed and bobbed a curtsy. "Here is your wrap." She settled a sapphire blue shawl over Grace's bare shoulders before exiting the room.

Grace gave herself one more look before heading to meet her sisters. Giddy butterflies flitted about her stomach, and for the first time, she understood what the fuss was all about.

They arrived more than fashionably late. Emmeline had taken longer than usual to complete her toilette, and then a carriage accident had stalled them in the streets. The collision brought to mind Damon's father and brother, robbing Grace of some of the joy and anticipation of the evening. How she wished she could lay into the previous Duke of Malford for having treated a child that way, especially his own son.

Then again, were it not for the deaths of his father and brother, she and Damon would never have met. He would still be roaming the moors of Yorkshire, and she'd be trapped in this hopeless cycle of Season events, but without the pleasure Damon Blackbourne had brought to them. Guilt picked at her over her momentary spot of gratitude for the Blackbourne family's misfortune, but she brushed it away. Silas Blackbourne did not deserve her pity, not when he'd so misused his second born.

The crush was thick when they entered. Emmeline and Rebecca disappeared into the crowd, leaving Grace standing with their cousin, Margaret, who'd come to town last week to join her younger sister, Daphne.

"You look fetching tonight, dearest cousin," Margaret said. "Do you perhaps have your eye on a certain someone?"

Grace's skin betrayed her by flushing even as she deflected the question. "Unlike you, I have never been the type to seek a full dance card. With whom do you most hope to dance this evening?"

"I would not mind if Lord Emerlin were to ask me. I met him this week at a dinner party. He has eyes to dream of. And have you seen that dimple when he smiles?" She sighed. "But alas, he is a marquess. Far out of the reach of someone like me, even if I weren't already firmly on the shelf."

Grace batted her cousin's arm. "You are hardly on the shelf, dearest cousin. You are scarcely two years my elder. And you outshine many a younger woman here. Enough to capture any man's attention, marquess or not. Though I do believe he might have his eye on a particular lady already. I hope that shall not leave you too brokenhearted."

A pout soured Margaret's face. "He does? Who? Oh, never mind. Don't tell me. I shan't want to know."

"And I shan't tell you, as I am not quite sure. It is merely a suspicion."

Margaret tapped her fan to her chin. "Then it must be someone of your close acquaintance, to raise such a suspicion. Unless . . . " She gasped and whirled toward Grace. "Are you saying *you*?"

"Heavens, no." She only had eyes—and feelings—for one black-haired, blue-eyed man. And Lord Emerlin, as kind as he was, was not him.

A man of rather hefty stature but pleasing features approached the women and cleared his throat nervously before bowing. "Miss Blackbourne, might I? I mean, would you? Dance with me, I mean?"

Margaret hesitated. "I should be delighted, Mr. Foote, but I cannot abandon my cousin."

"Nonsense! I am well enough here; please go ahead."

Margaret's briefest of frowns told Grace she'd guessed wrongly. Her cousin truly hadn't wanted to dance with this gentleman, but Margaret gave the man a kind smile and set her small hand in his. Grace had always liked that about her; her cousin had the kindest heart and would never slight anybody, no matter their position in society.

Grace stood at the perimeter of the room as men and women glided by each other on the dance floor. Having partnered twice with Damon, she understood now: dancing was the art of flirtation. Partners approached each other and then parted. At times they touched— fingers to fingers, or arms to arms—then parted again. Eye contact dominated most of the ritual, but occasionally they neared each other enough to speak a few words before they had to move again, circling among the other dancers until they could return to the person whose company they most sought.

At least that's how it seemed between those couples smitten with one another. Others worked to impress the crowd more than their partner or executed the steps as part of the routine, without any emotion invested. She had always been among the latter. Tonight, if she were to dance again with Damon, she'd be fully in the first group, craving the nearness, wanting to touch in one of the few ways permissible in society.

Where was he? She scanned the crush near the entrance, hoping to catch sight of him. He'd said he'd be here. After a few minutes, the music changed and a new dance began, an English country reel. A young gentleman neared her, but Grace gave a subtle shake of her head, and he moved off. She herself edged behind a large potted plant; the dancers remained visible through the leaves, but it gave her a bit of respite from the crowd.

Margaret had not returned; she was, in fact, dancing with James Bradley, Duke of Arthington. Not Margaret's original choice of peer, perhaps—Emerlin was dancing with Rebecca—but something in their expressions suggested potential attraction. Grace watched them a moment longer before a voice broke in from her side.

"You look exquisite."

Goose bumps erupted as the deep timbre of his voice echoed in her ear. He was close, too close for propriety, though the plant shielded them somewhat from view. She turned and gave him her best smile.

"Is it possible you attired yourself thusly in hopes of attracting a suitor?"

She rolled her eyes. *Fiddlesticks. Had she ruined the moment?*

He chuckled.

"My mother would certainly hope so," she said.

"As long as it's not me."

She grimaced.

His lips curled into a sardonic smirk. "I hold no illusions of how I am viewed in society, Grace. I am tolerated, but barely, mostly for the sake of my title, but also because of my sisters, who've managed, in spite of me, to maintain excellent reputations. From what I hear, they are quite witty and often sought out for parties."

He took a step back and made a show of admiring her dress. "Really quite beautiful. Might the lady be willing to wear a favor, a token, as the ladies of yore did for their champion knights?"

He pulled out a small brooch from a pocket in his ebony waistcoat, a delicate flower of sapphire with a diamond at its center.

Grace's hand flew to her mouth. "Oh, I couldn't. You know I can't. That is much too bold. And costly."

He grinned, that wolfish grin that rendered him far too alluring. "Would it help for you to know it isn't new? It belonged to my grandmother. And consider it a loan, if you must."

After a moment's hesitation, she took the pin and tucked it inside her bodice. She couldn't wear it openly; a man giving an unmarried woman a gift was highly improper. *Well, who had to know?* With Damon in front of her, his back to the dancers, and the plant to her side, she was pretty certain no one had noticed. She glanced down to ensure the piece was hidden.

"Never before have I been jealous of a piece of jewelry. But I may start now."

Grace laughed. The man was incorrigible.

"I do hope you have saved me a dance or two. Or all of them."

The power of his presence, of his focused attention overwhelmed her. How was it someone like her had managed to attract the notice of someone like him? He was so large, so masculine, so utterly, devastatingly handsome. And the way he made her insides feel! Memories of the kisses they'd shared spread a warm glow through her limbs.

"Perhaps one, Your Grace." From where had that sultry, teasing voice come?

He gave a little bow. "I may be Your Grace to everyone else, but *you* are *my* Grace. I would hope you would call me Damon."

"Yes. Damon."

"Damon, excuse me!" Damon's sister Cassie approached. "I'm sorry to interrupt, but I cannot find Sephe. I am concerned that she wandered off with Lord DuBois."

"That man is a rogue of the worst sort," Grace said. "He tried to foist himself on me at the Trahorn's dinner a few weeks ago."

Damon scowled, a muscle twitching in his cheek. "Excuse me, Grace," he said, his voice calm, though his eyes were not. "I must find her. If you could wait here for a few minutes."

"Certainly."

He gave a crisp nod before walking off with his sister.

After ten minutes or so, the heat from the numerous bodies began to get to Grace. She needed to step outside to garner some fresh air, but her sisters and cousins were busy dancing and her mother nowhere to be seen. Surely a moment alone on the terrace but in full sight of the ballroom would not be a problem. Damon would no doubt return any moment.

Grace threaded her way through the congested room, grateful once she reached the French doors. She waved briefly to Rebecca, who passed her on the arm of Lord Emerlin. A second dance this early in the evening? Grace's mouth tipped up, her suspicions confirmed.

Once outside, she drew in several breaths, appreciating the gentle May breeze. Several couples strolled or conversed at various places on the terrace, but she made sure to avoid contact, wanting to allow them privacy.

Something caught the corner of her eye. Or someone, rather. A tall man garbed in black stood a short distance from her. *Damon.* What other man wore all black? It had to be him. Why was he standing in such a poorly lit area?

Without giving it a thought, she raced to him. But as her eyes adjusted to the dimness, shock raised the hair on her skin. It was not Damon. This man was of similar height and frame, with black hair, but his eyes were all wrong. They were black. And sinister. Fear raced up her spine, and she whirled to go. The man's arm snaked out and caught her around the waist, pulling her against him as his other hand clasped her mouth, keeping her from making a sound.

"That's right, lady. You keep quiet an' I won' be hurtin' ya." He started to back them both out of the dim light, into the gardens.

Grace's panic rose. Where was this man taking her? Did he intend to harm her? What should she do? Her hands flew up and she pulled at his arm clutched about her midsection. He moved it higher, clamping it over her chest.

Damon's brooch pressed painfully against her breast before suddenly springing from the garment. The man paid it no attention.

Mortified this stranger was touching her in such an intimate way, she tried to open her mouth to bite his hand.

"I wouldn't do that," the man hissed, yanking harder against her. Her teeth bit into her cheeks before both his arms suddenly loosened, sliding up to her throat, grasping firmly. She wanted to scream, to beg for help, but as his fingers pressed into either side of her neck, her mind spun and everything went dark.

CHAPTER 19

SMYTHINGTON BALL, LONDON
MID-MAY, 1814

*D*amon hurried to the main ballroom. They'd found Sephe, safe and unharmed, playing billiards with several female friends. It had taken more time than he'd wished, as they'd first checked the more private areas, fearing she'd been spirited away to one of them. He'd disrupted a number of amorous couples, but luckily his sister hadn't been part of one of them.

Cassie had insisted on accompanying him, delighting in making pointed jests about the people they'd spied in compromising positions. "I mean, truly, Lady Chesterson? With Lord Plumperset? Widow or not, is he not thirty years her senior?"

"Please don't tell Mother," Damon implored. "I would never hear the end of it for having furthered your education in such a manner this evening."

"Fear not, dearest brother; this is not the kind of information a lady shares freely. At least not with elders."

He'd raised an eyebrow at that, but they'd hurried

along until they reached the billiards parlor. Cassie had pressed him to check it, though he'd insisted they'd find only gentlemen present.

"Women do not play, do they?"

Cassie had rolled her eyes, throwing open the door her only other response. It'd been full of ladies, Sephe at their center.

Damon was glad to have been wrong in this case, since it meant his sister was unharmed. That hadn't stopped Cassie from giving her a tongue lashing, however.

"Bother!" Sephe had exclaimed with a pout. "Why am I never allowed any fun?"

Her friends had quickly scuttled out of range, casting furtive glances at Damon. He scowled for extra effect, as Sephe reluctantly took his arm to return to the ballroom. One of the ladies had yipped, a noise so high-pitched she might have been a frightened pup.

Now, as they entered, he looked to the spot where he'd left Grace, but she wasn't there. Not entirely surprising; he'd been gone far longer than intended. He searched where the matrons sat to see if she were speaking to someone there, and when that yielded no results, he scanned the dancers. Her blue dress wouldn't be hard to pick out in this sea of white, but she was nowhere to be found.

"Do you see Grace?" he demanded of his sister Cassie.

"Grace, is it?" she teased him, before joining in on searching the room.

Spying Rebecca, he hurried over. "Lady Grace? Have you seen her?"

Rebecca gestured toward the terrace. "She stepped outside a moment ago. I think she wanted some air."

"And she hasn't come back in?"

"No, not that I've seen, but it hasn't been long. Why?

Is something wrong?" Rebecca's blue eyes rounded in apprehension.

"No, no. I'm sure everything is fine. She had promised me this dance, is all. I will check the terrace." He gave Rebecca a smile meant to put her at ease, though his own gut twisted.

Rebecca nodded, making to follow him until the young woman at her side distracted her with a question.

Damon sauntered to the terrace door, not wanting to give Rebecca cause for alarm. Two missing women in one night was too much. *She is merely outside and all is well.* He repeated the thought over and over. All had been well with Sephe, and all would be well with Grace.

But when he exited the ballroom to no sign of Grace, his heart began to pound. The terrace was deserted. Surely she wouldn't have ventured onto the garden paths? Perhaps Rebecca simply hadn't seen her return. He turned to reenter the ballroom when something sparkling at the edge of the terrace caught his eye.

He neared it, squatting down to retrieve the item. It was the flower brooch he'd given Grace. What was it doing here? Fear crawled its way up his throat, robbing him of breath as he looked around for further evidence of her. A bush nearby had a number of bent branches. Hooked onto its bottom was a jagged piece of a silver-shot gauzy material. *Grace's dress.* Terror engulfed him. He ran partway into the gardens, but couldn't see much in the inky darkness. He raced back to the terrace, where Rebecca was peeking out from the ballroom in concern.

"Did you find her?"

"No." Damon's voice was hoarse with panic. "It may be that something has happened. I need a lantern."

Emmeline came up behind Rebecca, a pleasant smile on her face. "Good evening, Your Grace." Her mouth fell at his ragged breathing. "Is something wrong?"

"We don't know where Grace is," Rebecca said.

Damon held up the brooch and the piece of fabric he had found. "She was wearing these. I found them near the bushes. I am concerned something nefarious has happened."

Emmeline looked at the brooch. "I don't remember Grace having a piece of jewelry like that."

"I gave it to her," Damon bit out. "Now if you'll excuse me, I need to get a lantern, a torch, something so that we can search the gardens."

"What should I do?" Rebecca interjected.

"Stay here in case she comes back; Emmeline, go and find help. I need men and lights."

Damon sprinted out into the darkness, a lantern he'd pulled off a terrace table in his hand. Holding it high, he scanned the terrain for Grace. Nothing.

Soon other lights joined his.

"What has happened?" said Arthington as he appeared by Damon's side.

"It's Lady Grace. She's disappeared."

Arthington's face whitened.

Emerlin dashed up to them both. "How can I help?"

"I . . . don't know." Damon pinched his nose with his fingers, willing Grace to come back, to be unharmed, to be safe.

"I shall alert the local night watchman," Arthington said, his tone brisk and authoritative. "We will find her, Malford. We will find her."

Additional guests filtered out onto the terrace as rumors of Grace's disappearance spread like wildfire. A number of the gentlemen combed the gardens, but besides flushing out a few cats and one clandestine couple, they found nothing more.

When Damon neared the house again after a fruitless search, Rebecca scurried over, a female servant in tow.

"She saw a man and a lady get into a carriage in the alley behind the gardens a short time ago. She noticed, she said, because the man handled the lady roughly."

"Was the lady wearing a blue gown?" Damon demanded, his eyes boring into those of the serving girl's.

"I—I think so, Your Grace," the girl stammered. "It were pale, I know."

"Did you see in which direction they went?"

"No, Your Grace, though the carriage were facing to go north on the street. I had to get back inside afore I saw it leave."

He nodded tersely. "Thank you."

The serving maid bobbed a curtsy and then looked at Rebecca. "Yes, you may go," Grace's sister said. "Thank you for bringing this to our attention."

Damon's lungs constricted as if clamped in a vise and he struggled to breathe.

Rebecca and Emmeline stood together, clasping each other's hands.

Arthington reentered the room, a night watchman in tow. "A carriage flew past him heading west on Piccadilly about fifteen minutes past," the Duke exclaimed.

"Carriages on Piccadilly are hardly an unusual site," Emerlin interjected.

"Yes, but this one was racing at breakneck speed," the watchman said. "Nearly crashed into a second carriage turning out of Berkeley Street."

All music and dancing had ceased as everyone circled around Damon and the Mattersley sisters. Speculation as to what could have happened was rife, and a number of ladies swooned at the idea of being taken from a ball in such a manner.

"What if he means to kill her?" one young woman exclaimed.

"Or worse," said another. "Dishonor her?"

Damon closed his eyes, willing himself to breathe in and out. He couldn't lose her. Not his Grace. Not now, when he'd finally found someone with whom he'd made a true connection.

The jostling of the crowd thrust Rebecca against him. He needed to take action, needed to end this spectacle as best he could. And he needed to find Grace.

"Arthington, Emerlin," he called. "I shall escort the Mattersley ladies home. Alert me if you hear of anything."

"Of course." Arthington's face was a mask of grave concern. He cast his eyes at Emerlin, and the message they conveyed infuriated Damon.

"We *will* find her," he roared. "And she will be all right. She will be." He would find her, *alive*, if it was the last thing he did.

Disregarding the looks—some curious, some frightened, some suspicious—around him, he offered an arm to each of the Mattersley sisters, and they clung to him as he led them to their carriage. After assisting them inside, he leapt in and took a seat next to Emmeline. The carriage sped off to Claremont House.

No one spoke. At length, Emmeline said, her voice tremulous, "Do you think we will find her? Truly, Damon? Who could have done this? *Why?*"

"Yes. Yes. I don't know. And I don't know." He closed his eyes. His head wanted to move, wanted to jerk, his body's reaction to extreme duress. He fought it with all he had. Concentrating on controlling his body helped keep the panic at bay. Temporarily. For he was panicking. He had no idea who had taken Grace, or why. Nor did he have any clue as to where, except somewhere west. But in town? Or worse, out of London? He clenched his jaw, willing his body to stay in control.

Rebecca began to weep, not the loud, obnoxious wails he'd heard from young women, but more a quiet shuddering. The sound closed around his heart, crushing it like a piece of soft fruit.

After arriving at Claremont House, the two girls flew from the coach and into the house, calling for the dowager, who, Emmeline had said in the coach, had claimed a headache and remained behind that evening. Damon followed more slowly, averse to facing Grace's mother, given the situation.

He waited in the hall. The servants were in too much of a dither to pay him any mind. Matilda Mattersley, Dowager Duchess of Claremont, came flying down the broad staircase, clothed only in her nightgown and wrapper. Her face was white, her mouth pinched. Anger erupted when she spied Damon.

"What has happened? What have you *done*?" she burst out, marching up to him. She was a good half a foot shorter than he, but at that moment Damon Blackbourne, Duke of Malford, felt about two inches tall.

"I—" he began, but Emmeline cut him off.

"Mother! His Grace had nothing to do with Grace's disappearance, and you well know it. He has been most excellent in his response, enlisting the aid of all he can and sending men out to search."

"Then why is he here instead of with them?"

"I came," Damon said, an edge to his voice, "to see your daughters home safely and to break this news to you. I came because I care for your daughter. And she for me."

The dowager's shoulders sagged at his words. It was as if the reality of Grace's disappearance had suddenly sunk in. "Who would do this?" she asked, her voice a shell of what it had been moments earlier. "Who would harm my child?"

"We shall find her, and justice shall be served. I promise you that, Your Grace."

"Have you sent for Deveric? He should be here. We need his help."

"Of course," Damon said, beckoning to a footman. "Send a carriage for Claremont, as quickly as possible."

Though the man was not in his employ and this was not Damon's house, the servant instantly obeyed the barked command.

Grace's mother's face had aged twenty years in five minutes. She clasped her arms around her waist, teetering as if she might fall over. "Thank you," she managed to say.

"Mama, let me lead you to the parlor. Let us sit down," Emmeline said, reaching for her mother's elbow.

"Yes," was the dowager's only response.

Rebecca turned to Damon. "Find her. Please. Find my sister."

"I will. *I will.*"

With that, he headed out into the night.

Chapter 20

*D*amon sat in his study, nursing a tumbler of brandy. He'd searched the streets for hours, questioning nearly everyone he saw, but had received no additional information. Grace had been snatched, thrown in a carriage, and bundled off somewhere west. More than that, he didn't know.

He hurled the glass at the wall. He'd come home only on the insistence of Arthington, who'd accompanied him on his quest. Although he had known the fellow duke only a short while, Arthington was proving quite a friend. Damon trusted him. Emerlin, too. How powerful to have other men of similar age and rank in whom he could put faith. It was a strange but welcome experience.

"We will help however possible," Emerlin had assured him. "Deveric will come to London as quickly as he can, and we will find Lady Grace."

But would they? How? They had no clue as to her abductor or her location. And if—*no, when*—they did find her, in what condition would she be?

Despite the grand wealth and polish of the West End,

there was a darker side to London. Women could and did disappear, though not usually a member of the aristocracy from a ball.

That was the one thing that gave him hope. This seemed too premeditated to indicate a random crime. A crime of passion was a possibility, but Grace had never mentioned any other suitors, nor had he seen anyone pursue her. He shook his head.

"Idiots," he muttered.

She was a beautiful soul, inside and out. How did others not see it, not rush to simply be in her presence? Perhaps that was intentional on her part. Like him, she didn't care to let people in, preferring instead to stick to her quiet routines, her close circle of intimates.

His eyes welled up with tears. He let them fall. There was no one here to see anyway, and it was a crushing despair that weighed on him, this fear that just as he had found someone with whom he could see sharing a life, whom he could even love, she'd been taken away, perhaps never to return.

Love. There was a powerful word. Did he love Grace Mattersley? They had had only a few encounters, but each had been significant, meaningful. In their conversation in the carriage that afternoon in Hyde Park, they'd not wasted their time on pleasantries and trivialities, but had dived right into substantive conversation. He loved that about her; she wasn't about surface. She was depth. She was intelligence. She was kindness. She didn't judge him for his ticcing movements.

Hell, yes, he loved her.

Hobbes appeared in the doorway. He must have heard the glass shatter. "Is there anything I may do for you, Your Grace?"

Damon nearly snickered at his valet's formality.

Hadn't they moved past that? He shot Hobbes a grin so wide, so crazed, he was sure he resembled Lucifer himself.

"Bring her back to me, Hobbes. Bring her back."

Hobbes nodded, sympathy radiating from his eyes. "Perhaps you should rest for a few hours."

Damon shook his head vehemently. "No. I cannot sleep. I must find her. I must." He stood and strode to the fire, which blazed with welcomed warmth, for he was frozen inside. Staring into the flames, he repeated the words over and over.

"I must find her."

THE ROCKING MOTION of the carriage jostled Grace to consciousness. She lay on her side, trying to gain her equilibrium. A horse whinnied. The violence of the rocking indicated they were traveling at a fast rate of speed. But to where? Why?

She set her hand to her head to steady it as dizziness and nausea overtook her.

"Ah, good. You're awake."

Her eyes flew open. A man sat across from her, though not the same one who'd pulled her from the terrace. Grace had never seen this man before. He was a portly fellow, with a shock of thinning white-blond hair and thick, bushy eyebrows. Beneath the eyebrows lay narrow-set eyes of an indeterminate color, perhaps hazel, perhaps brown. One of his feet was propped on a small stool.

"Who are you?" She forced herself upright. To her surprise, she was not bound in any way. Then the pistol nestled on the seat next to the man caught her eye. Clearly he had ways to keep her in line. Deadly ways.

"Do you not know me?" The man's lips pinched into a tight smile. "You know my nephew, most certainly. That despicable excuse for a human being."

His nephew? Who? Oh— "You are Damon's uncle."

The man nodded. "Good to see you have a brain."

"What are you doing? Why have you taken me? Where are we going?"

"Typical female, full of questions." His eyes bulged, a vein in his forehead visibly throbbing.

Was he mad?

"Damon has taken what is mine. He should not be Duke. I should. So I have taken something of his."

Grace frowned. "Me? I am not his. We are not—"

"Don't try to fool me, missy. I've seen the way he looks at you. I've watched you from afar. It's clear as day." He gave a self-satisfied chuckle.

"But," Grace began, before biting her lip.

"But what?"

"But why have you kidnapped me? What could you possibly hope to achieve?"

"He will give me what's mine. Oh, not Thorne Hill. It is entailed and no court would allow it. Unless I kill him."

Fillmore cackled at that, a high-pitched nervous keening. *Yes, the man was not in his right mind.*

He whisked out a flask from inside his jacket and took a large swig. "Oh yes, he will give me what is mine. I have creditors bearing down on me, men to whom I owe debts. I am an honorable man; I settle what I owe."

She stifled an unexpected laugh. The man considered himself honorable? When he'd kidnapped the sister of a peer, absconding with her to who knew where? The wildness about him made it clear, however, she needed to tread carefully.

"This is about money?"

"It is about *honor*," he roared, and Grace's head pounded from the force of his voice in the cramped space. "The man has none. He is a devil. He is possessed by a demon. He. Is. Not. A. Duke."

If anyone is possessed, 'tis you. Grace remained quiet, rubbing at the painful spots on her neck. What should her next move be? She glanced out the window, but it was still dark. She had no clue what time it was or where they were.

"We are traveling to Bath," he announced, as if she'd asked. "My gout pains me something fierce. I need the waters." He took another swig from his flask. "I have sent a messenger to Damon, telling him to meet me there. He will bring me the money I need, and I will let you go."

Surely he couldn't think that's all that would happen? He couldn't think Damon would simply hand over the money and that would be that?

Fillmore wiped his mouth daintily with a handkerchief he'd pulled out of his other pocket. "Do not fear, Lady Grace; you will be well tended to."

She wanted to scream. Being well tended to did not include being rendered senseless at a ball, thrown into a carriage, and forced to go with a monster such as him. And what did he think would happen to her after this, assuming he did, indeed, let her go? Her reputation would be in ruins. She'd be shunned, all marriage prospects gone. She'd seen it happen to her sister. Amara had never fully recovered.

Not that Grace had wanted to marry, but it had been her presumed course. Truth be told, the idea had crossed her mind more and more since meeting the Duke of Malford, not nearly as repugnant as before.

But now? Damon had never spoken of marriage. Of courting, yes, for which marriage was the understood outcome should they prove suitable. It was far too soon, however—their association of too short duration. No formal promises had been made, no proposals accepted.

Would—*could* he want her after this? A woman whose honor was in shreds? It would taint his sisters' opportunities. Mar his own tenuous standing in Society. Her head throbbed. It was too hard to think. Her eyelids fluttered shut.

"Yes, rest now. It is a long trip. You and I have plenty of time to get better acquainted."

Bile rose in her throat and she fought not to cast up her accounts. She kept her eyes closed so as not to have to see the lunatic across from her, not to have to see the pistol, not to have to face the reality that this was a terrifying situation with a very uncertain outcome.

Damon. Tread carefully. The man is not in his right mind. Don't let him hurt you, Damon. Don't let him.

After a few more miles, she fell into a troubled sleep, her mind still groggy from her bout of unconsciousness. Her last thoughts were of Damon's blue eyes, the fear in them mirroring her own.

Chapter 21

The note arrived at dawn the next morning, delivered by a street urchin who claimed no knowledge of who'd paid him to bring it. However, the instant Damon opened it and spied the flowery, uneven script, he knew.

Dearest Nephew,

You took what was to be my greatest treasure, so I have returned the favor. Rest assured, I shall keep your lady friend safe and unharmed.

You may retrieve her in Bath, a city to which I have lamentably had to return. I need the healing waters. My gout has flared, as it does in times of stress. Such as having to deal with a demonic upstart who's usurped one's rightful place in the world.

Bring me £30,000 to clear my debts and the girl is yours.

— F.

Damon roared with rage, balling up the note and throwing it against the wall.

How *dared* he? How dared his uncle snatch a lady of the *ton* and subject her to this harrowing ordeal, all for the sake of *money*? Had Fillmore come to him and explained the full direness of his situation, surely they could have worked something out. Now the only thing of which Damon was certain was that he wanted to kill the man.

And thirty *thousand* pounds? The sum was unheard of. How on God's earth had Fillmore run up such debt? Not that that was important now.

Damon bellowed for Hobbes, who scurried into the hall not two minutes later, Cerberus at the servant's heels. "I must go to Bath, Hobbes. My uncle has taken Lady Grace."

"I shall ready the carriage and our travel bags," Hobbes answered, unperturbed by Damon's foul temper.

"No. I'm going alone. I'll take my horse."

"Your Grace. I understand the delicate nature of the situation and the need for urgency. But you cannot ride to Bath on your own. It is two days' journey, perhaps a day and a half at breakneck speed, but you would have to stop to change horses often. And it would not be wise to encounter your uncle completely alone."

Damon paced, running his fingers through his hair. Cerberus loped along with him, meowing at his master's obvious distress. Damon stopped, scooping up the cat. "I must get to her, Hobbes. I must get to her *now!*"

Cassie ran into the hall, her eyes sleepy, wearing only her nightgown and wrapper. Hobbes discreetly cast his eyes elsewhere. "What has happened, Damon? I could hear you from my chamber. Have you news?"

"Fillmore has *taken Grace*, that's what's wrong," he bellowed. Cerberus butted his head against his chin.

"But that makes no sense. Why would he do that?"

"Because he is mad. A lunatic." Damon gave Hobbes a curt nod. "Have the carriage readied. We leave at once."

With a dip of his head, Hobbes left the room.

Cassie clutched her wrapper against her lean frame, her face pinched and troubled. "Should you not alert Grace's family? Perhaps wait for Claremont? You sent word to him last night, did you not?"

"There is no time. I do not trust that bastard to keep his word and not harm Grace. I don't trust him at all."

"Please, Damon." Cassie walked over and set a hand on his arm. "I understand your concern. I am concerned, too. But you must slow down, must plan."

"What is there to plan, for God's sake?" he yelled again, pointing a finger at the crumpled paper on the floor. "He's demanding thirty thousand pounds, Cassie. Should I summon the solicitors so that we may deliver it to him on a velvet pillow?"

"Certainly not. But should you show up alone and empty-handed, what do you think he will do? Hand her over sweetly with apologies? If our uncle is insane enough to take Grace in the first place, he's insane enough to kill her."

At that, the blood drained from Damon's face. "No. No, no, no." He sagged against the wall, sliding into a heap against the baseboards. Cerberus pawed at his face.

Cassie crouched next to him. "I am sorry, brother. But we shall find a solution. We shall save her."

Damon had held the tics back as long as he could, but now they exploded, his head whipping back and slamming into the wall behind him. Cerberus hissed in displeasure and scampered away. Cassie gasped and then tried to tug him away to stop the battering. "What is happening, Damon?"

He pushed at her arms, letting his head hit the wall again. "This—is me," he bit out after a moment. Slowly, painfully, he rose. His shoulders jerked as if he were sobbing, but there were no tears in his eyes. "This is why he took her, sister. Why Father rejected me. Why you all abandoned me. Because of this! The demon inside me!"

Cassie threw her arms around him. "We would never abandon you, Damon. Never. Do you know how many times Mother fought to go see you? Father never agreed, but nevertheless, she persisted. She tried to keep it discreet from Sephe and me. I heard her tell Adam once she hoped we'd forgotten you, because she'd failed you. She'd lost you. But I didn't. I never did." Tears seeped out of her eyes as she clutched her brother, whose shoulders still spasmed.

"I am a beast," he whispered, the fight going out of him. "I bring pain and sorrow wherever I go. He's right; it would be better if I were dead."

Cassie gasped. She grabbed hold of his chin and forced him to look into her eyes, blue reflecting back on blue. "Don't you say that. Don't you *ever* say that."

"But it's true, Cass. If I hadn't paid so much attention to Grace Mattersley, she'd be here now, safe and protected. Not being hauled all over England by a madman."

"Damon, you're talking nonsense. The fault lies not with you, but with Fillmore. With our father. *Not* with you."

"But you've seen me now. What kind of man can't control his body? Not exactly acceptable behavior in polite circles. *I'm* not acceptable. I never have been."

Hobbes popped his head in again. "The carriage is ready and waiting out front, Your Grace."

Damon fought to hide his pain and remorse and despair. But it was no use. Every inch of him felt hollow.

Defeated. Ice cold. No tears fell, but it wasn't for lack of sorrow. He simply had nothing left to give.

Cassie squared her shoulders. "You can do this. I have faith in you. You will get her back. You are an honorable man, a good man. You will rescue her, Damon. You will. But you need to get Claremont first. His family will want to help their sister. You need him."

He stared at her blankly before giving a short nod. Then he stalked out the door.

THE CARRIAGE RUMBLED through the streets of London, which were increasingly cluttered with mail coaches, delivery wagons, and men of business milling about, setting up for the day's trade. It was not far to Claremont House, though Damon did not wish to stop there. He didn't want to lose time, but in all honesty, he also didn't want to face Grace's family. He had let them down. He had brought their daughter and sister into harm's way.

Still, Cassie was right. He owed them the information he had.

When he arrived at Claremont House, Emmeline answered his knock, instead of the butler. Her red eyes and disheveled hair revealed her frazzled state of mind—a state matching his. She burst out, "Any news?"

He nodded tersely.

"Do come in." She backed up a few steps. "Mama will want to hear this, too."

"With all respect, Lady Emmeline, time is of the essence. My uncle has taken Grace. To Bath. He is waiting for me there, or soon will be. Honor dictated I tell you the details in person, but I must set out at once."

"Wait!" she cried as he turned to go. "My brother. He

will arrive shortly, I know it. The messenger will have ridden all night, and Deveric would have set out as soon as he knew."

Damon frowned.

"Please," Emmeline pleaded. "I know she means a great deal to you, Your Grace, but she means the world to us. Deveric will want to go with you. Please."

Damon closed his eyes. He wanted nothing more than to race off after Grace this instant. But it was this family from which his uncle had stolen her. Damon could not in good faith go against their wishes, seeing as how it was his fault that Grace was in danger. He signaled to the carriage driver. Hobbes emerged and ascended the steps, nodding to Lady Emmeline.

"Come," she said, motioning to them. "Rebecca and Mother are in the breakfast room. Let us plan."

GRACE STARED out the coach window, awake again now that the sun was high in the sky. On any other day, under any other circumstances, she would have admired the gorgeous English countryside. Now she sat, her back rigid, stewing in anger. How dare this heathen steal her, as if she were some medieval princess he wished to shut up in a tower? Her family was undoubtedly sick with worry. *The dastardly, onion-eyed, villainous, toad-spotted, milk-livered, weaselly clotpole of a blackguard!*

Satisfaction filled her over the Shakespearean insults—the bard had always been the master of creative epithets—but it quickly disappeared in the face of her fury. If only she knew stronger words!

Damon would come for her. His honor would demand it, regardless of whatever attachment may or may not lie between them. Somehow she did not doubt she would get out of this. She also had no doubt she would kill Fillmore Blackbourne if she could.

The vehemence of her emotions startled her. Normally, Grace loathed harming even a spider, though they frightened her. But as Fillmore Blackbourne droned on about how Damon had wronged him, about how Damon was an evil man whom they should have rid themselves of years ago, about how Blackbourne had never got the respect owed to him, she was seriously contemplating murder.

The man was delusional. He sipped from the silver flask long after she was sure it must be empty. Was it the drink or true lunacy that kept him raving? Once, he picked up the pistol and waved it at her. Her heart had nearly stopped. A drunk man with a gun was like pouring oil on a fire. Luckily, he'd set it down again. He'd also stayed on his side of the coach, thank heavens. Had the man tried to touch her in any way, weapon or not, she would have gone for blood.

She schooled her features into a placid, nonchalant expression in hopes that Blackbourne wouldn't suspect the calculations going on in her mind. It normally took a good two days to reach Bath from London. Though the horses had slowed from their gallop—"It's too painful for my cursed foot," Blackbourne had bemoaned—the middle-of-the-night start might mean only a day and a half of full travel, since roads were less congested.

They had stopped at several coaching inns along the way to change teams. At each one, Grace had sought a chance to leave the coach, perhaps signal someone for help if she could, but Blackbourne had remained inside the coach every time and thus so had she.

The carriage swayed, its familiar rocking almost soothing. Maybe the rascal would fall asleep. Not that she knew what she'd do if he did. Would she fling herself out of a moving coach in the middle of nowhere? Painful as it was to admit, that would be a foolhardy move. It didn't matter, because the man hadn't slept a wink despite the length of time they'd been traveling. His eyes remained wildly alert, attuned to everything. *Damn.*

"I have to use the necessities," she said at one point.

"We shall stop in another few miles to switch horses. I will take you. Should you try to escape, should you try to get anyone to help you or alert them to this situation, I will first shoot you, and then them."

She swallowed, her throat going dry. She might be willing to risk her own life, but she couldn't harm another person. She was well and truly trapped. Perhaps it was better to wait for help. Damon would come and likely her family, too, and woe betide Fillmore Blackbourne when they did. If the Mattersley family was one thing, it was fiercely loyal to each other.

The miles rolled by excruciatingly slowly. It was preferable to travel by coach with friends or family; the jostling might be uncomfortable, but at least the company was good, which couldn't be said for now.

Surely they would stop for dinner, perhaps even for the night? Blackbourne's discomfort grew with each hour that passed. But although their pace slowed, the coach continued on as evening crept in. Still the odious man opposite her did not sleep.

Finally giving in to her own exhaustion, Grace nestled as best she could into the coach's seat. She would escape him. Escape this. She would.

Fantasies of a vengeful Damon, blue eyes blazing as he swooped into the coach to rescue her, lulled her into a fitful sleep.

Your Demon is coming for you was her final cognizant thought.

But did she mean for Fillmore, or herself?

CHAPTER 22

CLAREMONT HOUSE, LONDON
MID-MAY, 1814

*D*amon paced the front parlor of Claremont House, waiting impatiently for Claremont. It was a good fifty miles to Clarehaven. Though the messenger had set out yesterday night, the time it would take for him to arrive and then for Claremont to make it back to London was not insignificant. The waiting chafed.

Emmeline and Rebecca took turns looking out of the window. The dowager duchess sat in an uncomfortable-looking chair, never once moving a muscle. She'd not said much to Damon, but she watched him like a hawk did its prey. Or a dragon.

Was she waiting for him to break out into convulsions, to explode into flames, to do something to show he was the demon his uncle claimed him to be? Was she merely thinking of her daughter, determining the odds as to whether Damon and her son could bring her back? He didn't know. He didn't care. All of his thoughts were on Grace.

Matilda had initially protested Fillmore Blackbourne

could not have done this. "Though not a peer, he is a man of honor. We have been long acquainted. My brother and he attended Oxford together."

However, after perusing the crumpled note Damon had brought with him from his own residence, she said no more.

Emmeline and Rebecca vacillated between talking of Grace and chatting about more mundane matters. He didn't blame them. If his mind could go to anything else, he would let it, just to ease the pain. Controlling his body gave him something on which to focus; the urge was still strong to move, to tic, as if somehow his mind thought that would give him release. He longed to run. Even running in circles would be better than nothing, and the room was large. But that would raise eyebrows even further, so he settled for pacing.

Suddenly, a door burst open. Seconds later, a tall, imposing figure strode into the parlor, marching like a man on a mission.

"Mother," he said, nodding in greeting to the dowager before turning to Emmeline and Rebecca. "Sisters."

Familial greetings out of the way, he walked over to Damon. "You must be Malford," the Duke of Claremont said, extending a hand. "I would say it is a pleasure, but under these circumstances..."

Damon eyed the proffered hand warily. He'd half expected Claremont to club him. It was Damon's fault, after all, that the man's sister was missing. Kidnapped. He shook hands, then pulled the crumpled note once more out of his pocket and handed it to Claremont.

Claremont scanned the missive, then raised startlingly green eyes to Damon. "I never cared for your uncle," he said. "There was always something . . . not right . . . about him."

"Agreed. And now the man has clearly gone insane." Damon cleared his throat. "I had feared you would shoot me on the spot. I am to blame, after all."

"Nonsense. The fault lies entirely with your uncle." Claremont chuckled, a caustic sound. "In truth, I think he shall quickly come to rue this decision. Not because we're coming after him, but because of my sister. She may act the quiet lady, but I know within lies the ferocity of a lion."

An unexpected laugh erupted from Damon. "Did you know," he said, "I have had that very thought about her?"

Claremont grinned. "Come. I've had the horses switched on my coach. Let us go."

Damon nodded. The men bid adieu to the women and headed out the front door. Hobbes was waiting on the step. Damon sent him back to Blackbourne House, despite many a protestation from the valet-turned-friend.

The two dukes launched themselves up into the coach, and Claremont tapped on the roof. The conveyance took off.

For a few moments, neither man said anything. Damon ran his fingers through his hair, glad to finally be moving, to be doing *something*, even if it would be some time before they reached Bath.

Claremont settled back in his seat, extending his long legs to the side of Damon's and loosening his cravat. "So, tell me," he said. "What has your uncle got against you?" His green eyes bore into Damon's blue ones.

"He wants me dead."

"Why?"

"Because—" Damon's chest constricted. It was too soon. Perhaps after knowing each other a while, perhaps if they had been true friends, he would have willingly told Claremont of his deficits. But now it was as if he were being asked to lay his soul open to a stranger. A stranger who might bear great influence on his future relationship with Grace.

It was a risk Damon would have to take. He started again. "Because I am not normal. I have this compulsion to move, to shake my head, or other parts of my body, for no good reason." He didn't meet Claremont's eye, but rather gazed out the window as he spoke. "It's better than it used to be; now I only do it under times of extreme duress." He broke off with a bitter laugh. "Like this situation, I suppose."

Claremont studied him. "I don't see you moving."

"I can control it. Sometimes. For periods of time."

"Do you need to do it presently?"

Damon took a deep breath. "No, strangely enough, I don't. Now that we're on the way, now that I know we're going to get Grace back, I feel better. More in control."

Claremont nodded. "Are there other elements to this compulsion?"

He seemed genuinely curious, no judgment or derision in his voice.

"My temper. It flares up quickly and can linger. Though I have never physically harmed anyone. Just an old chair or two. Age has helped with this; I am happy to say it's been years since furnishings have been in any immediate danger."

When Claremont remained silent, his fingers calmly resting on his thighs, Damon added, "Occasionally, I find myself counting in rhythms, whether walking, or playing cards, or running. I don't know if there is a connection. It feels as if I have no control over my own body. So I have worked to instill order in my life."

"And this compulsion, as you call it; this is why your father sent you away?"

Damon's lips pressed into a line. "Yes. When he could not beat it out of me, he got rid of me. At least he didn't murder me, as my uncle encouraged him to do."

Claremont let out a low whistle. "I cannot imagine any father treating his child that way. Though my own father did not always stay his hand, either."

Silence enveloped the coach for a few moments.

"I am sorry to have pulled you away from your wife and family," Damon offered at length. "Grace said you are father to a new daughter. Congratulations."

Claremont's face softened at the mention of his wife. "Eliza will be fine; she, too, wants Grace home safely."

"Tell me about her," Damon invited, wanting to turn the conversation away from himself.

Claremont smoothed the edges of his waistcoat. "Eliza is like no one else I've ever met, or ever will. She is American, as you might know, and has quite a unique take on the world. We grew up in vastly different circumstances." His lips winged up in a smirk at that last sentence.

Damon got the sense he was missing part of the story.

"She saved my life," Claremont added. "Not literally. But before Eliza, I was merely going through the motions. I was dead inside in so many ways and I didn't even know it. She brought me back. She helped me to live again, to love again."

If Claremont felt embarrassed at admitting such strong feelings to a virtual stranger, he didn't show it. Perhaps this intimate exchange was a way of acknowledging the innermost pain Damon had just shared.

The men lapsed into an easy conversation, sharing tidbits of their formative years, of their likes and dislikes, even discussing estate management for some time. Claremont spoke of his sisters, describing each one, including Grace, and Damon soaked up tales of her antics when she was a child. For his part, he shared about life at the abbey and of his sisters. Soon, the men were on a first name basis. It was as if they had known each other for years rather than mere hours.

"It doesn't bother you?" Damon finally spit out the question that had been on his mind.

"What?"

"That I'm . . . not fully right?"

Deveric considered his words. "I don't see a thing wrong with you, Damon. What I've experienced so far is a gentleman quite to my liking. I suppose were I to witness these movements, I might at first be startled. But I don't get the sense they have anything to do with your intellect. It is clear you have a sharp mind."

Damon sucked in a deep breath. "I appreciate your honesty." After a moment, he admitted, "It was one of the first things that drew me to Grace. She witnessed a fit and yet never once did she seem to give it a second thought."

Hours and miles passed by as the two men discussed various options for dealing with Damon's uncle once they arrived in Bath.

"I don't know what he is thinking. He might intend to kill me when I arrive. I hope he still has enough honor—and sense—not to harm Grace. I don't see how he thinks this could possibly end well, this scheme to extort money from me."

"My guess is he isn't. Thinking, that is. But he will regret the day he took my sister."

GRACE PACED the confines of the chamber in which she'd been kept since they'd arrived late the previous evening. Its contents indicated a lady's bedchamber, perhaps Daphne's. It was a lovely room, with delicate furnishings in deep shades of rose and brown. Nothing in it indicated a mad person lived here. Though it wasn't Daphne who was mad; it was her father.

The single window looked out onto the rear lawn of the townhome. There was little to see and no way of drawing attention to herself, locked away upstairs. She searched the room again, seeking anything that could be used as a weapon, if need be. The writing desk held a quite heavy candelabrum that could serve in a pinch. Too bad there wasn't a dagger lying about.

A giggle escaped her. Perhaps she'd been reading too many gothic novels, to be imagining such things. At least now she had her own experience on which to base such a novel. She passed the time sketching out the story in her head of the dastardly uncle who sought revenge against his nephew by killing the woman the nephew loved.

Though I'd rather survive this whole ordeal.

As to Damon loving her, dare she hope for such a level of attachment? He'd never said the words, never even come close to expressing such a sentiment. His kisses proved he desired her, but the two were not one and the same. Amara's experiences showed that. Still, Damon must have feelings of a stronger nature, given his decision to court her.

Then again, love and marriage did not necessarily go hand in hand, as many a noble match proved.

She loved him, though. She did. It should have been impossible, given the brevity of their acquaintance. The depth of her affection had burst upon her in the carriage, when the chance of never seeing Damon again became a real possibility in the face of Blackbourne's pistol.

Yes, she loved Damon Blackbourne. His raw intensity, the ferocity of his emotions; here was someone who did not experience life in half measures. She'd never been prone to outward displays, preferring instead to keep her emotions well hidden. Seeing someone express themselves so openly, and a man at that, had stirred a great admiration.

She loved his concern for his sisters and his mother, his willingness to risk ridicule to do what was right by them in spite of all he'd been through. She loved that he had survived so much, been through so much, and yet wasn't a permanently embittered soul; she'd seen too many of those. Yes, he still struggled, but she admired that, too—a man willing to admit he wasn't perfect. So different from her own father.

She loved his intelligence. He'd confessed in Hyde Park that never having attended Eton or Oxford bothered him; in his eyes, it rendered him inferior to other men of his standing. But he was better read than most peers she'd met, able to converse easily on numerous subjects. What other man could discuss equally the writings of Plato and the best growing methods of the potato? Or knew Indian herbs as well as English ones without ever having stepped foot on Indian soil? His tutor, his library, and his own passionate thirst for knowledge had served him well.

She even loved his awkwardness in polite society. Given he'd spent so many of his formative years alone, it made sense he hadn't learned the social niceties and mannerisms others took for granted. Many of the expectations and rituals were silly and she herself had erred on more than one occasion. His disinterest in formalities, in polite talk over more serious conversation, endeared him to her from the start.

Then there was the way in which he said her name. *Grace*. Sensual and reverent at the same time, as if she were a most delectable gift.

She sat on the bed with a sigh. As she smoothed her hand over the faded quilt, an image rose, unbidden, of Damon and her on the bed, locked in a torrid embrace. Her skin tingled, half in embarrassment, half excitement, at the idea of his fingers skimming over her skin, stroking her cheeks, of him pressing kisses along her neck. Of her weaving her hands through his hair as she sank into the icy blue depths of his eyes.

She bit her lip. Never had she lost herself in fantasies over a man. Indeed, like anyone, she admired physical handsomeness, but picturing herself intimately engaged with a man was a foreign experience. She pressed her hand against her stomach.

This wasn't just any man, however. This was Damon Blackbourne, Duke of Malford.

And she knew without a doubt he was coming for her.

CHAPTER 23

BATH, SOMERSET, ENGLAND
MID-MAY, 1814

*U*nder different circumstances, Damon would have enjoyed this time getting to know Claremont. He liked the fellow. He'd taken a chance in revealing his malady, but soon they would all be family—he hoped. He hadn't voiced that to Deveric yet. But after his uncle's actions, he had no choice: he must offer for her, for her honor and his own.

The idea of marrying Grace stirred the deepest emotions in him. Including fear. What if her family wouldn't accept him? What if she rejected him?

Grace's reputation may be in tatters now, but that was no guarantee she would marry him. Grace's sister Amara had refused to marry despite her quite public loss of honor. The Mattersley family had rallied around her, but it hadn't been enough to save Amara from scandal. Only Claremont's powerful stature and the entire family's staunch defense of Amara had kept polite society from completely shunning her.

"We are prepared to do so again for Grace," Deveric

had said before they'd embarked on this journey, his sisters and mother nodding in affirmation. Had it been a warning? A way of saying Damon would never have Grace, owing either to his own shortcomings or the fact that it was his contemptible uncle who'd caused this problem to begin with?

Perhaps after they'd rescued Grace, the Mattersley family wouldn't want anything to do with the Blackbournes again under any circumstances. Could he blame them?

He could have asked Deveric. But he hadn't wanted to risk it. Not yet. Not until Grace was safe, not until he knew how she felt after all that had happened. He hoped, he prayed, she would forgive him. But he had to know for sure.

Every muscle in his body tensed as the coach rode into Bath fifteen hours after they'd left London. They'd pushed hard, changing horses only as necessary and traveling through the night, but the darkness had necessitated a slower pace, despite the moon's aid.

Fillmore had no doubt done the same. He couldn't possibly have been in Bath for more than half a day, if that. Was there a chance they'd beat Fillmore in getting there? Doubtful. The bastard would have wasted no time reaching his home, his 'castle,' where he'd make a stand.

The horses clattered their way through the relatively quiet streets. Dawn had broken a short while before. Neither Damon nor Deveric had slept in the carriage, too concerned about Grace and too deep in planning the best way to retrieve her. They discussed a number of scenarios, but finally decided the best choice was simply to arrive on his uncle's doorstep first thing and hopefully catch the older man off guard.

The sights of the city didn't even register, so eager was Damon to get to No. 3 Crescent Circle, the town house in which his uncle lived. Silas had gifted the house to him upon Fillmore's marriage. Though Arbour Manor was to have been his primary residence, Fillmore had long made his home in Bath to be close to its healing waters. It'd been years since Damon had set foot in the city, and he had only the vaguest memories of chasing his cousins Margaret and Daphne around on the grounds in front of the crescent one warm summer day.

The coach edged down Upper Church Street, coming to a stop near the crescent.

"Should we make for the front or rear entrance?" Damon asked as they alighted from the carriage.

"Front," Deveric said, gesturing toward several gentlemen conversing on a nearby doorstep. "It might help to have witnesses should Blackbourne burst out in a crazed state."

Damon had tucked his pistol into his breeches, as had Deveric, but both were hoping it wouldn't come to that.

Damon rapped sharply on the door. After a brief moment, a young woman answered. Had the man no butler? "Malford, with the Duke of Claremont, here to see Blackbourne. My *uncle*," he commanded.

The woman stepped back to allow in the two men, her fingers shaking as she adjusted her cap. "Beggin' your pardon, sirs, I mean, Your Graces. I will fetch Lord Fillmore."

After what seemed an interminable amount of time but in fact was probably no more than five minutes, the serving girl returned. With a quick curtsy and eyes that wouldn't quite meet theirs, she said, "Lord Fillmore has invited you up to the parlor. If you'll follow me."

As they climbed the stairs, sweat pooled on the back of Damon's neck and his stomach knotted. If his uncle had done anything to Grace, anything at all . . .

"I'm right behind you," Deveric said, and a calm

overtook Damon. Thank God for the other man's presence. They would get through this together. They would rescue Grace, and everything would be all right.

They entered the room to find Fillmore Blackbourne ensconced in a large, heavily padded armchair, his left foot propped up on an intricately carved stool. He was sweating profusely, his face swollen and ruddy from either disease or alcohol. Or both. A crystal tumbler filled with amber liquid rested on a marble table next to Fillmore. His uncle had started early, or perhaps hadn't ceased from the night before. For a second, Damon longed for a drink himself. A quick scan around the room showed Grace wasn't there.

"Where is she?" he barked, using all of his self-control to keep from throwing himself on his uncle.

"Tsk, tsk. Where are your manners, boy? You haven't even introduced me to your companion." Fillmore waved his left hand in Deveric's direction.

"Claremont. Grace's brother." Deveric's voice was surprisingly relaxed.

"Ah," was Fillmore's only response. He adjusted his leg on the stool. "My apologies for not rising to greet you, but as you can see, traveling has exacerbated my gout. I hope to take the waters later today."

Damon stalked forward until he was standing directly before his uncle. "*Where is she?* Bring her here. Now."

Fillmore's eyes grew instantly cold. "Take one more step, dearest nephew, and it will be your last." He moved part of his jacket to reveal a pistol in his right hand, cocked and aimed directly at Damon.

Blood pounded through Damon's veins. It took everything in him not to whip out his own pistol, but he was close enough that, even as quick as he was, his uncle would be faster.

Deveric broke in from behind Damon, his voice still

preternaturally calm, though laced with steel. "Lord Fillmore, I should like to see for myself that my sister is fine, if you don't mind. At that point we can settle accounts."

"It is not from you that I want money," Fillmore snarled. "It is from this . . . this . . . usurper."

"Usurper?" The word was out before Damon could stop it. Deveric stepped quickly to him and pulled him back, putting more distance between him and his uncle.

"Understood. Damon promised me he would do whatever was necessary to get my sister back. But I need proof you have her to begin with. The only word I have to go on is Damon's."

Fillmore grinned, an evil sideways meandering of his mouth. Like a weasel. An apt descriptor. "Wise of you, Your Grace, to be wary of this one. The Devil incarnate, he is."

Damon cast a despairing look at Deveric, who ignored him, his gaze steadfast on the other Blackbourne.

Fillmore picked up the bell that rested next to the tumbler and rang it. "Very well," he said. "I'm sure Grace would like to see her brother."

The same serving girl who'd shown them to the parlor scurried into the room.

"Bring us the young lady," Fillmore barked at her.

The girl dropped a hurried curtsy and raced out again.

"I knew you would come for her," Fillmore said, addressing Damon. "I could see it in your eyes when you looked at her. You lust for her."

Deveric cleared his throat.

"It's true. My apologies, Your Grace, for such frank talk. Your sister is an attractive woman." Fillmore licked his lips.

Damon wanted to retch.

Deveric tensed next to him, but his words belied his reaction. "She is, indeed. A gentleman would know how to treat such a lady. Don't you agree, Lord Fillmore?"

Damon glanced at Deveric. The statement could cut two ways. The flinty look in his green eyes suggested the barb was aimed at his uncle.

Fillmore hooted. "Indeed. And we all know Blackbourne is no gentleman, regardless of what title he claims." He waved an arm dismissively. "He's not even fully a man."

Fury filled Damon's head, spawning rivers of rage that flooded his mind and wouldn't let go. He was one second away from losing control and going after the man, regardless of the pistol Fillmore pointed at him.

The door swung open. All three men turned toward it as Grace walked through. Her eyes widened upon seeing them. She cast an anxious glance toward Fillmore.

"Come here, my dear," he commanded.

She obeyed, walking over to stand next to his uncle on his right side, near the fireplace. Her eyes met Damon's, but he was still so lost in his own haze of anger he couldn't read them. She gave a weak smile.

"I was just saying, Lady Grace, that Damon here is not only not a gentleman, he's not even fully a man!" He hooted again, clearly amused by his own statement.

Grace said nothing. She gave the tiniest of head shakes, invisible to Fillmore, as if telling Damon not to respond. He focused on her, on those luminous chocolate orbs, fighting with all his might against the tics struggling to erupt, against the desire to charge his uncle and strangle him barehanded, regardless of the consequences. He used every scrap of strength to focus on Grace and ignore all else around him.

Until Fillmore spoke again. "He's a demon. The thorn

in my side. An embarrassment to the family. He shouldn't be here. He shouldn't *be* here."

Fillmore's hand shook. At any second, his uncle could accidentally shoot at him. Or intentionally, for that matter. With how unsteady Fillmore was, there was a chance he'd miss, but it was a chance Damon wasn't willing to take. They were too close.

"You seem rather disgruntled with your nephew," Deveric broke in with that relaxed voice. It sounded almost as if they were chatting over a game of cards, or tea. "Why is that?"

"Haven't you seen? Or perhaps he's managed to hide it from you, his true self." Fillmore frowned, but his hand steadied. "He twists and contorts himself in ways no human should. He ought to have been committed to an asylum years ago. I always told Silas that. No Blackbourne loses such control."

Damon looked to Grace. She betrayed no emotion, made no sounds, but edged slightly away from his uncle and closer to the fireplace. Was she preparing to run?

"Indeed," Deveric said, drawing Fillmore's attention back to him. "It must have been hard for you, growing up with such a beast."

Grace's eyes widened but she said nothing.

Deveric's words stabbed Damon in the back. Though part of the plan was to convince Fillmore he had an ally in Deveric, the statement still hurt. Despite the hours in the carriage, their acquaintance was brief. Could Damon trust that Deveric truly did not believe what he'd said?

Fillmore cackled. "Exactly. I pleaded with that idiot brother to get rid of him. He wouldn't listen. Said he could reform him. He failed. My stupid brother. Never could see the bigger picture."

"You were the brains in the family, I take it?" Deveric's voice was smooth, encouraging.

Fillmore took a swig from the crystal glass and set it back down on the side table. "With certainty. My mother always saw it. She said it was a shame that I'd never inherit. That I was the better man. The better Blackbourne."

Damon had never met his grandmother. She'd died before he was born. But were she alive now, he'd kill her for the seeds of discord she'd sown in her son.

"I've always known it," Fillmore continued. "I made my peace with it, best I could. Until—" He broke off, his eyes flying to Grace. "Where are you going?"

"My apologies, Lord Fillmore," she replied, her voice steady. "I was cold and thought to warm myself by the fire."

Fillmore harrumphed.

"You were saying?" Deveric prodded, commanding the man's attention again.

"Until he threatened to cut me off! Just like you did, you cur." He pointed at Damon with his free hand, spittle flying from his lips. "As if I were disposable, a responsibility he could wipe his hands of. Yes, I had gotten myself in a bit deep at the tables, but I always get back out. And a Blackbourne pays his debts!" His voice shook with rage. "I knew then what I had to do, what I should have done a long time ago."

Damon's brow creased.

Fillmore crowed. "Haven't you worked it out?" He flashed his teeth at Damon, a manic grin in a face contorted with glee. "The only thing between me and the vast Malford wealth was my brother. And my nephew."

"My brother. The heir," uttered Damon. The pieces were falling into place.

"Exactly! Adam hadn't married; there were no other Blackbourne males. It was easy enough to arrange for a carriage accident."

Grace gasped.

Fillmore shot her a quick glance before turning back to Damon. "But I never thought you still lived. That your mother would send for you. That whore, turning to a mongrel when she could have had me. All those years I pined for her, even after she married Silas. Married him because he had the title and the wealth. And then to reject me in favor of *you!*"

He raised the pistol, aiming it straight at Damon's heart. Damon cast one final glance at Grace. The terror on her face burned into him even as he reached for his own pistol. He'd never make it in time, but he had to try.

Suddenly, Grace whipped her arm around over her head, the fireplace poker clutched in her right hand. She brought it down on Fillmore's skull, the impact making a sickening thud. The pistol dropped from his hand, and he slumped over in his chair, blood oozing from the side of his head.

Grace stood behind him, cheeks slack, her eyes huge orbs. "Did I kill him?"

Deveric kneeled next to Fillmore, searching for a pulse in the inert man's neck. "No. He's alive."

Damon remained rooted to the spot, a cascade of emotions sweeping through him. Fear from having nearly been shot by his crazed uncle at close range, disbelief that it was his uncle who'd caused his father's and brother's death, anger that Grace had endangered herself by attacking Fillmore, and relief, oh such intense relief, that she was safe and his uncle neutralized—at least for now.

"Grace," he whispered, his blue eyes seeking hers. She dropped the poker and ran to him, crashing into him full force and wrapping her arms around him.

"I knew you would come," she said, her head resting against his chest. "I knew it."

He brought his hands up, momentarily breaking her grasp. He took her face in his hands, his thumbs stroking her cheeks as he leaned in and caught her lips in a fiery caress. She ran her fingers around his back, holding him to her as she returned the kiss, all the emotions of the past few days burning between them.

Deveric cleared his throat behind them, and Damon reluctantly broke off the kiss.

Grace turned around and gave her brother a sheepish grin. "Sorry, brother."

Deveric shrugged. "It was well earned by both of you." He walked toward his sister and enfolded her in a hug of his own. "I'm so glad you are safe."

"Did he—did the bastard mistreat you in any way?" Damon's gaze ran up and down her person. Though her hair was askew and her crumpled ball gown rimmed around the base with dust and dirt, she showed no other visible signs of injury.

"Not at all. Unless you count being subject to the ravings of a mad man—and intense alcoholic fumes—abuse. I was well cared for, all things considered."

The two men heaved sighs of relief.

"Still, we must marry at once."

Both Mattersleys turned to stare at Damon.

"We must," he insisted. "Her reputation has been irreparably harmed, and it's my fault."

Grace snorted. "I think it was your uncle's," she said before she grew quiet, biting her lip, her eyes unreadable.

Deveric looked back and forth between the two. "Still, Grace, Damon is right; there is no chance you will recover from this with your reputation intact. You've been in the company of an unmarried man for a night."

"A widower more than twice my age! I can't believe you're making that argument, Dev. You, who were always such a staunch supporter of Amara."

He grimaced. Her words had hit their mark. "I know. But look at what it cost her, Grace." Pain flitted across his face. "I don't want you to suffer in such a way."

Before she could respond, Deveric turned to Damon. "My apologies for having to say those things, Damon. They gave me no pleasure."

A myriad of emotions flitted through him at Deveric's words. He *had* doubted, even if momentarily. Guilt hit him for his own lack of faith. He studied the plush Oriental carpet at his feet.

"Malford," Claremont said, his voice troubled. "Damon. You didn't believe me. Did you?"

Damon didn't respond.

Grace stepped forward, touching his chin with her fingers, forcing him to look up. "I didn't believe him," she said. "Not what he was saying, and not that he meant it. Anyone who gets to know you at all knows you're nothing like what your uncle claims you to be."

Fillmore groaned.

"Not wishing to be a spoil-sport," Deveric said, "but I think it is time for us to leave. We can finish this conversation elsewhere."

Damon and Grace nodded, and the three exited the room. The maid hovered outside. From the look in her eyes, she'd heard at least some of what had transpired.

"Is he—Is he dead?"

"No. But he'll have a mighty fine headache when he awakens."

The maid nodded, her lower lip trembling.

Damon studied her a moment. "Do you wish to remain in my uncle's employ?"

The young woman burst into tears. "No, but I haven't anywhere else to go. He says if I leave, he'll turn me out without a reference. And then what would I do? I've got no one else. My ma and pa, they died."

"You will come work for me," Damon said. "I will double your wages."

The maid hiccupped. "Truly, Your Grace?"

"Yes. Unless the distance is too far? Thorne Hill lies some seventy miles from here."

She shook her head. "That be fine, sir. I mean, Your Grace." She bobbed a curtsy. "Thank you, thank you."

"Gather your things and meet us at the front of the house as soon as you can. I don't think it will be long before Fillmore awakens."

She nodded and scurried out of the hallway, presumably to her chambers.

Tears brimmed in Grace's eyes. "That was a kind and generous thing you did. I had not thought of it myself."

He nodded. "Let us go. We shall continue this discussion about our marriage in better quarters."

She stiffened but without further word descended the stairs, her brother following close behind.

Damon took a moment to breathe. He'd come so close to losing her. And now she was to be his wife.

He'd never lose her again.

CHAPTER 24

"*H*e's gone! Lord Fillmore is gone!"

They spun at the sound of the maid's frantic voice. She raced to them from the front door.

"Gone?" Grace exclaimed, bile rising in her throat. She'd truly killed him, then? No matter her fantasies of doing so a few short hours before, she'd never thought of how it would feel in reality to take another's life. Her hand flew to her mouth. *I've killed a man.*

"He must have gone out the back while I was packing. There was blood on the step, an' his horse is missing." The maid swallowed, her small satchel banging against her legs.

Damon swore.

Deveric grasped Grace's arm. "It will be all right," he whispered. "He can't get you now. You are safe."

She hadn't given a thought to her safety, only to her sin. But surely the man wouldn't come after her a second time? Then again, he was clearly insane—and had committed murder before.

"Damn him. *Damn him!*" Damon paced in front of the carriage, his strides like those of a prowling panther. "I should have finished him off. I should have—"

"No," Deveric interjected. "Your sense of honor is greater than that. As is mine. But should we encounter him again, when he is conscious . . . " His lips pulled into a grim line.

Damon stilled. "He had better hope he never sees me again. For if he does, I shall call him out."

"Indeed," Deveric said, laying a hand on Damon's shoulder. "For now, shall we make haste? I am sure my family wishes to know Grace is unharmed."

"Of course." Damon quickly aided Grace into the carriage, then Daisy, before climbing inside himself. Deveric followed.

Grace took the seat next to the maid, forcing the two men to sit side by side. In no way was she prepared to ride next to Damon, not with the way the touch of his hand had sent her pulse aflutter, even as Damon's declaration—"*We must marry at once!*"—pounded through her head.

"Would you prefer I get a room? Allow you some rest after recent events?" Deveric asked, as the carriage left the Crescent.

"No, dearest brother. I wish to leave this city as soon as possible in order to put these foul memories behind."

Grace fell silent, her emotions a jumble as the streets of Bath flew by. Deveric yawned and then tucked his head into his corner of the carriage, settling his hat over his eyes. A soft snore emanated from him less than a minute later. Shame spilled through Grace; she'd been so absorbed in herself, in all that had happened, she hadn't taken into consideration that the two men had ridden all night to get to her. She, at least, had slept a few short hours in Bath. They must both be exhausted.

She looked across at Damon. "I'm sorry," she said. "Should we stop after all?"

"No. I, too, want nothing more to do with Bath or my uncle. Ever again."

He fell silent and she followed suit. With the maid—Daisy was her name—riding with them in the carriage, it was not the time or place for a more serious discussion.

Luckily, Daisy did not feel the need to chatter, or perhaps sitting amongst peers in the interior of such a lavish coach intimidated her into silence. She'd attempted to clamber up next to the driver, but Grace had stopped her. "It will be more comfortable for you inside, Daisy, and you deserve it after having to put up with Fillmore Blackbourne."

True courtesy had motivated Grace, but also the knowledge that with Daisy and her brother there, she could avoid a more intimate discussion with Damon. The intensity of her newly acknowledged feelings, the terror of Fillmore Blackbourne nearly shooting Damon—all of it was such that she had not the strength for anything at the moment. She needed merely to exist, grateful the unexpected drama of the last twenty-four hours was now behind them.

Did Damon feel the same? He directed his attention not at her, but out the window, seemingly lost in thought. She took the opportunity to drink him in. His thick, black hair was tousled from the day's travels. Stubble dotted his jaw, which only enhanced his raw masculine appeal. His lips were slightly pursed, but that didn't hide their sensuality. If only they could repeat their kiss in Fillmore's parlor here, without Dev or Daisy, just she and Damon, locked in a heady embrace as the carriage rocked on.

Her skin flushed. *And then what, you ninny?*

"We must marry at once." Damon's assertion echoed

repeatedly in her mind. She couldn't ignore the tendrils of excitement the notion aroused. Damon Blackbourne, hers, forever?

She'd given lip service to the idea of marrying for her family's sake, but until Damon, never had anyone moved her to make a lifelong commitment seem reasonable.

"If I *were* ever to marry," she'd insisted to her family on more than one occasion, "it would only be for love. A grand, passionate love. Not for duty, or honor, or expectation."

Nothing less than the kind of love Deveric and Eliza shared made giving up what little freedom and independence she had make sense.

But what choice did she have now? Though thankfully nothing untoward had transpired, she was ruined in the eyes of society. Damon saw no other course than for her to marry him, immediately. Deveric clearly felt the same.

It was Lord Fillmore, not Damon, who'd dishonored her, however. How would wedding Damon save her? Save her sisters? Could it?

The *ton* would see no other option; she must marry or live in permanent scandal. The most logical course of action was to marry Malford.

Was it such a bad notion? She loved him, after all. And he felt something for her. Could it be love?

She sighed. It was all too much. *Let me think of lesser things. For a little while, at least, while there is respite in this carriage.*

The coach hit a rut in the road, and she bounced in her seat, clasping at the cushion as her eyes dropped to Damon's long legs, which rested on the floor across from her. Black boots led to equally black breeches, breeches which revealed the fine musculature of his thighs. She should not linger there. It was most improper.

Her gaze moved up to his lean midsection and over his chest. The light speckling of hair peeking above the top button of his shirt aroused her curiosity. He was cravatless. How had she not noticed before? When had he removed it? She'd never seen a gentleman in such a state of undress—at least not one to whom she was not related.

Her eyes rested there before moving up to his bare neck, where his pulse beat, slowly and steadily. What would it be like to press her lips there, as he had done to her? To taste his skin?

Her cheeks tingled and so she shifted her gaze further up, to his chin with its slight cleft, then to his lips. Which were grinning. She gasped and her eyes flew up to his. His cheeks crinkled in amusement.

"Like what you see?" he said, his voice soft.

She looked to Daisy beside her, but, like Deveric, she'd drifted off into sleep. *Thank goodness.* She needed no additional witnesses to her wanton behavior.

"I—" she began, but stopped, having no excuse for her blatant perusal.

He leaned forward and beckoned her to do so, as well. She did, hesitantly. Their faces were mere inches from each other. "This way we can whisper," he said, "and not disturb the others."

She nodded.

"Although if you'd like to kiss me, I wouldn't be adverse to that, either."

She tried to give him a severe look, but ended up biting her lip to keep from laughing.

His eyes twinkled in delight, but then grew moist. "I am so sorry, Grace. If I could have done anything—"

"—You couldn't." She broke him off with a shake of her head. "He is not right in the head, Damon. You are not at fault for that."

"But he is *my* uncle. If not for me, for your knowing me, you would not have been taken. You would not have been compromised. It *is* all my fault."

"I am not compromised!" she hissed, her voice causing Daisy to mumble in her sleep.

"Not in that way, thank God," he said. "But in the eyes of society, yes."

The words irritated her, though she'd acknowledged the same sentiment earlier. "Why do you care? It's not as if you value what the *ton* thinks."

"No. But I value you. And I must make this right. We must marry."

Her heart sank, a coldness creeping in. There was no emotion in his voice beyond perhaps resignation. No hint that any feeling other than guilt and a sense of honor drove his insistence that they wed.

At her silence, he went on. "We would be well-suited. Do you not think so? Our interests are not dissimilar, our temperaments compatible. I have no love of London, nor do you. We could spend our time in the country, at Thorne Hill, or Blackwood Abbey. When I must be in London to take my seat in the House of Lords, I would understand if you remained behind, far from the stresses of city life. We each do value opportunities for solitude, after all. It need not—" He swallowed. "It need not be a full marriage, if you do not wish it. But a marriage of convenience, a marriage for appearances' sake, would at least save you from the dishonor you have endured."

Grace's throat constricted, a sour taste rising in her mouth. Now he didn't even want her with him? He'd abandon her so easily? This was his idea of marriage—of lives lived apart?

Her mother had suffered through that; years of her husband gallivanting around London while she'd been stuck at Clarehaven.

"You should stay for the sake of the little ones," Samuel Claremont had insisted. "They need a mother's influence."

Little did it matter that plenty of other couples left their children to the care of nannies and governesses during the Season. And as Grace and her siblings had grown and he'd still left Matilda behind, it'd become apparent to all he'd not wanted her with him.

Had her mother wanted to go? Grace suspected so. Matilda Mattersley had never spoken openly of her feelings, but occasionally the mask of respectability and honor she wore like armor had fallen. Once, when a note from Grace's father had come, promising to return at some point in the future, that business had delayed him a little longer, her mother's face had crumbled, revealing the hurt underneath.

One evening shortly thereafter, as a young Grace passed the study, she overheard Deveric tell their brother Chance it wasn't business that kept Father away; it was his mistress.

Grace hadn't quite known at the time what a mistress was. When she'd asked her mother the next day, Matilda's face had gone ashen and she'd struck Grace across the cheek, the only time her mother raised a hand to her.

"Never mention that again!" her mother had commanded.

And she hadn't. But the anguish in her mother's eyes spoke volumes. It was one of the reasons Grace had apprehensions about marrying. She did not want to experience the pain her mother had, no matter how well Matilda hid it from the rest of society.

Damon continued before she could respond. "You have been raised in the ways of society, in the ways of the *ton*. You could help me with the rules and regulations.

As smart as you are, you could help in managing the estates, as well. I'm sure you've been taught the duties of a wife."

Grace's eyes pricked with tears. How had she mistaken Damon so badly? She had not thought him, of all people, to speak of marriage in such cut and dried terms, as a business transaction. She had thought that he, too, having suffered such loss and isolation as a child, wouldn't settle for anything less than a full union, driven by love.

She was wrong. How foolish she had been.

Was this why he had courted her? Not out of affection, out of attachment, but rather as a tool for his betterment?

Oh, to turn back time! To be back in Bath, in the bedchamber in which she'd acknowledged the myriad ways she loved him, in which she'd fantasized about him being her knight in shining armor. Though she'd been a prisoner, the future uncertain, it'd been less painful than this, this harsh reality that Damon did not love her. Not like she loved him. For if he did, wouldn't he have said so? Yet no such declarations had come from him, despite the passionate moments they had shared.

Or would she turn it back farther, to before they'd met? Would she wish to return to a time before she'd known this level of emotion? Before she'd fallen for the Duke of Malford?

Pain wracked her chest and she clutched her arms around her ribs. She was not interested in being his tutor, in training him in the ways of anything. She wanted to be loved and respected, not seen as a means to an end. She forced herself to sit up, to breathe regularly. She would not let him see how his words wounded her, would not reveal how her heart was breaking.

Amara had refused to marry without love, despite

years of ostracization after her dishonor. Grace could endure the same.

She looked him squarely in the eye, hers unblinking. "No."

"No? You haven't been trained to be a wife?"

"No, I will not marry you."

CHAPTER 25

*H*is chest constricted as if she'd stabbed him. Of all the things he'd expected her to say, that quick, decisive "no" wasn't one of them. He exhaled slowly, fighting to keep his face stoic.

"I see," he said, his voice calm. But his stomach rolled. Why didn't she wish to marry him? Could she not see what a position she was now in? Polite society would scorn her, a woman fallen.

His uncle's voice echoed in his mind. *You're only half a man.*

Of course. Of course she didn't want to marry him. Who would want someone whose body betrayed him as his did? Who would want to risk having children who might suffer the same affliction? And his uncle, his blood relative, had kidnapped her and dragged her across England. The man was mad. And Damon damaged. Perhaps she feared bad blood ran through the family. He wouldn't blame her.

He'd offered a marriage free of its normal obligations

so that she'd not feel forced, but still had the means by which to rescue her honor.

The natural progression of their courtship would have led to this point, to a proposal, would it not? Given her response to their kisses, he was certain she desired him as much as he her. He'd hoped with time, she'd wish for, insist on, a full marriage. A consummated marriage. Hoped she could be happy with him and might even come to love him.

It was her choice to make, whether to marry him and save her honor, or to refuse him, thereby ending their association. For if they didn't marry now, there was no future for them. They could not go back as they'd been before his uncle's actions, and because of those actions, there was no other reasonable path forward.

And she'd refused him.

He could tell her he loved her. He could risk it all.

But if she refused again, if she rebuffed him in that moment of most intimate exposure, he didn't think he could survive it. Too many people had rejected him to risk revealing himself in that way, and none for whom he'd felt the half of what he felt for Grace.

Still, he owed her. He owed her his name, not only because Fillmore had robbed her of her honorable status in society, but also because she'd likely saved his life when she'd attacked his uncle with that poker.

He stared out the window. The scenery passed by, an indistinguishable blur. Much like his emotions.

"Damon," she said, her voice the softest whisper, but he ignored her.

She did not try again.

After a few moments, Deveric stirred, his hat falling into his lap. He yawned, rubbing his eyes. "Sorry, sister," he said. "Between running after you and helping care for the baby, I'm a little short on sleep."

Grace gave a half laugh, though a quick glance revealed her eyes were on Damon, not her brother, her fingers nervously pulling at her gown. "You're up at night with Isabelle?"

Deveric shifted in his seat. "Occasionally. When Eliza will let me; she mostly wants to tend to Belle herself. Refuses the nurse, even."

"She is a wonderful mother. And you a wonderful husband."

Was that wistfulness in Grace's voice? Damon closed his eyes as the two conversed, fatigue seeping into every pore of his body—and his heart—though he listened carefully to their words.

"Are you all right?" Deveric asked Grace after a few moments.

I will not peek. I will not look to see her face.

"Yes. Though overwhelmed by all that has happened, I suppose."

"We should go to Clarehaven for a while, to let you recover."

"And because you want to see Eliza, I'm sure."

"Always. Unless you'd prefer to return to the family in London?"

There was a pause. "No. I do not wish to be the subject of further gossip, the next nine days' wonder. Let them find something new to obsess over. In time they shall forget me."

"Understood." Deveric fell silent. A minute later, he asked, "Damon?"

Damon reluctantly opened his eyes. He turned toward Deveric so as to avoid Grace. He could not look upon her just now, not with his soul in a thousand pieces. He had offered for her and she had rejected him, despite the situation in which she now found herself, despite the moments they had shared. "Yes?"

"Do you wish us to take you to Thorne Hill? It's rather on the way, from what I understand."

Damon ground his teeth, a muscle popping in his cheek. "I would prefer to stay with Grace. We have unfinished business."

Grace coughed. Deveric raised an eyebrow.

"I have asked your sister to marry me. She has refused. Given all that has happened, I feel I must convince her otherwise."

For he must. Though she had slain him with her refusal, he could not leave her to a life of dishonor, devoured by scandal. She deserved far better, even if it be a marriage in name only. Something to rescue her reputation. The protection of the Malford wealth, the Malford name. *Though the Demon Duke had sullied that in the eyes of the ton, as well, no doubt.*

Both of Deveric's eyebrows rose as he studied his sister. "You refused him?"

Damon could not help but look to her, to gauge her response to her brother's challenge.

Grace's cheeks blazed bright red, her eyes darting to Daisy. "This is neither the time nor place to discuss it."

Was it Damon's imagination, or did Grace elbow Daisy in the side? The maid squirmed and then blinked, sitting up straight in the seat.

"Oh, I'm so sorry, Daisy," Grace said, her voice all too innocent. "I didn't mean to wake you."

Damon's mouth tipped up in a sardonic grin. He caught her eye and dipped his head briefly.

Well played. But this isn't over yet.

THE REST OF THE TRIP to Clarehaven passed more quickly than Grace had expected. With Daisy awake, they'd dropped all intimate conversation, thank heavens. Her feelings were entirely too raw to discuss.

Instead, Deveric and Damon spoke of managing an estate the size of Clarehaven. Though her brother's discussion of farming methods and crop yields nearly lulled her to sleep, Damon asked numerous questions and compared how things were done at Thorne Hill.

"I look forward to implementing a number of your suggestions, Deveric. It is good to have the counsel of someone with, er, more years of practice."

"Any time," her brother responded. "I must say, for a man not raised as the heir, you have done a remarkable job of it, Damon. You have my respect."

Damon had swallowed, his throat bobbing, but made no response beyond a curt nod. Grace's heart, however, swelled in gratitude toward her brother. No matter that currently she and Damon were in a mess, surely Deveric's acceptance, the affirmation of a fellow duke, must assuage some of Damon's self-doubt. And Damon deserved as much.

After a short silence, Damon addressed Daisy. "Do you mind if we don't go to Thorne Hill immediately? I know I promised a position there."

Daisy's eyes bulged in her head at a duke asking her opinion. "It is no problem fer me, Your Grace," she squeaked. "I am sure I can be of help in the kitchen."

"I don't suppose you have any experience as a lady's maid?" Grace asked.

Daisy swallowed. "No, milady. But my sister was lady's maid to Daphne, afore she died. I sometimes watched her."

Grace's eyebrows knit together. "I am so sorry for your loss."

Daisy clutched her hands together. "She sickened and died within a week. Same as Mum and Da."

Grace fought the urge to hug the poor girl; it would likely overset her. "Well, if you are willing to try, I find myself in need of a lady's maid, at least until Bess returns from London."

Daisy nodded, a hesitant smile on her face. "I would be right happy to help you, milady."

"Good. That's settled, then."

All four occupants fell to their personal thoughts, a quiet with its own peace infusing the coach.

But Grace knew it would not last. No, she still had her family to face. And Damon.

IT WAS LATE in the evening when the coach finally rolled up to Clarehaven. They had stopped occasionally to change horses and for a fine cold lunch from an inn along the way.

Grace exhaled in relief as she exited the coach, guided by Deveric's hand. She looked up at the tall columns framing the doorway and smiled. "It is good to be home." How she had missed it.

"Yes, it is," Deveric agreed.

Helping Daisy from the carriage, he transferred her to his waiting butler, Mulder. "Please take Daisy to Mrs. Wiggins." The butler gave Daisy the barest of nods, his bearing stiffly erect.

To Daisy, Deveric added, "Mrs. Wiggins is Clarehaven's housekeeper. She will see you settled."

Daisy nodded her thanks and left with the taciturn butler.

A squeal emerged as the grand front door flung open and a short blonde woman raced down the stairs, launching herself into Deveric's arms. She kissed him once, twice, and then pulled away to greet Grace, enfolding her in a warm embrace. "I knew he'd find you. I knew it! Thank God!"

Grace beamed. The light, loving manner of her sister-in-law was the perfect balm to the heaviness of the last days. "Eliza, you are always such a delight."

Eliza giggled and turned back to Deveric. Damon stood to his side, and Eliza, upon seeing him, exclaimed, "Hello! I'm Eliza Mattersley. And you are?"

"Ah, my dear, bold wife," Deveric said, stroking a hand down her arm. "Still American in every way, too impatient to wait for an introduction."

She elbowed him, but her cheeks cracked into a smile.

"Eliza, the Duke of Malford." Deveric's eyes twinkled. "Malford, this is my wife, the Duchess of Claremont."

She dropped him a curtsy. "It is my pleasure, Your Grace. Thank you for rescuing our dearest Grace. Rather like a chivalrous knight of old—or the hero of a modern gothic novel, don't you think?" She winked at him.

Grace nearly laughed out loud at her cousin. Dearest Eliza, indeed; she brought joy wherever she went.

Eliza hooked her arm through the young woman's. "Come, let's get eat something while you regale me with this crazy adventure. Some of Cook's cherry tarts?"

"Save some for me!" Deveric called after them.

Eliza flashed a saucy grin over her shoulder. "Your treats come later."

Grace looked back, as well, not wanting to miss her brother's reaction to his wife's suggestive banter. Instead, her eyes locked with Damon's. His were burning, hungry, devouring her so fully she shivered.

If pure physical passion were a reason for marriage, she'd wed him in a moment. For she liked nothing better than imagining herself the tart, the object of his appetite, and him consuming her. It was quite the vision, indeed.

But it wasn't enough. It wasn't enough.

ELIZA AND GRACE sat in the kitchen, cups of hot chocolate resting on the wooden table in front of them. Eliza took a bite of a tart, a delighted noise escaping from her as she licked the cherry filling.

"Exquisite, as always," she said after she'd finished chewing. "I have never understood how you stay so slim with treats like these in the house!"

Grace looked down at her own lean frame. She rather envied Eliza's curvier figure, truth be told, whereas Eliza often bemoaned her own proportions, stating on more than one occasion she wished for Grace's willowiness. Did women always want what they didn't have?

"Too many more of these and Dev is never going to look at me again. I haven't even lost the baby weight, and here I am, stuffing my face."

Grace snorted. "I cannot foresee any circumstances in which my brother would not be totally besotted with you, Eliza. The rest of us, either. Clarehaven hasn't been the same since you arrived, and for that, I am eternally grateful."

It was hard to remember Deveric as he had once been: stoic, reserved, dedicated to duty but keeping people, including his own son, at arm's length. He'd lost his first wife and infant daughter in childbirth, and his guilt over their deaths had nearly consumed him. Until Eliza. He'd fallen madly in love with her and the American had turned him around one hundred percent.

No wonder. Eliza's exuberant personality and sparkly wit, her entrancement with everything she saw, everything she experienced, as if it were all new to her, endeared her to all. Oh, to approach life with such curiosity and zest!

It was Eliza who'd most encouraged Grace to write.

"Mark my words," she'd said. "Women writers are going to become more and more well-known. I have no doubt that authors such as Mary Wollenstonecraft, Fannie Burney, Ann Radcliffe, and Jane Austen will be remembered for generations to come. Your name could be among them!"

It had been some time since their last visit to Chawton for tea with the Misses Austen, however. Since the autumn before last, in fact. When Deveric had learned Eliza was with child, he'd practically forbidden her to breathe, much less travel, so terrified was he of losing the baby and his wife with it. Eliza had grumbled but mostly acquiesced.

"Though I don't bow to all his demands, that one was a small price to pay for Dev's peace of mind," she'd said recently. "Besides, it gave me lots of time to spend with Frederick and Pirate."

Frederick was Deveric's son, and Pirate the one-eyed puppy he'd adopted shortly after Eliza had come to Clarehaven. The boy and the dog were inseparable, and the same was now true for her nephew and his father, too. Eliza was to credit for that, the reconciliation between father and son. They owed her so much.

Grace sipped the chocolate, its liquid deliciousness coating her parched throat. She was tired—exhausted, in truth—but she didn't wish to be rude to her sister-in-law, especially considering Eliza was choosing to spend time with her, rather than Deveric or her own children.

"Thank you, Eliza."

"For what?"

"For letting Deveric come when baby Isabelle is so new and you wanted him here."

"Are you joking? You're his sister. You're *my* sister. We'd do anything for you."

Grace's eyes welled up.

"Oh! I didn't mean to make you cry!"

"No, no. It's fine. I'm merely tired."

Eliza hopped up from her chair. "Absolutely right. How silly of me to keep you here after all you've been through. You go up to bed. We'll talk again in the morning. Just know I'm here if you need anything."

Grace stood up, cup in her hand. "Thank you." With a grateful nod, she headed to her chamber and hopefully for blessed sleep, where she could forget everything that had happened over the last two days. At least for a little while.

What I need is love like you have found, dearest Eliza. Or the ability to forget Damon Blackbourne existed. For the Duke of Malford had seeped into her soul, and she feared no exorcism was strong enough to ever remove him.

But half measures were not enough. A marriage of convenience, of distance, was no marriage. She wanted all of him, or nothing at all.

CHAPTER 26

CLAREHAVEN, HAMPSHIRE, ENGLAND
MID-MAY, 1814

*G*race woke late the next morning. Bright sunshine streamed through the window, but she had no clue as to the hour. She sat for a moment in the familiarity of her old chamber. How different everything felt from the last time she'd been here. Now she had met a man, the first man who'd made her insides flit about like feathers in the wind. Not only that, she'd spoken with him at length on a number of topics. Including her beloved books. She'd kissed him. She'd fallen in love with him. He'd asked her to marry him, and she'd refused him.

She pulled the covers over her head, burrowing into their warmth. Should she have said yes? Maybe he could learn to love her, to forge a true partnership. But she couldn't predicate her life on a maybe. Her mother had done so in the hope her husband would come back to her, would love only her. Look where she ended up. The fairy tale had never come true. Grace refused to find herself in the same position, in love with a husband who never returned the feeling.

But he *did* care for her. Valued her. He'd made that clear. Was it possible he loved her and didn't know it? It wasn't as if he'd had many examples of love in his life. Rejected by his father, torn from his mother, living the greater half of his life essentially alone—What man could know love from that?

She groaned. Her mother, her sisters, even her brother would no doubt lament her turning Damon down. At least now, after recent events. Her mother may not be fond of Damon Blackbourne, but she was even less fond of scandal, and another slur on the family name might be too much for her mother to bear.

A knock came at the door. Daisy poked her head in. "Milady?"

Grace yawned. "I'm here."

"My apologies, milady. The Duchess wanted me to ensure you were all right."

"Yes, fine. Why?"

"You've been sleeping for nearly fourteen hours."

At that, Grace sat up bed. "I have?"

Daisy bobbed her head. "I am sorry for waking you. Lady Eliza would like you to know she is in the nursery, should you want to visit today."

Grace rubbed her eyes. That was Eliza's way of saying she wished to continue their conversation from yesterday evening. Grace would much rather escape to the library for some much-needed solitude, but she didn't wish to hurt her sister-in-law's feelings. "Thank you."

Daisy helped her dress—a plain, unfussy morning gown that did nothing to accentuate any of her positive aspects, but she didn't care. She needed to feel comfortable with herself again.

Reluctantly, she made her way to the nursery. What was Damon doing? Was he still here? Would she run into him? Or would he have chosen to return to Thorne Hill—or London, to rejoin his sisters? Doubtful. In spite of her refusal, he'd insisted they weren't finished. He would not have left.

A tingle ran up her spine at the image of Damon as a black panther, pursuing his prey, prowling around her with that hypnotic gaze, waiting to pounce. She pressed her hand to her belly as she walked. The idea of being captured by Damon Blackbourne wasn't unpleasant. To the contrary. *But if he takes you, he will devour you. Consume you. And unless he loves you, you will find yourself spit out, unwhole.*

That was the kind of love she wanted, the kind that might bring Damon to declare, as Fitzwilliam Darcy had, "In vain I have struggled. It will not do. My feelings will not be repressed. You must allow me to tell you how ardently I admire and love you."

She sighed, pausing outside of the nursery door. Behind it, children giggled and Eliza's happy voice murmured. That was the kind of marriage Grace wanted, if she were to have one at all: a marriage built on love and respect. Not one cobbled together out of scandal and potential usefulness.

Taking in a breath, she pushed open the door. Thoughts of Damon would have to wait; now she needed to spend time in the company of her delightful nieces and nephew.

"Gway!" cried Rose, a charming, chubby little thing. Nearly two, she was quite precocious with an advanced vocabulary—when one could make out what she was saying. She ran over from her mother and threw her arms around her aunt's legs, causing Grace to stumble, but not before she laughed at her niece's exuberance.

"Rose, one ought not to bowl over their elders," spoke a rather serious voice from behind Eliza. Frederick,

Deveric's eight-year-old son from his first marriage, poked his head around Eliza's side. "It isn't done."

"It isn't?" Eliza said. She carefully lay baby Isabelle in the cradle, then scooped Frederick up in a big bear hug, tickling his sides. "Is this done, then?"

The boy whooped with delight. Eliza held him a moment longer before letting him go. He stood up and smoothed out his clothing, but gave his stepmother a mischievous grin.

"Eight years old and he already thinks he's in charge," she said to Grace.

"I can see that. He is the spitting image of my brother."

"Yes. Yes, he is."

Grace settled herself on the floor, Rose clambering onto her lap.

"How are you?" Eliza asked.

"I am well. Much refreshed. My apologies for oversleeping."

"Oversleeping? Don't be silly. You needed the rest after that ordeal." Casting her eyes toward her son, Eliza said, "Freddy, why don't you take Rose to see the new puppies? Mr. Sayers said it would be all right today for a short while. Take Nurse Pritchett with you."

"Yes, Mama," he replied in a dutiful voice, but his eagerness showed in his racing to grab Rose's hand.

"Bye Gway," Rose called, waving her other chubby hand as they exited the room.

Isabelle fussed in the crib, and Eliza scooped her back up. "Will it bother you if I nurse her?"

"Not at all," Grace said.

"Plus, in here we have privacy; I doubt the men will wish to disturb us." After she settled the baby to her breast, she reached over and clutched Grace's hand, giving it a light squeeze.

"So, tell me about this Damon Blackbourne. This Malford."

Grace bit her lip as blood rushed to her cheeks. "There's, um, not much to tell."

Eliza hooted. "Given the color of your face, I doubt that to be true. Also, this Fillmore scoundrel would not have taken you if he thought you'd meant nothing to Malford. Right?"

Grace fingered her sleeve, unsure how to respond.

"So, did you kiss him yet?"

At the unexpected question, Grace started, nearly falling backward.

"Aha! So you have! Tell me, is he as good a kisser as he looks? A man like that, all lights and darks, all sensuality and shadows?" It was Eliza's turn to flush. "Not that *I* am looking in that way," she amended. "You know I only have eyes for Deveric."

Grace laughed. "We *all* know that."

"But you have to admit, Malford is something. Quite the brooding Adonis. If Adonis were dark, like Hades. I want details. Tell me all about your duke."

"He is *not* my duke."

Eliza's eyebrows rose. "Do you usually go around kissing gentlemen? Do gentlemen usually race after you in the dead of night to rescue you from a precarious situation? No? Well, then. I would say he was yours."

"I rescued myself," Grace muttered. "In a manner."

"Yes, I heard you were the one to conk Fillmore over the head with a fireplace poker. How perfectly Gothic."

"Conk?"

"Sorry. Another American word. But stop trying to get me off of the subject. Did you enjoy kissing Malford?"

Grace closed her eyes. "Immensely," she admitted.

Eliza squealed, which caused Isabelle to stir. "Sorry,

sweetheart," she whispered before turning back to Grace. "So what's next?"

"He has asked me to marry him." The shocked expression on Eliza's face was comical. "But do not make too much of that; it is only because I am now the object of scandal, and he seeks to absolve my reputation."

Eliza's eyes narrowed. "Are you sure of that?"

"Quite sure. He told me such. Offered a marriage in name only. He said he owed me that much for what his uncle put me through. He said I would undoubtedly make a good wife, having been trained as I have. I could help him as he learns the ins and outs of society, having been away from it so long himself."

Eliza's jaw dropped. "He said that? In a marriage proposal?"

Grace nodded glumly.

"Well, I can see why you refused him. But lousy proposal aside, how do you feel about him?"

Tears flooded Grace's eyes. "I love him. With all my heart."

Eliza nearly dropped the baby. "Are you serious?"

"Yes. I wish it weren't so."

"Why ever not?"

"Because . . . because he doesn't return the sentiment. Because I thought I'd never find someone who would interest me, someone who had depth and character, who had concern for more than merely societal niceties and proper form. Someone who wanted to do more, *be* more." She paused for a moment, considering. "He has been dealt much misfortune in his life, Eliza. He has struggled with things most of us have never had to face."

Should she tell Eliza of Damon's tics, of the reason for the battles? *No.* It wasn't her secret to tell. She wouldn't dishonor him by doing so. "And he has persevered. Did you know he read the entire library of the abbey in which he grew up? Hundreds of books, Eliza. And he's read them all. Because he wanted to educate himself!"

Eliza chuckled. "Books, you say? I see why you fell madly in love. But Grace, my dear, why do you believe he's not in love with you? His actions to me do not suggest a man who feels any other way."

"He has never said as much, never even hinted."

"Actions speak louder than words. Could he be afraid? From what you have told me, it does not sound as if he has had much acceptance in his life, much less love. It would be quite risky, especially for a man, a proud man, to express feelings he fears might not be returned. No wonder he offered you a marriage of convenience; it was a way of doing right without risking a greater rejection."

Grace stilled. She had thought the very same thing only an hour ago. Did Damon love her but was too scared to admit it?

Or was *she* the one frightened? If she accepted his offer, even without professing her love for him, her life trajectory would change. Instead of the spinster aunt, living out her days at Clarehaven, writing stories, she'd be a duchess. Duchesses held a huge amount of responsibility in the home, in the management of estates, and in society. Could she handle that? Did she want to?

If she *did* marry, she'd thought she'd be happiest the wife of a gentleman of lower rank, perhaps a member of the gentry. Were there not fewer obligations and restrictions for those not of the peerage?

But Damon hadn't wanted the dukedom either. It'd been thrust upon him by the family that had rejected him, and rather than abdicate his responsibilities, he had taken them up. Given his tics, his solitary tendencies, his isolated upbringing, and his strained relations with his family, it would have made more sense for him to refuse his mother's summons and to have stayed in Yorkshire. Yet he hadn't. That spoke volumes as to his good character. Not that she'd doubted it, given the way he'd behaved with her sisters, the way he'd rushed to her rescue, even the way he'd offered Daisy a position.

"But if he truly loved me, if he truly wished to marry me, wouldn't he have confessed his feelings after my refusal?"

"Did you confess your feelings after his botched proposal?"

Grace sucked in her cheeks in dismay.

"Perhaps you should seek him out? It sounds like a frank conversation may be in order."

Grace's heart leapt at the suggestion. "But what if you're wrong? What if he doesn't love me and is only trying to make the best of a bad situation?"

Eliza gave her a tender smile. "But what if I'm right?"

DAMON HAD SOUGHT Grace out that morning intending to convince her the only course of action was to marry him. But she hadn't been at breakfast—still sleeping, Eliza had said. And then Deveric had invited him on a tour of Clarehaven. Damon hadn't wanted to refuse his host. Indeed, he'd lost himself in Deveric's able discussions of the estate and all that was required for its upkeep. He asked numerous questions, to which Deveric gave thorough responses. Now they'd ridden out to the lake.

Grace had several times professed her love for this lake, for its waters. No wonder. It was a beautiful spot. He indulged in fantasies of bringing her here for a picnic. They would spread a blanket out under that huge weeping willow and dine to their hearts' content on a fabulous spread of cold chicken and potatoes, green beans and apple dumplings. He would read to her, perhaps a volume of poetry, or a novel, using his voice to exaggerate each character's actions. She would laugh in that pretty manner she had and lay her head in his lap as he read, his back against the willow tree. After a few pages, he would set the book aside. He'd look down into her spellbinding brown eyes, trace those delicately arched eyebrows with his finger, and touch the errant freckle on her cheek. He'd run his fingers through her hair, releasing the hairpins one by one to let the locks fan out over his legs.

Her pulse would beat in her neck, the rhythm picking up speed as he stroked his fingers along her ear, down to her collarbone, then over her dress, tracing the shape of her through the layers of fabric. What would it be like to take her breast into his hand? She was rather small, but he'd never cared for buxom women anyway—a handful sufficed. He dreamt of rubbing his thumb over her nipple, of watching as the nub came to attention. He'd then dip his head and kiss those luscious lips of hers, stroking her with his tongue the way his fingers were stroking her breast . . .

Deveric cleared his throat, snapping Damon back to reality. He shifted in his saddle, grateful Claremont was riding in front of him and thus spared the evidence of Damon's imaginings about his sister. "It's growing late. Shall we return to the house?"

Damon nodded, struggling to clear his head of his lustful thoughts. He had to get her to marry him. He had to.

After they'd ridden in peaceable silence a few minutes, Deveric spoke. "I take it you are going to ask Grace to marry you?"

"Again, you mean?"

"Ha, yes, again. I'm sorry I missed the first proposal. I should have liked to have heard it, or at least Grace's response."

"It did not go well."

"Obviously, since it's clear by your demeanor that she refused you." Deveric grinned over at Damon, who now rode by his side. "I'm torn, you know."

"What?"

"I am. On the one hand, all would agree it's the right thing to do, you marrying her on account of recent events. On the other, I wouldn't force anyone into a marriage they don't want, whether it be you or Grace. I endured that in my first marriage, and given its disastrous results, it's a fate I wouldn't wish on anyone."

"Though now you have your Eliza."

"Yes, exactly. Now I have my Eliza. And I want everyone to have what Eliza and I have. Lord knows it's rare in these times."

Damon merely nodded, unsure of what to say.

"And yet I have this feeling," Deveric continued, "that a union between you and my sister would be more than merely an effort to avoid scandal. Not that a scandal can be completely avoided as is."

Damon remained silent.

"As I was saying, I wouldn't be in favor of a match between you and my sister if I didn't suspect that you had feelings for her, feelings beyond friendship and, well, honor."

"I do," Damon conceded at length.

"And I believe she has feelings for you, too."

"That I cannot answer. That she so roundly refused me makes me think not. One can hardly blame her." He gave a derisive snort.

Deveric frowned. "What do you mean?"

"Come, Claremont. Let us speak plainly. I am no

great catch. Yes, I am a duke now, but titles are of no consequence to Grace. And it's not one I should hold. Were it not for my uncle, I would still be in the Yorkshire wilderness, the unwanted and forgotten son."

He ground his teeth, steeling himself against the pain of his own words. "I did not receive a proper education. The one tutor my mother hired I drove out. My library was thus my tutor, but in ways it was lacking and incomplete. Through Hobbes, I received guidance on successfully negotiating polite society, but there was only so much he could teach. I was not prepared to shoulder a ducal title and its corresponding duties."

He paused for a moment, but this time Deveric was the one who said nothing.

"I don't enjoy polite company. I rarely know what to say or what is expected," Damon added as the silence stretched on.

"All of those are things that can be overcome, Blackbourne. Indeed, you've already overcome a number of them."

"But there's one thing I can't overcome, and you well know it. This demon inside, this devil on my back. This betrayal of my own body, forcing me into movements and sounds I don't want to make, but cannot control. At least not for long. I thought they were gone, or I wouldn't have returned. I see now they were merely dormant, roused again by the challenges of the last month." His lips pulled into a thin line, anguish slumping his shoulders. "What woman would want that? What woman? What woman would risk having children that might be afflicted in a similar manner? Is it not better to let this die with me?"

If Deveric noticed the sheen in Damon's eyes, he did not comment on it.

"That is why I offered the option of a marriage of

convenience—in name only, lest she worry over the same things."

Deveric laughed out loud, a long and hearty bellow. "You offered my sister a marriage of *convenience*? Do you not know her at all? She finds marriage anything but convenient. No, nothing but a grand love would bring her to the altar—not even a scandal such as this. And if you believe Grace would reject you for any of the other, you have sorely misjudged her."

Damon scowled, his face burning. He did not care to be laughed at. And it was clear he'd miscalculated quite thoroughly. He needed a drink, needed to think over all Deveric had said.

They reached the stables and dismounted, handing the horses over to the stable master. As they walked toward the house, Deveric turned the subject to his children. Damon was grateful for the respite; he was worn quite raw.

It was only temporary, however. As the lights of Clarehaven welcomed them in, Damon braced himself, for he would need to speak with Grace again.

Tonight.

CHAPTER 27

CLAREHAVEN, HAMPSHIRE, ENGLAND
MID-MAY, 1814

*G*race rolled over and opened her eyes, confused by the darkness. She had lain down for a mere moment before dressing for dinner. Why was it pitch black? She sat up. The fire in the fireplace was reduced to glowing embers. She got out of bed and walked to the window, pushing aside the curtain. The moon hung in the inky, star-filled sky.

She must have slept through dinner, the excitement and anxiety of the past few days catching up with her. Her stomach grumbled. Would there be anything in the kitchen at this time of night? It must be after midnight, given the fire. Perhaps Cook would have left something out on which she could nibble.

Pulling on her wrapper, she crept into the hallway. All was quiet and dark as she padded toward the stairs. In which chamber was Damon? Was he, in fact, still here? She hadn't seen him all day. Would he think she was avoiding him, since she'd appeared at neither breakfast nor dinner?

Her earlier conversation with Eliza echoed through

her mind. Could Eliza be right? Was it possible Damon *did* love her?

A light flickered from under the library door. Who could be in there? She debated whether to pass by, but curiosity got the better of her. Perhaps Dev was up with the baby. He'd said in the carriage he liked to help with Isabelle at night. If so, she should apologize for missing dinner and assure him she was fine. She pushed the door and it opened with a mild squeak.

A man sat on the settee, facing the flames, but it was not Deveric, not with that raven hair. The firelight illuminated the sharp planes of his cheek. *Damon.*

He turned and their eyes locked. He blinked, then his cheek inched upward as he gave her a crooked smile. "Ah. The mouse emerges at last. I suppose it does not surprise me that books are your cheese. Irresistible."

He raised a glass to her in mock toast. Brandy, most likely—that's what her brother favored and kept well stocked. How much had he imbibed? He did not seem foxed.

"Damon," she said. "I'm sorry. I didn't mean to disturb you. I overslept and missed dinner."

He rose, all feline grace. "And you thought to find something to eat in the library?"

Grace clutched at her wrapper, embarrassment making her skin tingle. "No. I—There was a light. I . . . "

She stilled as he sauntered over to her, his eyes never leaving hers. He stopped mere inches from her body, far too close to be proper. She sucked in her breath. He raised his empty hand and she thought for a moment he was going to put it around her waist, pull her against him, but he merely pushed on the door until it clicked shut.

Grace stared at him, her eyes wide in apprehension and . . . something else. She shouldn't be here, in the library, alone with him, in the middle of the night. But he wouldn't hurt her. The apprehension wasn't fear. It was excitement. Nervousness. Desire. She licked her lip.

Damon groaned. "God, Grace, what you do to me. Don't do things like that."

"Like what?"

"Licking those damn luscious lips. It makes me want to lick them, too."

At her gasp, he smirked, his eyebrow rising. "But that would mark me for the beast I am, would it not? Taking advantage of a fair maiden in her own castle?"

Grace's brow knit. "What do you mean?"

"I mean," he growled, throwing his arms wide. "You make me want to do bad things. Things I shouldn't do."

She wrinkled her nose in confusion. "How is kissing me bad?"

He gave a short bark of laughter. "Because it makes me want to do more. So much more." He took a sip from his tumbler. His Adam's apple bobbed as he swallowed, and her fingers itched to touch him there.

"Stop looking at me like that," he growled.

"Like what?"

"Like the cat who wants the cream. I only have so much self-restraint, dearest Grace. And you've already made it clear that you don't want me."

She sucked in, hard. "Whatever gave you that idea?" She couldn't believe the words as they left her mouth. Who was this woman, freely admitting her desire for a man?

Damon leaned in very close, so close his breath caressed her lips, but he didn't kiss her. "You did. When you refused to marry me."

Grace gulped. The words were out before she had time to rethink them. "But that had nothing to do with me not wanting you, Damon. Exactly the opposite."

Perhaps she shouldn't have said as much. A proper lady wouldn't. And yet, despite the muddle in which they found themselves, there was something between them. She knew it. She had always known it. True, he hadn't declared his undying love, but for her to tell herself there were no feelings, no bond of some sort, was an outright lie.

It had felt safer to believe the lie.

Safer for whom? For her, she supposed. So that life would remain the same. So that she could go on with her plans and not have to risk anything, not have to risk *everything*, on a man. Not merely any man. This man. Because if she had said yes, everything would change. And she couldn't bear the idea of loving him without him loving her in return.

Damon slammed the tumbler on a table near the door. "What do you mean, it had nothing to do with me? I asked you to marry me, and you said no. I cannot see how that doesn't have *everything* to do with me."

He pinched his eyes shut, pain seeping across his face before he opened them again. "I understand, Grace. I am not what you would want in a husband, not what anyone would want in a spouse. I am damaged. I am a demon, just like they call me. I am unlovable. I've always known it." He jerked away from her and stumbled near the fire.

Grace let out an agonized cry and ran to him, locking her arms around him. "No, Damon," she said, tears leaking from her eyes. "Don't speak of yourself in such a way. Ever."

She ran her hand down his cheek, smoothing her thumb over his lips as if to keep him from saying anything further. "I refused you because I didn't want you to feel obligated on account of your uncle's actions. Because you offered me marriage, yes, but a marriage devoid of connection. Of affection. Of passion. Because the way you were speaking was not the way a woman wants the man she's in love with to propose."

She rose on her tiptoes and pressed her lips to his. "I love you, Damon Blackbourne," she murmured.

At first, he did nothing. Then it was as if a dam broke, and he clutched her to him, his mouth moving over hers, claiming her, devouring her. "Say it again," he pleaded. "Say it again, Grace."

"I love you," she said, a tear trickling from her eye. She did love him, for better or worse, whatever may come.

He opened his eyes, a blissful smile on his lips until he saw the tear. "Why are you crying, dearest?" He wiped the drop with his finger, then sucked it off his fingertip.

"Because. I am happy," she whispered. "And I am frightened."

He pulled her into him again, his arms wrapping her in his solid embrace. She rested her head on his chest and his breath stirred her hair. "Of what? Please tell me not of me. I would never hurt you, Grace. Never. I have this . . . devil inside of me, but I would never hurt you."

"I know that." She took a breath, squaring herself to admit her deepest fear, spurred on by Eliza's encouragement. "But I watched my mother give her life to my father. She loved him, loved him deeply. And he tired of her. She never meant as much to him as he did to her, and it ruined her, Damon. It ruined her. Only recently, only with the arrival of Eliza, could she see it, how she locked herself behind rigid propriety and rule-following as a desperate way to block out the hurt of my father's betrayal. She told me as much and warned me, warned all of us, not to do the same."

He leaned back, cupping her face between his hands. "But why would you think we would have such a marriage?"

"Because of what you said, Damon! In the carriage. You spoke of having to marry me because I was ruined. You spoke of me being a well-trained wife. You said I wouldn't have to come with you to London, that you'd be happy to leave me behind. Even that we need not have a full marriage. It was everything I never wanted!"

He closed his eyes. "God, I'm such an idiot, Grace. Come."

He moved to the settee, beckoning her. He sat and when she neared, pulled her on top of him. The intimate connection, so much of their bodies pressing together, was unnerving. Exciting. Arousing.

Cradling her in his arms, he gazed into her eyes, emotion roiling in his own. "I said those things because I thought they might convince you more than anything else."

He swallowed. "My feelings for you are deeper than anything I've ever known, Grace Mattersley. They're so intense, so complex, they terrify me. You accepted my movements right from the start, from that first moment in the library."

He stroked her loose hair from her face. "You're brilliant. I've never doubted women can be as intelligent, if not more so, than men, but for me, lacking any formal . . . education, it's intimidating." A sheepish grin spread across his face. "Not very manly of me, is it?"

Pulling her closer before she could respond, he feathered her cheek with kisses. "My whole life I've been told, been shown, that I'm unlovable. My mother was the sole person professing otherwise. But even she abandoned me. How could I think otherwise, than to believe I wasn't worth loving?" He clutched her to him, burying his face in her hair. "To hear you say it. Oh my God, Grace, you can't imagine how it feels."

He ran his arm around her middle and up her side,

under the wrapper. The heat of his hand soaked through her thin nightgown, and it made her shiver, but not from cold.

"I don't need a traditional wife. I don't care if you spend all day in the library reading. I don't care if I ever learn which spoon is correct, or which form of address goes with which person. I don't need you to teach me that. I don't want you to do anything you don't want to do. I only need . . . kindness. I need love."

He pulled back, gently tilting her chin up with his hand so that their eyes could feast on each other. He smiled, his eyes welling up. "I love you, Grace Mattersley. I love you. You have slain my demons. You have slain me. Will you do me the incredible honor of being my wife?"

Grace's heart nearly burst. He loved her? He truly loved her? As she loved him? She flattened herself against him, her lips capturing his in a scorching kiss. She poured all of her emotions into him, and he returned the kiss in kind, his hand running down her side. She pressed her breasts against his chest and he moaned, his hand sliding around to gently caress one of the small mounds. He broke off from her mouth.

"I take that as a yes?" he breathed, even as his thumb moved over her nipple, flicking it gently.

"Yes! Oh, yes, Damon!"

He shifted on the settee so that he was lying full-length on it, his head reclined on its arm, Grace on top of him. He ran his arms over her back under her wrapper, his touch arousing the most exhilarating sensations. He moved farther down, cupping her derriere as he pulled her against him, his arousal pressing into her. "Stop me, Grace. Stop me, or so help me God, I'll take you right here on this sofa."

She wriggled against him, delighting in her power.

"Why ever would I?" Her eyes sparkled with mischief. "I'm already a ruined woman, am I not? You said that's why I needed to marry you."

He groaned as she shifted against him. "Forget what I said. I'm an idiot."

He made to push the wrapper from her shoulders, and she sat up, aiding him, dropping it to the floor. The nightgown she wore was modest, a thick cotton not at all seductive in any manner, but he beheld it as if she were wearing a gossamer negligee. Hesitantly, he reached up and undid the long row of buttons at the front, his eyes never leaving hers as the gown dropped farther and farther open. At last he pulled it down past her breasts to her waist. And then he stared.

Grace fought the instinct to cover her chest with her arms. No, she would not show shame, for there was nothing of which to be ashamed. He reached up and cupped the small mounds in his palms. His pupils dilated. "You are so beautiful. So very beautiful."

He slid a hand around her back and tipped her forward so that one of her nipples grazed his lips. He opened his mouth, eagerly sucking on the tip. An unexpected bolt of electricity coursed through her, her eyes flying open wide for a second before she closed them and gave herself over to the sumptuous feelings he awakened in her. She braced one arm on the settee, trying to steady herself against the waves of sensation crashing over her. She pressed her hips into his, seeking the pressure, and he moaned against her breast.

"I want," he said, his breath coming in short gasps, "to see you. All of you."

Grace's skin flushed in spite of herself, but she stood up, instantly missing the heat of his body. "Only if you return the favor," she whispered, casting him a flirtatious glance.

Damon leapt up, his fingers flying to his cravat.

"No, no. Let me." She pushed his hands away and worked at untying the knot herself, the tip of her tongue peeking out between her lips as she concentrated.

Damon chuckled. "You are irresistible. The tip of that tongue drives me wild."

She leaned forward and licked his neck. He shook at the contact. "Mmm," she said. "I will have to think of other things to do with it."

Gracious, where had that boldness come from? She wasn't even sure what she'd meant, but he instantly responded. His hands flew back to her breasts, kneading them before feverishly pushing her gown down over her hips.

"Now that's not fair. I'm completely naked and the only thing I've managed to wrest off of you is your cravat." Her sauciness surprised her, but she gave a sultry laugh as his hands slid across her skin, once again clutching her derriere and pulling her flush against him.

Her hands moved back up and she pushed against him. He released her, a puzzled look on his face until she pulled at his shirtfront. He worked on loosening his breeches as she pushed his shirt up, her fingers running over the smooth muscle and light sprinkling of hair on his chest.

"Not so fast," she practically purred. "I want to undress you myself."

Damon stilled as she caressed his shoulders, then stroked her hands along his back. "Who is this siren?" he said. "She has most definitely bewitched me. I am her slave."

Grace giggled. Her boldness caught her unaware, as well. She'd had a kiss or two before Damon, but that was all. Yet this felt so good, so right, that she felt no guilt, felt no shame. They were one, bound together for all time. She reached for his loosened breeches and pushed them down. Where they caught on his boots.

"Bother!" she said. "I'm obviously a novice at this."

"Perhaps it is unfair to say, but I am happy to hear that." He sat and pulled off the boots one by one before rising again. The breeches followed the boots, and he stood there, clad only in his smalls. Black smalls.

Something about that made her smile. A wicked little smile, as her eyes ran up and down his muscular legs, so different from her own softer, fleshier ones.

"You are like a Roman statue," she proclaimed. There was no mistaking the solidness of his form. Her confidence faltered at the bulge in the front of his smalls.

"And you my Venus." His eyes raked over her. He did not touch her, though, merely waited. "If you wish to stop, Grace, so help me God, I will. I don't want to. But I will."

"No," she said. "I'm merely a bit nervous." Her cheeks burned with the admission.

"Truth be told, so am I."

At those honest words, she moved forward again, wrapping her arms around his waist, rubbing her naked breasts against his chest. What a strange sensation, warm skin on warm skin, his hard but yet soft with hair, hers delicately tender. His lips found hers and they lost themselves in a fervent kiss. Her hands snaked down and carefully pushed the smalls until they fell to the ground. Damon kicked them to the side. They stood, pressed full-length into each other.

He danced her to the settee and lay her down. He parted her legs and settled himself between them, the firmness of his length against her most private spot causing her to writhe in pleasure. He smiled at that before moving to suckle her breasts again, first one, then the other. "Such perfect beauties," he whispered.

"They are not too small?" she asked, trepidation lacing her voice.

"They are perfect." He rose up over her, making room for his hand to slide down her soft belly into the curls below. He traced his finger along her cleft and she made mewling noises, reveling in his touch.

"Here?" he asked as he found a most sensitive spot.

"Yes," she breathed. "Oh, yes."

He stroked her, his tongue and lips pressing caresses against her breast. A magnificent expectation built through her body, like waves lapping the shore, pulling back and surging forward again under the skillful ministrations of his fingers. Suddenly, she burst, her hips bucking under his hand as infinite tiny flames shot through her entire body.

"Damon!" The sensation was beyond exquisite, and she clutched him to her as wave after wave of pleasure washed over her, wanting to share it with him.

He said nothing, his eyes dark with need, but kissed her, thrusting his tongue between her lips as he moved between her legs. "I hope this doesn't hurt," he said.

She didn't have time to respond, because he was sliding into her, the huge length of him. It was the strangest sensation, but not entirely painful. He went slowly, pausing as he was able, his breath coming in harsh gasps.

"Are you—?" he said, but she broke him off, pulling his lips to hers. As he kissed her, she reached down and pressed against his buttocks, burying him deeper, as deep as he could go, inside her. He groaned with pleasure and began to move, slowly at first, then building up to a steadier, faster speed.

He was inside her. How could that be? It was peculiar. It was marvelous. She lost all thought, giving herself over to the experience. He pounded into her, his back slick with sweat, his neck taut with anticipation and need.

"Oh God, Grace," he cried, and she moved with him, her hips meeting his in an age-old dance.

"Yes, Damon." He was nearing the same precipice to which he had led her. "Yes."

At the sound of his name on her lips, he exploded, pumping into her a few more times until he collapsed on top of her, his head buried in the side of her neck.

They lay there for a long while. She ran her fingers languidly over his back, savoring the intimacy of what had just transpired. He pressed light kisses against her neck.

"I love you, Damon Blackbourne," she whispered, a contented feeling like she'd never known settling over her body.

His fingers intertwined with hers. "And I you, Grace Mattersley . . . Blackbourne."

CHAPTER 28

CLAREHAVEN, HAMPSHIRE, ENGLAND
MID-MAY, 1814

*H*e didn't want to move, but they couldn't stay there all night; not only was the settee becoming deucedly uncomfortable, but Damon didn't want to risk being caught in such a compromising position, whether betrothed or not.

Reluctantly, he stood, giving Grace's naked body an appreciative glance before reaching for his smalls and breeches. Her skin flushed pink as she rose, searching for her nightgown.

"Over there," he said, pointing. "But it's a shame you have to put it on. Such a dowdy thing for such a beautiful package underneath."

Grace grabbed the nightgown and whirled around to face him again, her cheeks nearly scarlet. She yanked the gown over her head, nimbly fastening the buttons up the front.

"Are you embarrassed, my love?"

Her fingers paused. "A little."

"Don't be. I plan to look at you naked as often as I

can in the future." He gave her a wolfish grin, which widened even further when her cheeks reached a color he'd heretofore thought impossible for human skin.

He stood, clad only in his unsecured breeches. "Do you find the sight of me distasteful?"

His voice was teasing. She hadn't stopped sneaking glances at him. His form was more muscled than what was currently fashionable among the dandies. Running and performing hard labor at the abbey had not only provided an outlet for his unwanted movements, but they'd honed his physique in innumerable ways. Never had he appreciated that so much as now, as Grace Mattersley shyly eyed his legs, her gaze moving up to his chest and then finally his face. He winked at her.

"No. You are glorious."

At her softly spoken words, he strode to her, clasping her head between his hands as he kissed her, a soul-searching kiss into which he poured all of his emotions for this woman.

Her arms wound around him, her fingers tracing the muscles in his back. One hand slid down, down, until it covered his backside. He jumped as she squeezed his buttock. She laughed against his lips.

He gave her a peck on the nose before stepping back a few inches. "Saucy wench. I see you are full of surprises. I like that about you. But I'm afraid I must depart, lest I keep you here, loving every inch of your delectable body, until well past dawn."

Grace sighed. "You are right. Though I'd far prefer the latter." She pulled the wrapper around her shoulders, then reached up with her right hand and smoothed his hair off of his forehead. "Thank you."

His forehead wrinkled. "For what?"

"For loving me."

His heart threatened to burst. This woman, this

glorious woman, was thanking *him* for loving *her?* Didn't she know it was he who should be groveling at her feet?

"Oh no," he said. "Thank *you*. I never thought—" He broke off as his voice caught. "I never thought I would find someone who would love me for me. Exactly as I am."

She stood on her toes and gave him a quick peck. "You took the words right out of my mouth." She giggled as he tried to capture her lips in another kiss.

"No, no, no," she teased, pushing against his chest. For a second her fingers lingered, running over the hard muscle, but then she stepped away. "I must return to my bedchamber, and you must get dressed."

She reached for the doorknob behind her and opened it, slipping out the door. Just before it closed he heard her whisper, "I'll see you at breakfast. Husband."

HE'D ONLY HAD an hour or so of sleep, but his mood was high and his steps jaunty as he entered the breakfast room the next morning. He homed in immediately on Grace, who stood at the side table, nursing a cup of tea. She was garbed in a modest gown of yellow muslin.

Sunshine. She is my sunshine.

It took all of his willpower not to run to her and enfold her in his arms.

He was so focused on her he failed to see the other people in the room.

"Good morning, Damon!" cried a familiar voice. His sister Cassie was seated at the table next to Lady Emmeline.

"Cassie? What? When?"

"We arrived last night, later than we had wished since

the carriage became bogged down in mud about half an hour out."

"But . . . "

"Yes, I'm happy to see you, too. And thrilled Lady Grace is back, safe and sound."

He looked to Grace, who peeked at him over the rim of her teacup, her eyes apologetic. *So much for having each other to themselves this morning.*

Emmeline piped up. "Indeed, we were so delighted to hear the news of her return, we simply had to see for ourselves that she was all right." She flashed a grin at her sister, who flushed a most becoming rose.

What was Grace thinking? The same as he, of their time in the library? Or of future private moments to come?

Sephe, who sat to the other side of Emmeline, muttered, "I'm sure they would have returned to London shortly. Did we really have to miss the Findlay ball?"

Damon chuckled at his sister's whining. "Two months in and still not exhausted by the Season? You were born to be a debutante."

"Yes, and now I'm missing my moment to shine. And a certain Lord M—."

"Oh, pshaw," interjected Cassie. "We only need stay a few days. Emmeline felt it best to leave for a bit, and we wished to show our support for dearest Grace."

Her hesitation on the word *leave* indicated there was more to the story than the women were letting on, especially given the pinking of Emmeline's cheeks.

"Has there been talk?" Grace's voice was sharp.

"There is always talk," Rebecca said.

"But some time away gives London time to find a newer object of interest," Emmeline insisted.

"Yes, and us a break from questions and looks!" Rebecca's mouth pinched.

Grace cast her eyes to the floor. "I am sorry."

Damon wanted nothing more than to wring his uncle's neck for the hurt the man had caused his future wife.

"But the shame is on Fillmore, not Grace," cried Cassie, mirroring Damon's thoughts. "And fear not. Lady Gilmore has run off with a certain Mr. Logan. A man of no standing. That shall have tongues wagging for some time."

It wasn't likely to stem all gossip and speculation, though, much to Damon's frustration. Still, they would rise above it. Together.

The door opened and Deveric entered, followed by Eliza, holding baby Isabelle.

"Good morning." Deveric nodded in greeting to Damon and then to the women at the table.

"Morning," Damon answered.

Would the whole neighborhood soon appear? How he longed to be alone with his love, to pepper her face with a thousand kisses, to fall at her feet and give thanks to God for bringing her into his life.

"How are you doing?" Eliza asked Grace.

Grace's cheeks pinked, much to his delight, her gaze darting to him and away again. Eliza's face took on a knowing expression at the exchange, but she said nothing. She did, however, wink at him.

He started in surprise. Had anyone else noticed? It seemed not, as they all busied themselves with their breakfasts.

"How is Mother? Did she accompany you?" Damon asked his sisters, trying to focus his attention on something, anything other than his adorable soon-to-be wife.

"No," Cassie said. "She did not wish to travel. She has never cared for long carriage rides. No offense to you,

Lady Grace, or you, Your Grace." She nodded to Claremont.

"None taken," Grace said. "You needn't have come; I am truly fine."

"And we are happy to see that," Cassie responded. "Thank you, Your Grace, and you, brother, for rescuing Lady Grace."

"Actually, Grace rather rescued herself; she hit our uncle over the head with a fireplace poker."

"Truly?" Sephe's face lit up with glee. "Did you kill him?"

"Tsk tsk," Damon chided. "Bloodlust does not become you, dearest sister."

Sephe gave a most unladylike snort.

"I did not kill him," Grace said, her tone earnest. "Though I rather fancied doing so at the time."

"My goodness," Deveric said. "Let me be sure never to get on the wrong side of any of you women."

Damon walked to Grace on the pretense of fetching a biscuit. He stopped within a respectable distance, though he longed to move closer. "Morning, wife," he said in a voice too low for the others to hear.

Grace choked on her tea.

"Perhaps we should tell them?"

"Now? Here?" Her voice was the lowest of whispers.

"Why not? Unless you have changed your mind?"

She gave him a dazzling smile. "Never, my love."

"Well, then." He set the biscuit down on the table and pulled her to him, kissing her as tea sloshed out of her cup and down the front of his waistcoat. He didn't care.

There came a collective intake of breath, then the sound of clapping. He broke off from Grace and turned to a sea of curious faces.

Eliza handed Isabelle to Deveric before hopping up and down in excitement. "Hooray!"

Deveric raised his eyebrows, but said nothing, waiting for them to speak.

Damon settled his arm around Grace's waist, pulling her in close. "I am proud to say that Lady Grace Mattersley has done me the utmost honor in consenting to be my wife."

The table erupted in cheers.

"When is the wedding?" Emmeline burst out.

"As soon as possible," Grace said, her eyes reflecting her happiness.

Deveric cleared his throat. "Do you think that wise," he said at length, "given recent events?"

Damon frowned. "How do you mean?"

"A hasty wedding may raise eyebrows, in that people may wonder if a worse ill befell Grace."

"You mean we should wait to prove to the world that I am not with Lord Fillmore's child?" Grace said.

The room fell uncomfortably silent.

"I do not care what the world thinks," she added, her voice strong. "I only care what Damon and my family think. But you know I was not harmed at Fillmore's hands. Right, brother?"

"I do, yes, but the rest of the *ton*—"

"—Does not matter to me," she interrupted.

Damon laced his fingers through hers, incredibly moved at her defense of him and her bravery. It *was* possible that after their night together she could be with child. *His* child. The idea both thrilled and terrified him.

"Very well." Deveric nodded his approval.

"You know, dear brother," Cassie said. "Mother will be devastated if you do not announce your betrothal in London. She will want to hold an engagement ball."

Damon's face paled. "But surely not while still in mourning?"

"I think all will understand if mourning is set aside

for this. It's not often a duke marries, after all. And she—we all—want to show our staunch support of this union. Of Lady Grace."

Grace rubbed her fingers over his at her waist. "I think it is a fine idea. We must face everyone sooner or later. Better in triumph and celebration than otherwise, is it not?"

Cassie smiled in thanks for Grace's support, as everyone else dipped their heads in agreement.

"Though perhaps my family should host," Deveric said. "To show our full support of my sister and to remove attention from you and your mother, Damon. She will no doubt be struggling with the news of these latest happenings."

Damon doubted anything would distract the *ton* from recent events, but he nodded in acquiescence.

"And if we should happen to disappear to the library for a period of time," Grace whispered in Damon's ear, "surely no one can begrudge two book fiends that?"

Her other hand slid behind him and lightly pinched his backside. It took all he had not to burst out laughing at her cheekiness. He liked this side of Grace. Yes, indeed.

Deveric nodded. "Then it is settled. I'm sure between Emmeline and your sisters, they will plan the grandest ball the *ton* has ever seen."

Damon swallowed. What was he getting into? *It's for the family.* Then he and Grace could escape to Thorne Hill or Blackwood Abbey. He squeezed her close, and she gave him the most beautiful smile. Yes, he could do this. *They* could do this.

It's for Grace. It's all for Grace.

The baby began to fuss. "Belle is tired. I think we shall return to the nursery," Eliza said as she took her daughter from Deveric. Moving toward the door, she paused near Damon's sisters. "I have planned a visit to Chawton today, to pay a long-overdue call on my friend, Miss Jane Austen. It has been ages since we've seen each other. Would you like to join me?"

Cassie and Sephe glanced at each other. "If it's all right with you, Your Grace, I believe we'd rather discuss dresses and such for the ball. And we shouldn't want to distract you from your friend."

"Emmeline? Becca?" Eliza tilted her head toward her sisters-in-law.

"I am of a mind with Damon's sisters—" Emmeline started before Rebecca interrupted.

"And I have plans to go riding. It's been an age!"

Emmeline poked at Rebecca. "But don't let us keep you, Eliza. You needn't change your plans on our account."

"I should like to go," Grace broke in. "Damon, would you?"

"Actually," said Deveric, "he'd asked yesterday evening to discuss the best methods for fertilizing crops."

Eliza chirped merrily. "If you'd rather talk manure, be my guest. Grace and I will enjoy a fine day together. I especially look forward to hearing about *all* of her adventures of late."

Her raised eyebrow made Damon shift uncomfortably. Surely Eliza couldn't know about last night?

"I shall meet you in the parlor in, say, an hour, Grace?" Eliza made for the door as Isabelle's fussing increased to wails. Deveric followed behind, making silly faces at the baby. Isabelle quieted as she stared at her father.

"That sounds delightful." Grace looked to Damon. "If you don't mind, my love, I should like to write for a bit?"

He'd have to get used to losing her to her stories

sometimes. He was fine with that, happy to see her doing what she so clearly loved. "Of course."

She beamed at him as she left the room, her step light. *I am the luckiest man in the world.*

A lucky man about to talk pig shit with one of the highest-ranking men in the land. A rank he now shared.

Life was strange. But good. Oh so good.

CHAPTER 29

CLAREHAVEN, HAMPSHIRE, ENGLAND
MID-MAY, 1814

*G*race frowned at the words on the page. They wouldn't come together, not the way she wanted them to, not with the apparent ease of Miss Jane Austen's writing. It didn't help that thoughts of last night continually distracted her. But to write of those intimacies was surely not appropriate for any sort of novel.

With a frustrated sigh, she set down her pen.

"Is everything all right?"

Grace jumped in her seat at Eliza's voice. When had she come in? How long had she been there? "Yes. Though I fret I shall never be as good a writer as Miss Jane."

Eliza laughed, a good hearty laugh. "My dear, I don't think most authors will ever rival the talents of Jane Austen. I have a feeling her influence and works will last for generations to come."

"Truly? Then perhaps I shouldn't even bother."

Eliza shook her head with vigor. "If all of us stopped doing what we loved because there existed someone in the world who did it better, civilization would have ceased a long time ago, don't you think?"

The American smoothed her hair, tucking loose strands inside her bonnet. "If you have a novel in you, then you must write it. No one else can. It shouldn't matter whether it earns you regard or brings you wealth. If you have a story that must be told, you must be the one to tell it."

Grace's shoulders rose at her sister-in-law's words. She lifted the pen again. "I suppose you are right." She scribbled rapidly across the page. "I have a story in me, the story of a man who conquered his demons."

She stopped for a moment, exchanging an understanding glance with Eliza. "As we all must do, whether they are visible or not."

Eliza nodded her approval. "Exactly."

AS THE TWO WOMEN seated themselves in the carriage, Deveric rushed over from the stables. "Is there room for two more?"

"Sure." Eliza patted the cushion next to her. "Tired of talking about dung already?"

"We decided we'd rather spend the day with you lovely ladies," Deveric said. "This one—" he pointed at Damon, who'd followed behind him, "—has been daydreaming over his betrothed too much to concentrate on anything I said."

"I'd like to deny that," Damon responded, the corner of his mouth tipping up. "It does not make me sound particularly manly. However, His Grace speaks the truth."

He settled himself in next to Grace and reached for her hand. How wonderful to be near her, to be able to show his feelings for her so openly. Why had he ever fought them?

The few short miles to Chawton flew by as the group chatted, a comfortable, companionable conversation that pleased Damon immensely. Not only Grace, but the whole Mattersley family seemed to have accepted him. *Except the dowager duchess, perhaps.*

He grimaced at the thought of Grace's mother, who, like his own, had remained behind in London. His next encounter with her was not likely to be pleasant, given it was his relative who'd taken her daughter, and this after the dowager had made it clear Damon was not a suitable match. *We'll cross that bridge—er, dowager—when we come to it. To her.*

While Grace and Eliza stopped for tea with Miss Jane Austen, Damon and Dev talked horseflesh as a group of boys kicked a ball around a nearby field. One smaller boy in particular caught Damon's attention. The boy hung back, mostly out of the action, as the larger children tumbled by. Every once in a while, the boy moved in a strange way. A familiar way.

Damon went still, his focus rigid on the child.

An older lad shoved the boy. "Idiot. You missed the ball. Shaking yer head again?"

The young boy blinked rapidly. The words had a hard time coming out of his mouth. "I—I'm sorry. I d—don't mean ta d—do it." His nose twitched several times and his shoulder shrugged up to his ear repeatedly.

"Sure," sneered the older boy. "Go away. We don't wan' yer kind here." A number of the other boys hurrahed in agreement.

The young boy didn't protest. His shoulders sagged and he shuffled off, head still twitching. No doubt that wasn't the first time the child had been cast out.

Damon's heart beat faster.

"Damon?"

He couldn't respond. A cold sweat broke out on his brow.

"What are you—" Deveric started to say, then stopped as he followed Deveric's gaze.

The young boy entered a rather dilapidated house a short way down the street. Mere moments later, he emerged again, sobbing and clutching his ear. A large, burly man with a mane of untamed hair followed him, shoving him between the shoulder blades.

"Get out. *Out*. Yer no son of mine." The man cuffed the boy on the head. "You ain't natural."

He narrowed his eyes and spit on the boy's threadbare shoes.

The boy whimpered.

"I'll have no devil livin' in my house, jerking and twitching and shoutin' out words. Get on."

The man kicked, landing a hard blow to the middle of the child's back. The boy fell in the street, sobbing.

Fury surged through Damon, the man's image conflating with that of his father. His hands balled into fists and before he could stop himself, he charged across the street. The first blow caught the large man unaware, a sharp jab to the chin that snapped his head back.

"He is but a *child*," Damon roared, his other hand coming out to crack a blow to the man's ribs. "He is no monster. He is a boy. A child."

The man growled and struck out at Damon, managing to land a punch on his cheekbone as Damon tried to help the boy up. He swiveled and kicked the man in the midsection, knocking him back onto the dirt road. Damon fell on top of him and landed another blow, this one on the man's head.

"Can't you see? He can't help it. *HE CAN'T HELP IT!*" He hit the man again, then again.

Suddenly, strong arms were pulling him off. "Malford, stop," Deveric commanded. "You must stop. You are killing him. Stop."

Damon stood, his chest heaving, his arms tensed for battle. He stared down at the bloody man, then swung a crazed glance back to Deveric. Grace stood behind her brother, her arm around the young boy, her face white.

Oh my God. What have I done? He looked back at the man on the ground, who by now was moaning and trying to crawl away.

"Grace, I . . . " His voice cracked, ragged and hoarse, as he lifted his eyes to her once more.

She smoothed the boy's hair, then, giving a glance to Deveric, left the child with her brother and walked to Damon, who was still gasping in large lungfuls of air. A small crowd had gathered to watch the scene.

"I know," she said when she reached him. She carefully put her hands to his face, her finger smoothing over the welt already rising beneath his eye. "I understand." She held his face until his breathing eased and his hands no longer shook.

"I'm so sorry, Grace. I—I let the beast out again. I will understand if you wish to be released from me."

She went up on her toes and kissed him, right there in the street. "Never. I wanted to beat the man myself. But I admit, I am glad you stopped. I would not wish you to carry the sin of murder on your shoulders."

She gestured to the man, who still lay on the ground, holding his ribs and making incoherent noises. "A demon such as that is not worth it, anyway."

She looked back at Damon. "For it is men like that who are the true demons, Damon," she whispered. "Not you. Never you."

He shook with emotion, his eyes filling with tears. One ran down his cheek. He didn't care, though they were in the middle of the street, onlookers observing their every move. "You are my own angel, God's own Grace delivered to me after all these years. I do not deserve you."

"I rather feel the same about you, Damon Blackbourne," she said. "But for now, there is a frightened child needing tending."

He nodded, looking over at the boy, who peeped at him from behind one of Deveric's legs. His eyes grew round as saucers as Damon approached, and he grabbed Deveric's thigh as if to use it as a shield. Had the situation been different, Damon might have laughed at the comical expression on the Duke of Claremont's face as he fought to keep his balance.

Damon bent down and addressed the boy directly. "I won't hurt you, lad."

He was met with stony silence, but he wasn't surprised; the boy had just witnessed him beat up his father. The child wouldn't know whom to trust, if indeed he could trust anybody.

"I have had the same struggles as you."

The boy's eyes narrowed even as his neck twitched.

Damon let his own head snap in return, again and again. The adrenaline from the scuffle was receding, but his body still pushed to move. Normally, he'd fight to control it in such a public setting, but he wanted the boy to see, to know, they shared the same affliction.

Grace bent down, as well. "Would you like to come with us? We could take care of you."

The boy looked uncertainly toward his father.

"Does he often beat you?" Damon asked.

The boy nodded. "But it's my fault, sir, I mean, my lord. He tells me ter stop, but I . . . "

"You can't." Damon said it as a statement, not a question.

Tears leaked out of the boy's eyes, flooding his face. "I c—can't," he repeated.

"Where is your mother?" Grace asked, her voice soft, soothing.

"She d—died. 'Cause of me, when she borned me." He cast a glance toward his father again. "He h—hates me fer that, and fer—" A hiccup of a sob stopped the boy's words.

"We won't make you come, lad," Deveric broke in as he pried himself loose from the child's grasp. "It is your choice. But if you do, you will have meals and a bed and be well cared for. I promise you that."

"And who be you?"

Damon had to admire the child's spunk, especially in the midst of all of this.

"I am Deveric Mattersley, Duke of Claremont. This is my Duchess, Eliza." He slung an arm around Eliza, who'd joined them from the cottage while Grace had been speaking to the boy. "And this is my sister, Lady Grace. The man who saved you from your father, that is Damon Blackbourne, Duke of Malford."

The boy's mouth fell open. "Two dukes?"

Eliza grinned. "Yup. Two dukes," she said, reaching for the boy's hand. "But on the inside, they're really just kids, regular people like you and me." She laughed at his incredulous expression. "I promise."

Grace and Damon rose at the same time, and Grace took the boy's other hand. "What's your name?" she asked him.

"Geoffrey," he answered. "Geoffrey Miller."

"Well, Geoffrey, there is a little boy at our home who is about your age," Eliza said. "His name is Frederick, and I think he would be most delighted to make your acquaintance. He is rather tired of being saddled with two sisters for companions."

"That is, if you should like to come," Damon added. "As Claremont said, it is your decision."

Geoffrey worried his lower lip.

Such a heavy choice for a child—to stay with the familiar, but awful, or take a chance on the unknown—and yet Damon knew the boy needed to make it for himself. And Damon needed to accept the answer, whatever it may be. At length, the boy nodded.

The man on the street stirred, sitting up with a groan. He held a hand to his head, but then bellowed in anger when he spied the group of them standing a few feet away.

Deveric walked calmly to the man. "Mr. Miller," he said. "We should like to take your boy into our care. Are you in agreement?"

The man spat, a wad of blood and phlegm striking the ground near the duke's boot. "Take me boy? Why should I agree? 'Specially with that nob near to killin' me?"

"Because we will give you a thousand pounds," broke in Damon, his tone solid ice. "No doubt more money than you have ever seen in your lifetime. On the condition you never seek the child out, nor breathe a word of what happened here. Should you do so, we will find you again. And I might just finish the job."

The boy's father flinched, his eyes not meeting Damon's. He remained quiet for a few minutes before nodding. "He's a nuisance, anyway. You'll see. Not right, is that boy."

Fury reared its head again, and it took all the restraint Damon possessed not to strike the man again. "He is no longer your nuisance. And that is all that matters."

Deveric fished out a few pounds from his coin purse, dropping them at the man's feet. "The rest shall be delivered from Clarehaven within two days' time."

"Clarehaven?" The man's face slackened. "The . . . Duke?"

"Indeed." Damon's grin was wolfish. "Be proud. Your son has now risen to great heights."

"Goodbye, da," Geoffrey said, his lip trembling.

Mr. Miller said nothing, refusing to acknowledge the boy in any way.

Without another word, the foursome, plus their new, young companion, headed back to Chawton Cottage, where their carriage was stationed.

"When Miss Jane writes of future heroes," Eliza whispered to Grace, "I should not be surprised if they bear some resemblance to our men." She gestured toward the window, where the author peeked out. The curtain dropped.

"Perhaps," Grace said as she helped Geoffrey into the carriage. "I cannot think of better hero material."

THE BOY WAS SILENT most of the journey, his attention jumping between the outside scenery and his companions in the carriage. Grace smiled at him in encouragement, but he looked away whenever their eyes met, his head jerking in a manner similar to Damon's.

She noticed Damon couldn't keep his eyes off the boy, either, but the expression on his face was pained, as though he were reliving his own childhood. Occasionally, he looked to Deveric and Eliza, as if to judge their reactions to the boy and his movements. They, for the most part, chatted quietly together, seeming to sense the other occupants in the carriage needed time to themselves.

Once at Clarehaven, the boy leapt out of the carriage with excitement, only to come to a skidding halt at the massive stone home before him. The boy's mouth fell open and he turned toward Grace, ducking his head into her skirts.

"It's all right," she reassured him, surprised and a little pleased she was the one he'd chosen to latch on to. Likely because she'd been the closest, but still, it touched her.

"Have you ever seen a house like this?" Deveric said, moving over and crouching down by the boy.

"No, Your Grace," Geoffrey responded. His eyes blinked rapidly.

"Well, it looks huge at first glance, I admit," Deveric said. "But I promise you'll determine the best places to play in no time. How about you and I go meet that other boy I told you about, my son Frederick?"

Deveric held out his hand, and Geoffrey released Grace's skirts to take it. The two walked up the steps to the front door and passed through.

Grace's heart swelled at her brother's tender dealings with the overwhelmed child, pleased he'd not bundled Geoffrey off to the servants' quarters to be tended to there. A boy plucked off the street, from a poor family in terms of both wealth and social status, Geoffrey had an uncertain position in the household. Over time, they'd determine the best course for him, no doubt.

Or perhaps she and Damon would. At Thorne Hill. She peeked at her betrothed. His gaze was still fixed on Geoffrey. Would he welcome the boy into their home?

Eliza approached Grace and Damon. "I have seen a child like him before," she said. "One of my neighbors back in Virginia."

"What do you mean, like him?" Damon asked, his tone sharp.

"One who made similar movements with his head and eyes. The boy I knew often made noises, grunts and such, and sometimes echoed the words people said." She crossed her arms, raising one hand near her face, her thumb supporting her chin while she tapped her cheek with her finger, her lips pursed.

Damon's posture went rigid, his face locked, the muscle in his cheek flexing. After a moment, he asked, "What happened to him? Did he—did he face ostracism and persecution because of these movements?"

"Sadly, yes. Though mostly from strangers. His family did what they could to ease his life. I wish I knew how he fared. The poor boy. He was the sweetest child, when one looked past the tics."

"Thank you for being willing to let us take him in, Eliza," Grace said.

"How could we not? It is not that poor boy's fault, and it hurts me so much to see people mistreated for things they cannot help or change." She moved toward the front door. "I should go check on the children."

After Eliza entered the house, Damon exhaled, a rough outpouring of breath. "It is hard to see such a boy. It is like looking into a mirror from a time long ago." His shoulders slumped.

Grace slipped her arms around his neck, hugging him closely. It was a tender embrace, one of intimacy, not of passion. He clung to her, pressing her head into his chest with his hand.

"If we can save him . . . " He broke off.

"We have. We will. He will have a better childhood than you, Damon. Because we can give him love, can we not? We can give him acceptance. And I think you and I should be the ones to do so. He should be *ours*."

He leaned back, his eyes soft, watery, as they met her own. "You would do that? Make a boy not of your own blood, not of your own station, part of your family? Love him?"

"Part of *our* family, and yes. I may not have the same struggles as he does, as you have, but I know what it is like to feel as if one doesn't belong."

He drew her close, nuzzling her hair with his lips. "I don't know what I did to deserve you, my angel, my own personal Grace, but I will never let you go."

She moved her head up, fastening her lips to his. The sweet kiss swiftly grew into something more, and his hands laced through her hair, holding her to him. He groaned as she pressed herself against him.

A moment later, he broke off, panting. "As much as I would like to continue this, perhaps the front lawn of Clarehaven is neither the time nor the place."

She giggled, looking behind her at the house.

"I suppose you are right." She grabbed his hand. "Come, Your Grace. Let us check on Geoffrey. And then," she said, "perhaps we could spend some time in the library."

Her cheeks flushed even as she said the words.

He threw his head back and laughed.

CHAPTER 30

CLAREHAVEN, HAMPSHIRE, ENGLAND
LATE MAY, 1814

A week later, Grace paused in the middle of selecting gowns for Daisy to pack. Sorrow filled her at leaving Clarehaven once more. It was her home and she'd treasured her time with her siblings. And Damon, of course.

But returning to London meant she and Damon were one step closer to being wed. Thank heavens! Despite multiple suggestions about the library and even an invitation to her chamber, Damon had put her off, insisting they wait until after they were married.

"I did not take you for such an old-fashioned gentleman," she'd said one night while stealing a kiss in the hallway.

"I did not either, to be honest. But I neither relish getting caught by your family, nor risking any more damage to your reputation should I indeed get you with child before we are wed."

"You did not care about that the first time," she protested. Having tasted Damon once was not enough; she was eager to try again.

"I was not thinking with the right appendage at the moment."

She bit her lip. "Do you regret it?"

"Heavens, no!" he exclaimed, dropping a kiss on her brow. "I am sorry if I led you to think that. In fact, I can hardly wait to repeat it. Again. And again. And again. But I have lived my life under the shadows of dishonor and rejection, and I will do all I can to lessen that for you."

"Even if I don't care about those things?"

"Even then."

"Damon, my reputation is already in tatters. Indeed, we do not even know what kind of reception I shall face upon our return."

"We will make it clear the fault lies entirely with my uncle."

"But you know yourself that will not be enough, do you not?"

He grimaced. "It must be enough. There are certain advantages to being a duke, even one rumored to be as demonic as I, and that is that we can get away with things others cannot. As ridiculous as that may be."

Grace chewed on her lower lip. "Have you had any word from your uncle?"

"No."

"Do you think—" She swallowed hard. "Do you think perhaps I did kill him after all?"

"Were he dead, we'd have heard. But, no—my man Hobbes sent a message that Fillmore had been seen in a gambling hell in St. Giles, so, no, the bastard still lives."

"He can show his face in London? Does this mean people do not know what he did?"

"It means certain gambling hells will look the other way in the name of lucre."

"Oh." She sighed.

"What I don't know is with what he has been gambling. Not Malford money; I cut off his funds weeks ago."

"Do you think Daphne and Margaret have seen him? He is their father, after all. Would he make contact?"

"I sincerely hope not, for their sake as well as his. They must know he shall never redeem his honor, must know it is better to sever all ties with him."

"Knowing in the mind and knowing in the heart are two different things, Damon. He was horrible to you, but you yourself said he doted on Daphne and was kindly enough to Margaret. I don't know how they have taken his most recent behavior, nor how they feel about breaking connection with him completely."

"We shall find out soon enough, I suppose."

Daisy moved about the room, retrieving hair ribbons and shoes, bringing Grace back to the present. The maid had taken a shine to Geoffrey, delighted when Grace reluctantly decided, given the great upheavals in both of their lives recently, it would be best for Daisy and Geoffrey to remain at Clarehaven while the family returned to London to finish out the Season.

Deveric and Eliza had elected to come to town, as well, to show support for Grace and Damon and to celebrate their wedding. Frederick had begged to stay behind with Geoffrey, thrilled to have a companion with whom to play, but the two younger girls, Rose and Isabelle, would accompany Eliza and Deveric in one carriage, while Damon, his two sisters, Emmeline, Rebecca, and Grace would ride in another, larger one.

An hour later, all was ready.

"Goodbye, Geoffrey," Grace said, her throat thickening with emotion as she knelt before the boy. "We will return as soon as we are able."

"'Tis all right. I have plenty to do here, especially with

Frederick and the puppies," the boy responded, though he threw his arms around her, his eyes watery as he hugged her.

He was a bright boy, and once he'd seen that nobody here teased him for the movements he made, he'd come out of his shell, proving himself to be a talkative, engaging young man. She'd even made progress with teaching him how to read, lessons she looked forward to continuing once they were together again.

But now it was time to go. Waving goodbye to Daisy, she followed her sisters into the carriage.

The coach was of good size, but three people squished into each side still made for close quarters. Not that Grace minded; she was nestled against Damon, Rebecca to her other side.

Both her sisters conversed easily with Cassie and Sephe, so Grace relaxed, happy to remain quiet herself. Damon slung his arm around her shoulders, bringing her closer into him, absent-mindedly rubbing his thumb along the fabric of her sprigged muslin at her shoulder. The motion was so soothing she almost hoped the carriage ride would never end.

Because the closer they got to London, the closer they got to her mother. And Fillmore Blackbourne.

MATILDA MATTERSLEY rushed down the steps of Claremont House, an unusual display of emotion and vigor for her. She enfolded Grace in her arms. "Thank God you are all right," she breathed into her ear.

After a moment, her mother stepped back. "I hope you were not upset by my decision to remain in London, my daughter. I wanted to combat any talk here, and knew you would return shortly."

Grace clasped her mother's hands. "It was fine, Mama. I was with Deveric and Eliza. And Damon."

At the mention of Damon's name, her mother's lips tightened, thinning even further as the Duke of Malford exited the carriage after the Mattersley and Blackbourne sisters.

"Malford," she bit out, barely dipping her head.

"Your Grace," he responded, his face implacable. Grace reached over and took his hand.

"Mother," she said as she drew him near her. "I assumed Dev sent word. Damon and I are betrothed. We have returned to London to show all is well and to celebrate our wedding."

"Indeed?"

Grace met her mother's hawkish gaze directly, refusing to give ground. "Surely after all that Fillmore Blackbourne has done, you can see that he, not Damon, is the true devil in the family."

Damon made to interrupt, but she stopped him. "I love him, Mama. And he loves me. And we will be married, and happy, whether you wish it or not." She finished her speech with a stomp of her foot.

Matilda was silent.

Grace's glance flitted to Damon, who betrayed no emotion, but kept his eyes on Matilda.

At length, the dowager duchess dipped her head in assent. "It is for the best, I suppose, to quell any lingering scandal."

"It is for much better than that, Your Grace," Damon said, his voice even. "Grace is the greatest treasure I have ever been given. I know I do not deserve her, but I will work every moment of my life to make her as happy as she makes me. I understand that your impression of me has not been a favorable one. That is true for many people. I hope, however, that over time you will learn to see me not as others do, but as your daughter does, so that I may prove to you I am no longer the Demon Duke, now that I have this angel by my side."

Matilda inhaled sharply, pursing her lips as she looked back and forth between the two of them, then at the siblings standing around witnessing the exchange.

At length, the faintest of smiles spread across her face and her spine visibly relaxed. "Well said, Malford." She gestured toward Eliza and Deveric. "If you make my Grace half as happy as Eliza has made my son, then I shall be indebted to you forever."

Grace heaved a sigh of relief. *Thank God.*

The siblings moved around them and up into the house.

"Have you heard anything of my uncle?" Damon asked the dowager.

"There are rumors." She frowned. "That he is in London. But he has not appeared at any social functions."

"If he is here, I shall find him."

"What will you do?"

Damon hesitated. "He killed my father and my brother. Justice shall be served," he finally said. "One way or the other."

THE NEXT WEEK evaporated like morning dew. Although news of Grace's return brought numerous callers to see her or at least find out the gossip, the Mattersleys refused every one, saying they were occupied planning a grand ball for the coming Saturday night.

According to Emmeline, members of the *ton* were speculating wildly as to the nature of the ball, especially since it had been added to the calendar at the last minute. Some thought it an engagement ball, while others insisted a Mattersley would never agree to wed the Demon Duke, scandal or no scandal. Many presumed it an attempt to show all was normal and to deflect attention from Grace.

Grace snorted when she heard that one. "If we wanted to keep attention from me, why on earth would we host a *ball?*"

Emmeline shrugged. "Though naturally everyone wishes to attend, and so are cancelling other engagements." The delight in her sister's eyes was unmistakable. Would she never tire of the social whirl, of the matchmaking opportunities?

Grace herself was less lackadaisical. Questions and rumors swirled about her disappearance and subsequent return. Would marrying Damon be enough to dispel them, to maintain her reputation? She wasn't worried for her own sake; being with Damon was all she needed, even if they were banished from polite society.

But her sisters, Damon's sisters, Damon's cousins— their own prospects could be tainted by the scandal. Or ruined. She didn't want that.

Her mother had proved a surprising ally, having gone from rejecting Damon to, if not exactly gushing about the match, at least announcing her staunch support.

"If he is what you truly want, my dear, I am at peace with it. I like the way he looks at you, much the same as Eliza looks at Deveric."

She'd waved off any concerns about Grace's reputation. "If there are any benefits to having been such a firm advocate for propriety and decorum all these years, it's that I have good relationships with my fellow matrons. I know who spreads gossip and who sets the tone for what is and isn't allowed."

That was certainly true. At one point, the dowager

duchess had even been invited to serve as a patroness of Almack's.

"I'm far too busy," she'd claimed.

Emmeline said the real reason their mother declined was that their father's mistress often frequented the place, working to get her own daughters launched onto the marriage market.

Grace had gained new appreciation for her mother this week. In the past, the two had often clashed over Grace's future, but now that Grace had Damon and knew the depth of her love for him, the pain her mother must have endured while her husband had cavorted with other women was unfathomable. If Damon were to stray, Grace didn't think she would survive it. And yet her mother had and had found ways to thrive.

As they decided the details for the ball, Matilda came alive, her face aglow with excitement as she discussed the dinner menu or the music or Grace's gown.

Maybe it was not too late for her mother to find the kind of happiness her children—at least some of them—had found.

Grace mentioned the notion to Emmeline and Rebecca after dinner that evening.

"Mother? Marry again?" Rebecca's puckered forehead expressed her views.

"I don't see why not," Emmeline said. "She's still a handsome woman. It sounds like a marvelous plan."

"You would," Rebecca retorted.

"I'm already generating a list in my head of available widowers. Oh, this shall be fun indeed!"

Grace and Rebecca exchanged a look as Emmeline clapped her hands and raced from the room.

"If nothing else," Grace reminded her sister, "it will keep Emme too occupied to find *you* a husband."

Rebecca laughed. "An excellent plan!"

CHAPTER 31

Her nerves on edge, Grace pulled at the sheer overdress fluttering down over numerous delicate ivory petticoats.

"Ethereal!" Madame le Bec, the modiste, had exclaimed at the final fitting for Grace's new ball gown. "A dress fit for an angel."

Madame le Bec, whose beaked nose fit her name, had insisted on a bodice in the deepest plum, a plum matching the flowers the dressmaker had added to the hem of the gown. "It does the most beautiful things for your dark eyes and hair, ma petite."

The sleeves of the bodice, if one could call such narrow bands of fabric that, hugged her upper arms, yet left her shoulders completely bare. The gown wasn't indecent compared to many dresses other ladies wore, but still, to have so much of her skin revealed, it was almost as if she were naked. Goose pimples peppered her skin at the thought, or rather at the thought of Damon's lips dropping kisses along the exposed flesh.

Bess, thrilled to have her mistress back, had spent

extra time on Grace's hair, weaving it into an intricate braid that she then pinned up into a bun, with a chain of delicate ivory flowers woven throughout. Soft ringlets, achieved with curling papers, framed Grace's face, accentuating her cheekbones.

"You look like a Greek goddess," the maid exclaimed.

Grace secretly felt like one, too. Aphrodite, perhaps? She smoothed her hands over the gown. What would Damon think when he saw her?

Damon. She hadn't seen him since their arrival back in London. What was he doing? How had he been? Were people assaulting him for information about his uncle? Laying blame on him for the whole situation?

She hoped not.

She knew the reasons for staying away from him, knew it was better not to draw attention to herself, or to him. Her mother was truly excited to announce their engagement at tonight's ball, and considering the difficulties Matilda had had in accepting Damon, Grace wasn't about to do anything to reverse that.

Still, oh, how she missed him. So many things she'd wanted to share with him, only he wasn't there. She read numerous novels during her week in hiding, but how it hurt not to be able to discuss them with Damon. She hadn't even had a chance to give him the Gibbon books. She longed for that winsome side grin, his incredible light blue eyes, the crinkling of his brow when he concentrated.

She squared her shoulders. Tonight. She'd see him tonight. In less than an hour.

She descended the stairwell to the foyer, where Emmeline and Rebecca spoke with one another. Emmeline was stunning in a frothy green concoction that emphasized her emerald eyes. Rebecca wore pure white to complemented her dark hair and blue eyes.

"Oh, aren't you lovely?" Emmeline exclaimed when Grace reached them. "Isn't she lovely, Rebecca?"

Rebecca nodded but couldn't get a word in before Emmeline went on. "I can't believe you are betrothed, dearest sister. Damon is quite the catch, handsome *and* titled. If I could, I'd steal him for myself!"

As if you could handle him. No, he is not the right one for you. Not like he is for me. "I'm glad you have decided to leave him to me," Grace said, giving her sister a smile. "I fear if I had to compete with your effervescent personality, I should no doubt come out the loser."

Matilda glided into the room, resplendent in a dress of evening primrose, its deep yellow hue accentuating her still-dark hair and hazel eyes. How wonderful to see her mother happy. The dowager duchess should reside in London year-round; it was obvious she enjoyed Town living far more than the quiet life at Clarehaven.

"Shall we, daughters?" Matilda ushered them into the ballroom.

Only minutes thereafter, the first guests arrived. The room was more than half full and the dancing had commenced before Damon appeared, his sisters and Cousin Daphne in tow. His mother followed behind, wan in her gray gown, but her chin resolute.

Grace only had eyes for Damon, however.

He wore his traditional black coat and pantaloons, but had swapped out his ebony waistcoat for one of a rich, cardinal red lavishly embroidered with golden thread. The effect was intoxicating, as the red in the coat magnified the ice blue of his eyes. His shirt and cravat were of a crisp white instead of the black to which she'd grown accustomed, and they deepened the tawny richness of his skin. At least he had kept his signature skull-headed stickpin, though this one, of gold, held a rose between its teeth.

A *charming touch.*

His hair had been carefully styled. Though Grace preferred the tousled effect, it didn't detract from his handsomeness. Her belly fluttered as he crossed the room. Reaching her, he executed a bow.

"My lady."

Grace bobbed a curtsy. "Your Grace," she said, enjoying the double meaning. For she was indeed *his* Grace.

He took her gloved hand in his and pressed a kiss against its back, his eyes never leaving hers. A gasp rose from somewhere nearby and voices murmured around them, but she hardly noticed. Never had she wished her hands were bare so much as she did in that moment. Oh, to feel the caress of those lips again.

"You look magnificent." His eyes dropped to the roundness of her bosom.

Her flesh tingled at the heat in his gaze. "Thank you. As do you."

Eliza sidled over to them. "Stop looking as if you're going to ravish each other right here on the dance floor!" Her teasing eyes softened the words.

Damon flashed Eliza a wicked grin. "Well, that would give people something to talk about, wouldn't it?"

"Other than my kidnapping, you mean." An unwelcomed glumness enveloped Grace. No one had yet approached her, but she'd been on the receiving end of curious glances. It was only a matter of time, or perhaps alcoholic spirits, before people commented directly.

"Never you fear." Eliza tucked her arm through Grace's. "The only thing anyone will be discussing after your mother's announcement is the marriage of the century."

At Grace's wrinkled brow, Eliza giggled. "I mean yours, silly!"

Across the room, the Dowager Duchess of Malford spoke to the musicians, and the music ceased. Matilda inclined her head toward Grace, indicating she and Damon should come to her. Damon extended an elbow to Grace. She took it as Eliza released her other arm and gave her shoulder a reassuring squeeze.

"It is my sincerest pleasure," Matilda said, her voice commanding the room, "to announce the betrothal of my dear daughter Lady Grace to the Duke of Malford. We pray the union of our two families will only strengthen both, leading to many years of happiness—and many grandchildren."

A chuckle went through the crowd at Matilda's words, but all eyes soon turned to Grace, and a rising tide of voices flooded the ballroom. If only the floor would open up and swallow her whole, like Jonah and that whale. The engagement wouldn't be enough to stem the gossip.

She looked to Damon. "I am sorry."

"None of it was your fault, Grace. I am to blame, not you." His words were whispered, so that only she could hear.

Turning to the crush, he addressed them in a firm, clear voice. "A familial dispute escalated, resulting in the unfortunate detainment of Lady Grace. While a lady's maid was always in her presence and she remained unharmed and well cared for, I take full responsibility for my uncle's actions."

He surveyed the room. "I am the luckiest man in the world to have secured this lady's hand in marriage, but let no one ever say it was for any reason less than that I love her, body and soul."

Voices murmured at his declaration. It was unheard of for anyone, much less a man, to speak so publicly of emotion. Damon took that moment to step closer to

Grace, tilt up her head, and press a quick but intense kiss to her lips.

One of the young debutantes burst into nervous laughter as a smattering of applause filtered through the room. Damon stood inches from Grace, his eyes fastened on hers.

"Well," she said, her ears burning, "you do know how to switch the focus."

He gave a devilish chuckle.

The music started up again on Matilda's signal. Just as Damon extended his hand to Grace, a commotion at the edge of the room drew their attention.

Fillmore Blackbourne stormed in, his waistcoat unbuttoned and his hair in disarray. His eyes were wild as he stomped his way toward Damon and Grace.

How had he gotten in here?

All other thoughts fled as the man pulled out a pistol. He raised his right arm and aimed directly at Damon's heart. Fillmore's arm shook, and the reek of alcohol emanated from his person.

"*You!*" Fillmore roared.

The musicians fell silent. Nobody spoke.

Damon said nothing, staring his uncle down.

"*You* should not be here! You should not be alive. It should be *me*. I should have been Duke. Not this miserable wretch of a human. *Infested by demons*, he is!" Fillmore shouted to the crowd, even as he kept his eyes, and the weapon, trained on Damon.

"Uncle." Damon's voice was measured, but a muscle spasmed in his jaw and his head jerked. Once, nearly imperceptibly. Had Fillmore noticed? "Put down the gun, Uncle. There are ladies present."

"Do not tell me what to do!" the man screeched, his eyes bulging.

He took a step toward Damon. Grace held her breath,

her heart pounding against her rib cage. The gun was now only a few feet from Damon's face.

Damon inched sideways, putting more space between him and Grace. He held up his hands in an apparent effort to diffuse his uncle's temper. It didn't work.

"I have nothing. Nothing! Because of *you*. You should have died. I should have killed you then."

"Like you killed my father and brother?"

Grace bit her lip so hard she drew blood. Why was he antagonizing him? *Stop, Damon.*

Fillmore blinked his eyes, as if not believing Damon had said what he'd said. "I had to." His voice squeaked eerily, more child-like than adult. "I had debts. And I was owed it."

Silence reigned.

He lowered the gun a few inches, his face falling. "I've failed," he said. "Failed. I have nothing left."

He scanned the room, then addressed Daphne, who stood to the side, her face ashen, her eyes pleading. "I have nothing for you, daughter. Or for Margaret, wherever she is. I've gambled it all away."

Damon took a step forward, but Fillmore instantly swung his gaze around, his arm popping up as his eyes narrowed. "I should have killed her when I had the chance," he sneered, flicking the pistol's barrel toward Grace. "Robbed you of any chance at happiness. Just as you have robbed me."

His eyes narrowed even further, into snake-like slits, and he moved the weapon up to Damon's face. His arm grew chillingly calm, no longer shaking. "No. It is you who must pay."

His shoulders drooped and in that moment, Grace knew. He was going to shoot.

She leapt toward Damon, shouting "*No!*" as the retort of the gun echoed through the room. They crashed to the floor in a jumbled pile, the gunshot ringing in her ears.

Oh my God. Damon. Oh my God. Did he hit you? Did he hit me? Damon. Oh no. Oh no.

She pushed herself up. Damon lay beneath her, unnaturally still. Copious amounts of blood flowed from the side of his head.

"Oh no! *No!*" she screamed, pressing her hand to the wound. The world faded away, nothing audible, nothing visible except the sight of Damon's blood flowing through her fingers. And those eyes, those beautiful blue eyes, closed.

Chaos erupted around her. Eliza fell to her knees beside Grace as Deveric ran to her side.

"No, no, no. He can't die. He can't *die!*"

"Let me see, Grace," Deveric commanded, his hand prying hers from Damon's temple. Blood still gushed from the wound.

Grace closed her eyes, nausea ripping through her stomach.

Eliza flung her arms around her. "It's going to be all right, Grace. It's going to be all right," she whispered over and over.

If Damon were dead, nothing would ever be all right again.

"The bullet grazed him," Deveric announced. He ripped off his evening jacket and wadded it up, holding it against Damon's head to stem the flow of blood. "It looks worse than it is, Grace. Head wounds bleed a lot."

"He's not . . . he's not dead?"

"No. Thanks to you." Deveric gestured toward the wall behind them, where a bullet hole marred the flowered paper. "Had you not pushed him, Lord Fillmore's shot would have been dead center."

The Mattersley clan hovered around them, as did Damon's sisters Cassie and Sephe and their cousin

Daphne. The ladies moved to form a barrier against the prying eyes of fellow ballgoers. Felicity fell to her knees next to Grace, her eyes locked on her son's still frame.

"I have sent for a doctor," Matilda announced. "Come, let us get him to a bedchamber. And Watson," she motioned toward the pencil-thin butler, "ensure our guests depart in orderly fashion."

"Yes, Your Grace." Watson nodded solemnly, gesturing to the footmen.

Thank heavens for her mother's military-style approach to the situation, for blackness swam before Grace's eyes. She might faint. Servants ushered guests out while several strapping footmen carefully lifted Damon and bore him out the side door.

"Where is Fillmore?" Deveric asked.

"I don't know," Eliza answered. "He ran right after he shot. In the commotion, I think he got away."

Deveric cursed under his breath.

"Emerlin," interjected Rebecca in a thready voice, her fingers clutching her skirts. "Lord Emerlin went after him. I saw him race from the room in pursuit."

"I need to be with him. With Damon," Grace said, struggling to rise. Eliza braced her at one elbow, and Cassie ran forward to hold the other. Together, the women helped her from the room.

It took the doctor less than fifteen minutes to arrive. Thankfully, the blood flow had lessened considerably in that time. Deveric had checked only briefly, maintaining pressure with his coat against the wound.

The doctor hurried him out of the way and leaned over to examine the patient.

"It is as you said, Your Grace," the man said as he fiddled in his bag. "A flesh wound. He should be fine once we stitch this up." He pulled out a needle and thread. "Did he hit his head when he fell?"

"I don't know," Grace whispered, her eyes on the needle.

"Wait!" Eliza cried. All heads turned toward her. "Is that needle clean?" She wrung her hands.

The doctor frowned.

"Please," she insisted. "If a short delay won't hurt him, I'd like you to boil the needle—and the thread—before you use it. And wash your hands thoroughly with soap. And maybe some brandy."

The doctor's eyebrows flew up at her words.

"Our American doctors believe it helps lessen the chances of fever," Eliza explained.

Deveric nodded his agreement.

The doctor shrugged. "As you wish, Your Graces."

He handed the needle and thread to Eliza, who rushed out the door.

Deveric turned to Grace. "Are you all right?"

Grace shook her head. "No. But I will be, once he is."

After a short time, Eliza returned, the needle and thread held on a clean cloth. The doctor scrubbed his hands in the water she'd brought in a pail, wincing at its heat but not complaining. He set to work.

"Perhaps you should go lie down," Deveric said to Grace.

"I'm staying with him."

"Damon will be well taken care of, Grace."

"Would you leave Eliza?" she asked, her chin jutting out.

"Understood," was all Deveric said.

The doctor checked the stitches and left laudanum for when Damon regained consciousness. "*If* he does," he muttered under his breath, but Grace heard, and her stomach climbed into her throat.

"Thank you for your services," Eliza chirped as she ushered the doctor out before she, too, moved to exit the bedchamber, dragging Deveric with her. "Call for us if you need us."

Grace merely nodded, taking a seat at Damon's side. Voices echoed in the hallway, but blessedly, no one disturbed them. Pulling off her gloves, she smoothed his hair, that beautiful mass of hair, with her fingers. His face was still unnaturally pale, but his chest rose and fell evenly. *Thank God.* She set her hand to his heart, burrowing in under his shirt, desperate to feel his flesh directly. Its warmth soothed her, as did the steady thump-thump beneath it.

"Wake up, Damon. Please, wake up."

CHAPTER 32

CLAREMONT HOUSE, LONDON
EARLY JUNE, 1814

*H*ow his head pounded. It throbbed in rhythm with the beat of his heart, which, for some reason, was extra strong. He wiggled his fingers. *Ah*. They were resting on his chest. No wonder every heartbeat was palpable. But why did his head hurt so?

Frenzied images rushed at him. *Fillmore. A gun. Grace.* Grace. He remembered her crashing into him, the report of the pistol, then falling. *Good God. Had Fillmore killed him? Had Fillmore killed Grace?*

His eyes flew open. Everything blurred at first, but came into focus after a moment and he found himself gazing into the most delicious chocolate eyes he'd ever seen. Even if they were currently rimmed with red.

"Damon?" Her voice croaked.

He said nothing, drinking in the beauty of her face. The finely arched brows, the long lashes, pert nose, and the most tempting mouth. Perhaps he was dead. It would make sense, with this divine angel floating near him.

The angel smiled. "Thank God," she whispered.

He felt the same way. *Thank God for the perfection before him.*

Her fingers stroked his brow. She leaned in and kissed his forehead, then turned to the side table. She picked something up. A cup. *Thank goodness.* He was so very thirsty.

He took a few sips as she held the cup to his lips.

"What happened?" His gravelly voice echoed in his ears, increasing the pounding at his temples.

"Your uncle shot you." She swallowed, tears welling in her eyes. "I pushed you and the bullet grazed your head."

He raised his fingers to the left side of his head, testing the bandage there. He grinned ruefully. "I don't suppose this adds to my devilishly good looks."

Grace half laughed, half sobbed. "I was worried you would never wake up. The doctor didn't know why you were out for so long."

"How long was I out?"

"Nearly a day."

A day? Yet she was still in her ball gown? He frowned.

A knock came at the door. Grace looked to him and he nodded. She rose and crossed the room to answer it.

"How is he?"

Claremont.

"Oh, Dev, he's woken up! Come see. He has returned to me!"

Deveric strode into the room. "About time, Malford," he chided. "I was beginning to think I was going to have to beat you back into consciousness."

Damon arched an eyebrow, wincing when it pulled at his bandage.

"Grace has been so worried, she hasn't left your side."

Damon reached out a hand for Grace's, and she caught it immediately, intertwining her fingers with his.

"My uncle?"

Deveric grimaced. "He is dead, Damon. Emerlin found him in the garden. Lord Fillmore had put the gun to his head and taken his own life."

"I can't say I'm sorry," Damon said after a moment. "Given what he did to Grace. To my family."

Grace squeezed his hand.

"How is Daphne? Margaret?" he asked.

Deveric and Grace exchanged a glance. "Overset, certainly. But I think they will be fine. They and their aunt have returned to Bath."

Not surprising. Daphne would want to escape the gossip and the scandal as much as she could. The poor girl. Fillmore had likely irretrievably damaged her prospects. Margaret's, too. He and Grace would support the two young women in whatever way they could.

"My mother? Sisters?"

"In the hall. Anxious to see you when you are ready."

He nodded in acknowledgment, then moaned at the pain the motion wrought.

"The bullet wound itself is not deep," Deveric assured him. "Though if Grace had not knocked you off balance, you would be dead. As it is, you'll have a scar. Probably make you that much more irresistible to the ladies."

"There's only one I care about." Damon looked over at Grace. "Grace Mattersley, as soon as I'm up and out of this bed—which will be immediately, if I have anything to say about it—I'm marrying you. After enduring your kidnapping and my being shot, I don't want to risk anything else happening before I can make you my wife."

She laughed, and the delightful sound warmed him to the core. "As you wish, my love. As you wish."

Deveric cleared his throat. "Sorry to interrupt, but shall I let in the other women now? Before my sister decides to join you in that bed?"

Grace's cheeks burst into delicious color. Damon merely grinned.

The door had barely been opened when the three Blackbourne women swarmed through it. Grace stepped away so the women could approach Damon.

Felicity, her hair mussed and likewise still clad in her now-wrinkled ball gown, dropped to her knees at his side. "Oh, Damon. My son. Thank heavens you are all right. Thank God!"

Tears streamed down her face. "I knew," she went on. "I knew he was dangerous. It's why your father never told him we'd sent you away; we both feared for your safety, even then. And to know now he was the cause—" A sob caught in her throat, cutting off her words.

How odd that in the end, his banishment had likely saved his very life. And cost Silas and Adam theirs, as Fillmore had seen the dukedom within his grasp.

Sorrow flooded over him—not so much for himself; having been estranged from his kin for so many years, his father's and brother's deaths had hardly affected him. He'd grieved for their loss long ago. No, this sorrow was for the fierce agony evident in every line on his mother's grave face.

"Mother," he said, taking her hand. "It is over. Finished. Fillmore bears the blame, not you. And he cannot hurt us—any of us—any longer." At those words, he reached out to Grace, who stepped closer and clasped his hand in hers again. He rubbed her palm tenderly.

Felicity swallowed, her eyes radiating love.

"Now, if you don't mind," he said with a grimace. "I believe doctor's orders were to rest. For today, at least."

"Of course," his sisters said, as his mother rose to her feet. With one last caress of her fingertips against his cheek, Felicity and the other occupants of the room exited, one by one, until only Grace remained.

"Shall I go, too, my love?"

He scoffed, despite the pain it brought to his temples. "You are the only medicine I need, love. I do believe your brother had the right idea." He patted the bed to his side.

She crawled in carefully next to him. "Are you sure I won't hurt you?"

When her breasts pressed against his arm, he groaned. She immediately withdrew a few inches.

"No, no," he protested. "That was not from pain, but from wanting more . . . medicine . . . than I can handle at the moment."

She moved closer, pressing a kiss to his cheek. "I do believe you are right. We are the cure for what has ailed each other."

With a sigh, she nestled into his shoulder and was lightly snoring within minutes, her arm draped possessively across his chest.

Yes, he thought as slumber overtook him, as well. *You, my dearest Grace, my saving Grace, are the only one who could exorcise my demons.*

WITHIN A DAY Damon was, indeed, up and around, though Grace and the other Mattersley women clucked over him so incessantly he was almost glad to escape to his own town house the day after—which he'd insisted on, so as not to inconvenience the Mattersleys further.

"But, Damon, it is not inconvenient. And I need you here," Grace had protested.

"And I need to be in my own home, dearest. For every time I see you, I want to pull you into my arms and do the things I oughtn't do, as much because we're not yet married as because of my injury, my love."

Begrudgingly, she'd let him go.

Yes, he was *almost* glad. Hobbes fussed over him nearly as much as his mother and sisters, and Cerberus had affixed himself to Damon's side, jumping on him whenever Damon happened to sit down. Like now, in his library.

He rubbed the cat's head absentmindedly. Cerberus purred and nudged him for more attention. Damon chuckled.

"Yes," he said to the cat. "That's how I feel about my Grace. No matter how much I have, I want more."

He had relived that night at Clarehaven a thousand times, reveling in the beauty of the emotional as well as physical connection with Grace. His few meager experiences with Yorkshire lasses hadn't been nearly as fulfilling. His loins tightened at the thought of being with her again, of kissing her luscious mouth, of wending a path down her front to her breasts, to her stomach, and lower.

The cat growled, disgruntled by the change in the state of Damon's breeches. He shifted his legs and the cat jumped down. It was just as well; these kinds of thoughts only led to greater frustration. Thank goodness the wedding was a mere few days away.

With Deveric's help, Damon had managed to procure a special license, and he and Grace were to be married three days hence at St. George's of Hanover Square, just as Deveric and Eliza had been.

"St. George's is a Mattersley tradition," Deveric had said with a wink. "A good omen, I should say."

Damon itched to see Grace. Instead, he threw himself into estate matters, the paperwork bringing back the headache that had gratefully dissipated. But the work occupied him, and busy was what he wanted until he could hold Grace in his arms again.

CHAPTER 33

HANOVER SQUARE, LONDON
MID-JUNE, 1814

*T*he wedding itself was a simple, sweet ceremony. Grace wore a white silk dress rendered all the more elegant because of its lack of ornamentation. Damon returned to his customary black waistcoat, though he donned a white silk shirt and cravat and added a small white rose to the lapel of his jacket. The black and white combination of bride and groom was most striking, everybody agreed.

Because of the recent events, Grace and Damon decided to journey immediately after the ceremony to Thorne Hill. They'd had enough of London's gossip about them; someone else could become the latest *on dit.*

As they entered the carriage, Damon sat next to Grace and drew her close. They waved goodbye to the Mattersley clan and as the horses pulled the carriage through the London streets, he simply held her. His wife.

Wife. The word infused his heart with delight and wonder like never before. This woman, this intelligent, unpredictable, amazing, brave woman, was his wife. And she loved him. Loved *him.* Damon. The Demon Duke.

He nuzzled her hair, dropping a kiss on the top of her head. She arched back to look up at him, a dazzling smile crossing her face. "I have something for you."

She leaned forward, breaking contact with him to pull a box from under the seat. *Where had that come from?*

"I had Hobbes put it in here before the ceremony," she explained as she handed it to him.

A gift? His new bride had gotten him a gift? And from the weight of the box, a heavy gift, indeed. He lifted up the lid, revealing a set of books stacked neatly within. It was the Gibbon set, the six volumes of *The History of the Decline and Fall of the Roman Empire*. He ran a finger over the bindings, swallowing back his emotions.

"When? Why?"

"That day at the bookshop on Pall Mall. And because I think I loved you even then, though I hadn't quite admitted it. And what better way to show love for someone than to give them books?"

"What better way, indeed?" He chuckled, even as his eyes moistened. "I will treasure it always. As I will treasure you. But—" He stopped.

"But what?"

"I haven't—I didn't get you anything."

"Oh, yes, you did," she answered, bobbing her head emphatically. "You gave me you. You gave me love. You gave me the power and freedom to make my own choices. And that's all I ever want."

Taking the gift box, she set it back under the seat before nestling into Damon again, her brown eyes capturing his. "Husband," she whispered.

"Wife," he replied before seeking her lips in an intense kiss. She wound her arm around his neck, holding him as she returned the kiss with enthusiasm, her mouth opening under his. His hand moved to her waist, kneading her flesh through her dress.

The rhythm of the carriage moved their bodies together, and for long moments the only sounds were the clopping of the horses' hooves and the occasional moan. Damon's hand had worked its way up to Grace's breast, which she eagerly pressed into him. She'd moved her own fingers from his hair to his chest, tracing the muscles through the front of his shirt.

He broke off, panting, resting his forehead against hers. "You don't know how often I've thought of that night at Clarehaven," he said. "Of how often I've wanted to repeat it."

"Yes, I do." A saucy smile brought dimples to both of her cheeks. "Because I've thought the same."

He took her mouth again, infusing every ounce of love for this woman, his *wife*, into this intimate connection. She groaned against his lips, clutching him to her. She, like he, wanted an even more intimate connection.

But not here. Not in the carriage. He would not take his new wife in a coach like a baseborn lad unable to curb his desires. She deserved better. A luxurious bed. A warm fire. A husband in control of his own urges.

He broke off from her, frustration surging through his veins. "God, Grace," he breathed. "I want you."

She gulped in air, her eyes shining pools of desire. "And I you. Husband." She snaked her arms around him, holding his head to her as she wove her fingers through his hair.

He was lost.

"Wait." He pulled back. "We should be in a bed. A real bed. I want your wedding, our wedding night, to be perfect."

"We have plenty of time for perfect," she said, her voice rough. "Besides, perfection is overrated. I prefer the less predictable. Much more interesting that way."

He laughed. What had he done to deserve this woman? He'd never thought he'd find someone who would accept him as he was, much less someone who'd love him. And yet here he was, ensconced in a well-insulated carriage with this gorgeous creature. His wife. He traced his finger down her arm.

"And if the driver should, er, notice?"

She dropped her eyes, chewing her lip. After a moment, she started untying his cravat. "Then we shall have to be quiet, I suppose. You know, ducal in behavior. Because dukes and duchesses never behave improperly. Don't you agree?"

The cravat slid out from behind his neck. He said nothing as she unbuttoned his waistcoat and then started on his shirt. As she exposed the skin beneath, she peppered his abdomen with soft kisses. His legs trembled, anticipation flooding his loins. He'd never made love in a carriage before. The rocking motion of the seats brought numerous scenarios to mind, each more delicious-sounding than the last.

Pulling her head up, he dropped kisses on her eyelids, her cheeks, her nose, before once again tasting her mouth, his tongue reaching out to lick her lips. She moaned in response.

"Shh," he whispered against her mouth. "We're being quiet, remember?"

Her only response was to push his jacket over his shoulders, taking his waistcoat with it. She tugged on his shirt, and he shifted forward, pulling it over his head with both hands and discarding it without care. As her fingers slid across his bare collarbone, electricity sizzled through his veins. He couldn't get close enough to her, wanting, needing to have bare skin on bare skin. His arms reached for the bodice of her gown, carefully undoing its buttons. The petticoats underneath were nearly sheer, so much so that the pale rose of her nipples shone through. He throbbed with anticipation and a ragged groan escaped from his throat.

She giggled, a husky giggle that did nothing to calm his roaring senses. "Quiet, Your Grace. I expect better from someone in your lofty social position."

He snorted even as his fingers loosened her petticoats, eagerly sliding them off her shoulders. He'd wanted to make a witty retort, but all words, all thoughts fled as her perfect breasts came into view, the nipples jutting up as if to taunt him.

"You are so beautiful, Grace." His hands slid over the precious mounds. "So beautiful."

He gently flicked one nipple and she squirmed, but leaned into his hand as if to ask for more.

"I am glad you think so." She covered his hands with her own, looking down at them on her chest. "I always felt I was the least comely one of the family."

"Never." He pulled her around and onto his lap so they were sitting face-to-face. Or rather breast to mouth, since she was straddling his thighs and thus positioned a bit higher. Positioned perfectly. He took one of the tips into his mouth and suckled it, thrilling in the soft mewling noises she emitted. He ran his fingers up her bare back, caressing the soft flesh. Her hands came to his hair, grasping him close. She rocked her hips into his, aided by the movement of the carriage, and the friction made him buck up, seeking more.

She must have felt the same, as she pressed against him again and again. He reached for the bottom of her skirts and slid his fingers underneath, trailing them up her calf, then her thigh. He moved his hand around to the front, to the curls he sought and then farther down, farther in, until he'd found that delicious spot. He rubbed it lightly, and she writhed against his hand, her sudden inhalation letting him know he'd hit the right place.

"Damon," she breathed. His lips released her breast momentarily and he looked up. The sight of her, of Grace, of his wife, her eyes closed and head thrown back, giving herself over to the movement of his fingers, the feel of his tongue against her skin, fired his blood. He took the other breast in his mouth, laving the nipple as his fingers kept up their steady movement below, slow circles that had her clawing at his shoulders.

He wanted to tear his breeches open and thrust himself into her. He wanted to push her onto the other carriage bench and fall between her legs, to taste the very essence of her, to thrust his tongue inside of her. He groaned against her breasts at these erotic fantasies. There would be time for them. Lots of time. The rest of their lives. For now, he wanted to bring her to the edge and watch her fall apart in his arms.

She was close. Her legs tensed and her back arched as she leaned into him, holding his head against her breast. Her breathing came in short pants now, and she ground her hips against his thigh, against his fingers. "Oh God. Damon. Oh . . . oh . . . Damon!" She screamed his name as the waves of pleasure overtook her, her hips rocking into his hand, her fingers wild in his hair.

He released her breast as her movements slowed, dashing kisses against her ribs. "So much for keeping quiet," he teased.

Her cheeks shot through with red, but she wiggled backward on his thighs, reaching for the top of his breeches to loosen them. He hefted his hips up off the seat, taking her with him as she worked his breeches and smalls down over his derriere. She laughed as they bunched at her legs. How utterly delightful that she could find humor in this most intimate of moments.

She half stood and he instantly missed the heat and pressure of her. His brow furrowed until she pushed at her gown and skirts, dropping them to her feet. He instantly shoved his breeches farther down, but they stuck at the tops of his boots. He growled in frustration.

"Again?" Grace looked down, considering.

He reached out and drew her back to him. "Sit down," he said, as he pulled her thigh over his. She did, leaning back so that she could look down at him. She swallowed as she took his length in her hands, her fingers stroking the velvety skin. He feared he might spill his seed then and there, so hypnotically seductive was it to see his wife touching him in such a way.

"You look so very different from a woman," she said.

He made a noise, part laugh, part moan. "Good God, I should hope so!"

She stroked him up and down a few more times until he caught at her hand.

"You are quite the temptress, my sweet wife," he whispered. "And I long for the time when you use only your hands—or your mouth." His eyebrow cocked up wickedly at the flush that spread over her skin. "And I shall most definitely return the favor. But for now—"

He lifted her hips and pulled her forward until he nestled in her curls. "—I want something else. I want you." Using his hand, he guided himself into her, slowly, as she enveloped him inch by inch. The intense pleasure nearly undid him.

"I had no idea one could—" Grace murmured. She wriggled her hips so that he was fully within her.

He groaned at the sigh of pleasure that escaped her, clutching at her hips as he bucked up into her.

"Yes," he whispered. "Yes. Move with me, Grace. Together."

She braced her hands against the backboard of the

carriage and practiced raising herself and lowering, again and again. "Oh my Lord," she moaned, her eyes closing.

"Yes. Isn't it beautiful?" He grabbed at her rear, kneading the fleshy orbs as she moved against him, up and down, up and down. Her pace increased and he matched it, their breath coming in short, harsh grunts now.

The release he so sought snaked through his loins, and he pounded into her even as she sank down. At the last minute, he took her nipple into his mouth, sucking hard as the world exploded around him and he spilled himself into his wife.

"Grace," he cried out, once, and then held her against him, skin against skin, flesh against flesh. They sat that way for who knew how long, the rocking of the carriage making both cognizant that they remained joined, loath to move, to lose that connection.

It wasn't long until he stirred again. He wasn't surprised. He didn't think he'd ever get enough of her, of Grace. His wife. His love.

But he would have to wait. The next time he made love to her—for that was definitely what this was, a more intimate connection than he'd ever known—it *would* be in a real bed. His bed. Their bed. He gently disentangled himself from her and pulled her close into his side.

"I love you, Grace Blackbourne," he said as he ran his thumb over her bare shoulder.

She shivered. "I love you, too. But do you think we could get dressed again? I'm feeling a little . . . exposed."

He chuckled as she rose to retrieve her dress. "I guess it's one thing to consummate a marriage in a carriage," he said. "It'd be quite another to show up at Thorne Hill naked."

She made a show of throwing the dress at him, and he ducked, pure joy rising up in his throat, bursting forth in gales of laughter. She laughed, too. Together, they dressed, then she settled into the crook of his arm, her head on his shoulder. He rubbed his thumb on her arm over the fabric of the dress. He liked it much better when he was touching skin. He was about to ask her a question when a soft snore rose to his ears. He grinned.

His wife had fallen asleep.

CHAPTER 34

*G*race dozed for much of the rest of the way to Thorne Hill, waking only in the last half hour. Bleary eyed, she looked up at Damon in dismay. "I'm so sorry!"

"Nonsense. It's clear you were exhausted. Besides, this way I can keep you up all night and not feel guilty." His devilish grin made her giggle.

"Tell me more of the history of Thorne Hill," Grace asked as they neared the estate.

"In truth, I don't know as much as I should. Many of my childhood memories are hazy, and while I spent the winter months here before coming to London, much of that passed in a blur as I acclimated to new surroundings." He grimaced. "And new people."

He shifted in his seat as he looked out the window. "It's been in the family for at least a century. I admire its architecture, but with my experiences here, I don't feel attached to it. Not as Cassie does."

"Cassie?"

"Yes. When I first arrived, it was she who taught me

the ins and outs of the house. She knows everything about it, every servant's name, every piece of silverware, every furnishing—even those in storage."

Grace ran her hand over his thigh. How taut his muscles were. "Perhaps *she* should run it."

He didn't speak for a moment. "I've considered that, actually. In truth, I'd rather return to Yorkshire. To the abbey. But I couldn't think to ask such a sacrifice of you, to take you so far away from your family."

"I would miss them," she conceded after a short silence. "But my home is with you."

The tender smile on his face showed her words had moved him. He gave her a quick kiss, his eyes smoldering.

"I wonder if you might consider living part of the year in Yorkshire and part of the year here—at Thorne Hill, or in London."

"Like Persephone and Hades?"

He flinched. "I should hope Yorkshire would not seem the equivalent of the underworld, nor you feel a prisoner in it."

"I was teasing, my love."

His muscles relaxed.

"I rather like the idea of Yorkshire," she said.

"But you've never been."

"No. But anywhere with you and a fine library cannot be anything less than paradise."

His pupils flared as he drew her face up for another deep kiss. "Keep talking like that, wife, and we shall certainly arrive in a state of undress. Thorne Hill is only a few minutes more."

As they rounded a bend in the road, the house came into view. It did not match the grandiosity of Clarehaven, but she immediately loved its precisely symmetrical façade and the sizable windows that covered the front of the house. Sunlight always buoyed her spirits while reading, and such windows no doubt allowed many a warm ray.

A large stone staircase descended from the front door, on which the servants had lined up to greet the returning master and his new wife. As the carriage pulled to a stop at the front, a smile split Grace's face; Daisy and Geoffrey were among the persons assembled there.

"Geoffrey!" she exclaimed, turning to Damon with a quizzical expression.

"I sent a carriage for them," he said with a shrug of his shoulders. "I thought we ought to have them with us, not leave them at Clarehaven. I hope you approve."

"Of course! I am so glad to see him. Both of them."

A footman stepped forward to open the door. Damon exited first, then held his hand out to assist Grace. She watched Geoffrey as she descended. He still made his movements, but they seemed less pronounced. His face was unsure. Were people being kind to the boy?

The butler stepped forward and introduced himself and each of the servants in turn. Grace walked the line, greeting each person warmly. When she got to Geoffrey, she enfolded the boy in a hug. "I'm pleased you are here. I hope you have been made to feel welcome."

"Yes, ma'am, I mean, Your Grace," he said, but he still seemed sad.

Grace frowned. She leaned in near his ear. "Is anyone being mean to you?"

His ears flushed red. "Not really, ma'am. I miss Freddy, 'tis all."

"Then we shall have to visit him soon. And get to know some of the other children nearby."

Damon touched her elbow and she stood, lacing her arm through his. Together, they walked through the front doors.

"Thank you again for letting Geoffrey come here," Damon said as they entered the foyer.

"Me?"

"Yes, you, wife. I don't think many women would want to take in a stranger's child, much less one of lower birth and with his, um, differences."

She stopped at the foot of the stairs, turning to face him. Servants milled about, but she ignored them, focusing her complete attention on her husband.

"A child is a child," she said, her voice low so that only he could hear. "All deserve kindness." She touched her hand to his cheek. "All."

Her heart swelled as his eyes moistened. He swallowed.

"I have been thinking," she went on. "Could we help more children? Children like Geoffrey, or others without parents at all."

She looked down at the tiled floor. "I know we couldn't help every one, Damon, but wouldn't it be wonderful if we could save at least a few? Give them the love—and education—every child deserves?"

He pulled her to him, lifting her chin to capture her in a kiss so bold, so fiery she could only clutch at his jacket sleeves as she succumbed to the fervor of their embrace. It was more than physical lust driving his passionate action, and indeed, when he broke off the kiss, he murmured against her lips.

"My God, you are indeed my saving Grace. If only I had . . . " he said, and this time a tear did fall from his eye. "If only I'd had someone like you when I was small. Someone who could have helped me."

"You did," she said, her own eyes welling up. "You told me. Your Mrs. Hardy. Remind me to thank her when we are in Yorkshire. And Hobbes. And Cerberus. That is more than some ever get."

Hobbes and the cat had left in a separate carriage that morning. "I wanted my wife to myself," Damon had explained. "And Cerberus does not exactly travel well."

She'd spied the two in the hall a moment ago. Who looked more frazzled, the valet or the animal, she wasn't sure. Only one had borne scratches on his arms, however.

"Indeed." Damon nuzzled against her neck. "Though I think both prefer never to ride in a carriage again. At least not together."

She glanced around. The servants had discreetly exited the room. Had they witnessed the kiss? She should probably be embarrassed. Proper ladies did not engage in amorous embraces with their husbands in public. Then again, she'd never much valued being a proper lady.

Damon brought his hands to her face, holding her cheeks gently as he fixed his eyes on her. "I love you, Grace Blackbourne. Thank you for all you have given me. You have healed my tortured soul, tamed the wild beast." He sighed, closing his eyes. "I can't promise you my movements won't ever come back. I wish I could."

"And I can't promise you I won't run around with ink-stained hands, or won't forget to eat sometimes because I've gotten lost in a book, or won't hide away in the library whenever possible to avoid callers."

He laughed, a great booming laugh that echoed through the foyer.

"As long as you let me hide with you." His blue eyes flashed in wicked delight. "I have an even greater fondness for libraries now. And carriages. Definitely carriages."

"Perhaps we could consider adding a bed to that list," she said with a saucy grin. Her fingers ran down his chest and then lower, to his stomach, then lower still.

His eyes widened, but he grabbed her hand, pulling her toward the stairs. "The house tour will have to wait. The only room I'm interested in seeing right now is my chamber. *Our* chamber."

She giggled as she stumbled after him. "Indeed, my husband."

Reaching the top, he swung her up into his arms and carried her down the hallway, planting kisses all around her face as they went.

"And then the library, my beloved wife," he said. "Most definitely the library."

The

End

AUTHOR'S NOTE

Authors often talk of the book of their heart, the book they just had to write. This is the book of my love. Namely, my love for my son, who, like Damon Blackbourne of *The Demon Duke*, has Tourette Syndrome (also called Tourette's or simply TS). It was he who inspired this duke.

The Tourette Association of America defines the syndrome thusly:

> "Tourette Syndrome is a neurodevelopmental disorder that affects children, adolescents and adults. The condition is characterized by sudden, involuntary movements and/or sounds called tics. Tics typically emerge between the ages of 5-7 years, most often with a motor tic of the head and neck region. They tend to increase in frequency and severity between the ages of 8-12 years. Most people with TS show noticeable improvement in late adolescence, with some becoming tic-free. A minority of people with TS continues to have persistent, severe tics in adulthood.

> Tics can range from mild to severe and, in some cases, can be self-injurious and debilitating. Tics regularly change in type, frequency, and severity—sometimes for reasons unknown and sometimes in response to specific internal and external factors, including stress, anxiety, excitement, fatigue, and illness. Individuals with Tourette often have co-occurring conditions, most commonly

Obsessive-Compulsive Disorder (OCD), Attention Deficit-Hyperactivity Disorder (ADHD), anxiety, and learning difficulties."

Anybody who's "different" knows the challenges of being so, especially when one's differences manifest themselves in a visible manner. My son often insists he's never getting married, because nobody will ever want him. While much of that is (hopefully) typical teen self-doubt, it breaks my heart. The first time he said it, I decided right then and there I'd write a book in which the hero has TS but finds true love—and acceptance.

I patterned this story somewhat after Beauty and the Beast not because I think people with TS are beastly in any way, but because (1) it's my favorite fairy tale, and (2) many in the past (and present) have viewed people with Tourette Syndrome negatively.

Tourette's is still not well understood, but at least we view it today through the lens of science. Medical advances allow us to understand it as a neurological disorder, not a psychological disturbance, much less the work of dark forces. In earlier centuries, when science was less advanced, people attributed many medical maladies to sinister causes. The first known mention of a person with tics—a priest—came in the *Malleus Maleficarum*, that infamous handbook for witch hunting published in 1486. It attributed the priest's symptoms to possession by a demon.[1] Not an auspicious beginning for anybody suffering from these unwanted behaviors.

Though people have speculated 18th century notables writer Samuel Johnson and composer Amadeus Mozart

---

[1] Tourette's syndrome: from demonic possession and psychoanalysis to the discovery of genes. Francisco M.B. Germiniani; Anna Paula P. Miranda; Peter Ferenczy; Renato P. Munhoz; Hélio A.G. Teive. July 2012. (http://dx.doi.org/10.1590/S0004-282X2012000700014)

had Tourette's,[2] the first medically documented case was that of the Marquise de Dampierre, a French noble-woman whose tics physician Jean Marc Gaspard Itard chronicled in 1825. It was this case Georges Gilles de la Tourette used in 1885 as his primary example of what he called a "maladie des tics." Tourette went on to study others who exhibited similar symptoms. From him, the syndrome took its name.[3]

Today in the United States, one out of every 160 children (0.6%) between the ages of 5-17 has TS. Males are affected three to four more times than females. Though coproralia, or "the involuntary utterance of obscene and socially unacceptable words and phrases," is a common stereotype of people with Tourette Syndrome, less than 10% of those diagnosed with TS exhibit this symptom.[4]

I am not a medical doctor. This book is a work of fiction and expresses my own research and experiences of someone with Tourette Syndrome. I have endeavored to accurately reflect how people in the Regency might have reacted to someone with tics, as well as to give a realistic portrayal of how the syndrome affects a person. However, as with many neurological disorders, TS can and does present differently in different people.

My hope in writing this book was to raise awareness of and compassion for an oft-misunderstood syndrome,

---

[2] Famous People with Neurological Disorders.
http://bandofartists.org/about-tourettes/famous-people-with-neurological-disorders/

[3] Kushner, Howard I. A Cursing Brain? The Histories of Tourette Syndrome. Cambridge, Massachusetts: Harvard University Press. 1999.

[4] Tourette Association of America. https://www.tourette.org/about-tourette/overview/what-is-tourette/

one that continues to perplex the medical community and the general public today.

As a show of support for my son and all people with Tourette Syndrome, I will donate 20% of my profits from each sale of *The Demon Duke* to the <u>Tourette Association of America</u>.

For Further Reading

(These are a small sample of the books available, though information on the history of Tourette Syndrome is scanty)

Basic history of Tourette Syndrome:
<u>https://en.wikipedia.org/wiki/History_of_Tourette_synd rome</u>

Chowdhury, Uttom. Tics and Tourette Syndrome: *A Handbook for Parents and Professionals*. London: Jessica Kingsley Publishers. 2004.

Kushner, Howard I. *A Cursing Brain? The Histories of Tourette Syndrome*. Cambridge, Massachusetts: Harvard University Press. 1999.

Marsh, Tracy. *Children With Tourette Syndrome: A Parents' Guide*. Bethesda, Maryland: Woodbine House. 2007.

Tourette Association of America.
<u>https://www.tourette.org</u>

Don't miss Margaret Locke's Best-selling, Award-winning Magic of Love series!

A MAN OF CHARACTER
MAGIC of LOVE Book One

Fall in love with the magic in *A Man of Character*.

http://bit.ly/MLAMoC

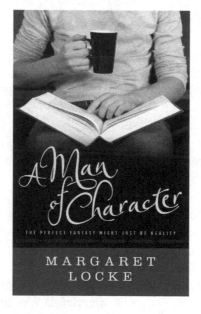

The perfect fantasy might just be reality.

What would you do if you discovered the men you were dating were fictional characters you'd created long ago?

Thirty-five-year-old Catherine Schreiber has shelved love for good. Keeping her ailing bookstore afloat takes all her time, and she's perfectly fine with that. So when several men ask her out in short order, she's not sure what to do . . . especially since something about them seems eerily familiar.

A startling revelation—that these men are fictional characters she'd created and forgotten years ago—forces Cat to reevaluate her world and the people in it. Because these characters are alive. Here. Now. And most definitely in the flesh.

Her best friend, Eliza, a romance novel junkie craving her own Happily Ever After, is thrilled by the possibilities. The power to create Mr. Perfect—who could pass that up? But can a relationship be real if it's fiction? Caught between fantasy and reality, Cat must decide which—or whom—she wants more.

Blending humor with unusual twists, including a magical manuscript, a computer scientist in shining armor, and even a Regency ball, A Man of Character is a whimsical-yet-thought-provoking romantic comedy that tells a story not only of love, but also of the lengths we'll go for friendship, self-discovery, and second chances.

An excerpt from *A Man of Character*:

W hat was wrong with her? A week ago she'd insisted to Eliza that she wasn't the least bit interested in a man, and here she was, having gone out on a date with one, and now fantasizing over another, thinking thoughts that reminded her of the smutty story Eliza had found. She hadn't paid attention to men for six years; what had her reacting to two in such a short time period?

Make that three. You can't deny Ben Cooper caught your attention, too.

The door opened and an older couple walked through. At the sound of their voices, the man looked up and then checked his watch.

"Oh, I'm late." He gave her a wolfish grin. "Gotta scoot."

Tucking the book back onto the bookshelf, he winked and sauntered out the door.

Cat stood there, breathing slowly to calm her flaming senses. Anyone would react to that man, right? Right? That mouth. She'd wanted to touch it, to feel those lips on hers. Goose bumps prickled her skin.

She didn't understand what was happening to her, why she was suddenly so aware of men, when before she'd managed to convince herself they were just part of the scenery. No doubt her sister would say it was her biological clock, tick, tick, ticking away.

Cat wasn't so sure. Maybe it was her stories, the ones Eliza had unearthed from that box. She had written them, after all. Perhaps reading them again had sparked something within her, made her realize that at one point, at least, she'd been very, ahem, interested in men and sex. And love.

A MATTER OF TIME
MAGIC of LOVE Book Two

The magic continues!

Don't miss *A Matter of Time*—Eliza and Deveric's story.
(Featuring some familiar faces from The Demon Duke!)

http://bit.ly/MLAMoT

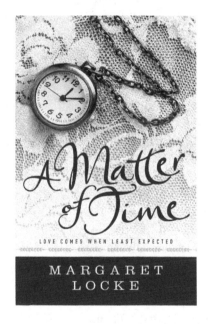

Love Comes When Least Expected

**Can a man with a past and a woman from the future
forge a love for all time?**

Nobody would blame widowed doctoral student Eliza James for giving up on Happily Ever After; at twenty-nine, she's suffered more loss than most people do in a lifetime. But Eliza's convinced her own hero is still out there, waiting for her, just like in the beloved romance novels she devours. Every Jane Austen-loving girl deserves a Darcy, right?

Only Eliza doesn't dream of a modern-day affair: she wants the whole Regency experience. When a magical manuscript thrusts her back two hundred years into the arms and life of one Deveric Mattersley, Duke of Claremont, however, Eliza realizes some fantasies aren't all they're cracked up to be, especially when her duke proves himself less than a Prince Charming.

Convinced he's at fault for his wife's death, Deveric Mattersley has no interest in women, much less marriage. Determined to atone for his sins, he focuses on running his family's estates, and on raising his son–until the mysterious Mrs. James appears. Who is she? What does she want? And why does she make Dev's blood run hot in a way no woman ever has?

A charming time-travel Regency romance full of wit and humor, A Matter of Time reminds us that, like books, you can't judge people by their covers, and that love often comes when least expected.

An excerpt from *A Matter of Time*:

J anuary 1st, 2012. Or not.
It is a truth universally acknowledged that a woman who's just traveled across an ocean and back two hundred years in time might find herself in a bit of a pickle. Unless that woman discovers herself to be trapped in the arms of a man in possession of a good fortune . . . and in want of a wife.

Eliza blinked her eyes as that corny perversion of Jane Austen's opening line to Pride and Prejudice flitted through her mind. She looked down at the man in whose arms she was awkwardly wedged. He was half-sitting, half-leaning on a settee sofa, out cold. His arms, however, held her firmly, and even as she attempted to shift to survey her surroundings, he clutched her to him. His warmth and size enveloped her, a strange energy humming between them.

Peeking out over her left shoulder, Eliza could see she was in a library of some sort. Not a public library, but rather an old-fashioned personal library, like the ones she always read about in her novels. Built-in bookcases lined the two walls, filled with volumes of books in antique-style bindings— only in pristine condition. A fireplace separated the shelves on one wall, and a large portrait of an older gentleman in a white curly wig hung on the oak panels over it.

Turning to the right, she lifted her head a bit in order to see over the back of the sofa. A large, heavy, ornately carved desk, which was covered with papers, sat near a back wall containing more bookcases. A real inkstand rested on top of the desk, and next to it, several quill pens. An old clock ticked forlornly from the wall behind the desk. She couldn't see the entryway into the room— it must be behind her— but the distant strains of a violin and the low murmurings of conversation drifted in from somewhere close by.

She closed her eyes. If the furnishings were any indication, she was in Regency England. For real. It'd worked. It had actually worked.

The man shifted, but didn't relax his grip. Eliza's eyes flew open again as the enormity of the situation hit her. She was trapped in the arms of a duke. A duke her friend Cat created for her. An authentic Regency duke.

A SCANDALOUS MATTER
MAGIC of LOVE Book 3

Revel in the magic again in *A Scandalous Matter,* Amara
and Matthew's story.

http://bit.ly/MLSMatter

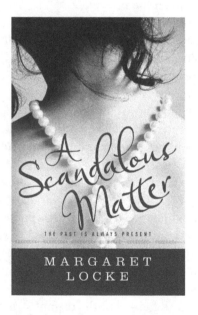

The past is always present.

**What if your soul mate doesn't want happily ever
after?**

Independent, spirited Amara Mattersley may live under scandal's shadow, but at least the nineteenth-century Regency society judging her is familiar. That's all about to change when she finds herself in twenty-first-century Charlottesville, Virginia—and locking horns with one very befuddling, very male, UVA professor.

Computer science professor Matthew Goodson has no time for love—no time for anything, actually, but his quest for tenure and his obsession with the screen. The last thing he expects is to get side-swiped by this adorably odd British miss. Yet something in her calls to him, pulls at him, in a way unknown—and uncomfortable.

Can the past and the present blend together into a mutual future? Or will old wounds and new complications sabotage any chance at a twenty-first century happily ever after?

An excerpt from *A Scandalous Matter*:

H e held up a hand to quiet her as he strode toward the left side of the room, the side from which the noise had come. As he neared the Romance section, he could swear he heard scuffling, then a low moan. A low, female-sounding moan.

Rounding the corner, he stopped short at the sight of a young woman sitting on the floor, cradling her head. She wore a long white dress, a maxi dress, his sister Taylor would call it, with some sort of short red jacket over it, and she had a bonnet— a bonnet, of all things— on her head.

He frowned. What was going on? Some sort of cosplay gone bad? His brow furrowed as he studied the woman. A second moan knocked him out of his reverie, and he rushed to her side.

"Are you okay?" He'd figure out why and how she'd gotten here later; for now, he needed to ensure she was all right. His EMT training never fully left him, though he hadn't gone on runs in years. He crouched down next to her and reached for her hand to pull it away from her head. At his touch, the woman yelped and yanked her hand back. She looked up, affording him his first full view of her face.

My God, she's stunning. A pair of hazel-green eyes peered out of a face that was both delicate and strong at the same time. Her curvaceous lips flattened into a line as her eyes widened. But there was no doubt about it, this was one gorgeous woman.

She shook her head, then glanced wildly about the room, her eyes darting to and fro before settling on him again. The panic in them made him want to reach for her, but at that moment, Cat approached from behind him.

"What's going—" She broke off as Matt stood and moved to the side so she could see the newcomer. Cat's hand flew to her mouth before she dropped it and pasted an unnatural-looking smile on her face. "Amara?" she said, taking a step closer to the woman.

The bonnet wielder's eyes flew open even wider, a feat he wouldn't have thought possible. She gave a nod. "Miss Schreiber?"

Huh. A British accent. He hadn't expected that. Maybe it was part of the role.

Cat nodded enthusiastically, crouching down by the woman. "Yes! It's Mrs. Cooper now, but please call me Cat. I'm so glad you're here. I know you must be—" She broke off and glanced up at Matt. "I know you must be overwhelmed, Cousin Amara. We have much to talk about. But first," she gestured toward him, "you must meet Matthew Goodson. This is *he*."

Something in the way Cat spoke caught Matt's attention. Why had she emphasized his name in such a weird way? Why wasn't she wigging out that this woman, whom Matt would swear was not here before, was sitting on the floor in the middle of the bookstore? The store had been closed for more than an hour. Had this Amara person been in the room the whole time, and he hadn't noticed?

It wasn't entirely implausible. His family teased him that when his face was in a screen, the rest of the world didn't exist. "And your face is always in a screen," Taylor claimed. "You're such a geek, Matty. An adorable geek, but a geek nonetheless. Come up for air sometime!"

"Well—" he started to say, wanting to return to Ben and his food. He wasn't needed here; the two women knew each other. Though at least one of them wasn't acting like it. In spite of them being related?

Something was off.

ACKNOWLEDGMENTS

"Appreciate good people. They are hard to come by."
-Unknown

I am blessed beyond belief to have such great people to work with and cheer me on. Thank you. Thank you. Thank you.

To the Shenandoah Valley Writers Critique Group for their support and suggestions, as always.

To beta readers Phyllis A. Duncan, Josette Keelor, and Annette Will, for their wonderful feedback.

To Kary Phillips, for her brilliant editing and proofing skills. And her affection for the Marquess of Emerlin.

To my amazing editor, Tessa Shapcott, who takes my messy slab of clay and helps me fashion something beautiful (or at least readable!) out of it.

To Joy Lankshear of Lankshear Design, for this gorgeous book cover. I could stare at it all day.

To Emily June Street, for working her formatting magic – she is a wizard, y'all!

To RWA's Beau Monde, for constantly offering helpful answers to my many naïve questions. I quest to get it right, but of course any errors remain my own.

To my kids, for putting up with mom working—*again*.

And to Brett. Because "you gave me you. You gave me love. You gave me the power and freedom to make my own choices. And that's all I ever want."

ABOUT MARGARET

Don't tell anyone, but Margaret Locke started reading romance at the age of ten. She'd worked her way through all of the children's books available in the local bookmobile, so turned to the adult section, where she spied a book with a woman in a flowing green dress on the cover. The back said something about a pirate. She was hooked (and still wishes she could remember the name of that fateful book!).

Her delight in witty repartee between hero and heroine, in the age-old dance of attraction vs. resistance, in the emotional satisfaction of a cleverly achieved Happily Ever After followed her through high school, college, even grad school. But it wasn't until she turned forty that she finally made good on her teenage vow to write said novels, not merely read them.

Margaret lives in the beautiful Shenandoah Valley in Virginia with her fantastic husband, two fabulous kids, and three funny cats. You can usually find her in front of some sort of screen (electronic or window); she's come to terms with the fact that she's not an outdoors person.

LET'S KEEP IN TOUCH!

Margaret loves to interact with fellow readers and authors! You may find her here:

Blog/Website:
http://margaretlocke.com

Facebook:
http://www.facebook.com/AuthorMargaretLocke

GoodReads:
http://www.goodreads.com/MargaretLocke

Pinterest:
http://www.pinterest.com/Margaret_Locke

Twitter:
http://www.twitter.com/Margaret_Locke

Instagram:
http://www.instagram.com/margaret_locke

BookBub:
https://www.bookbub.com/authors/margaret-locke

GET A LOCKE ON LOVE:
JOIN THE VIP EMAIL CLUB

Interested in being the first to know about Margaret's upcoming releases or hearing other insider information?

The key is signing up for her VIP Email Club, through which you'll get exclusive excerpts, giveaways, info on new releases, and more!

Sign Up Here:

http://margaretlocke.com/vipreaders

THANK YOU FOR READING

What did you think of *The Demon Duke*?

Would you kindly consider leaving a review on
BookBub, GoodReads, or the retailer site of your choice?

Word-of-mouth is the best way for authors to reach
readers,
and the online version of word-of-mouth is reviews.

Thanks so much!

Margaret

CPSIA information can be obtained
at www.ICGtesting.com
Printed in the USA
LVHW01s1655080518
576441LV00001B/30/P

9 780996 317085